*For My Dear Husband:*
Thanks for believing.

*For My Sons:*
Thanks for your help and love.


## MY GRATITUDE TO:

MARGARET WESTHAVEN—for delightful hours reading our manuscripts aloud, and for recording this one with me.

VIVIENNE GRIFFIN—for extending your hand of friendship across the ocean, and giving me visions of the 19th-century Shipston.

PETER DRINKWATER—for British historical tidbits of great worth, and for all your artistic jewels.

William Wordsworth
Lord Byron
The duke and duchess of Wellington
Mr. Stultz
Lady Sally Jersey, Countess Lieven, Emily Cowper, Mrs. Drummond Burrell
Prinny, or the Prince Regent
Lady Caroline Lamb
Harriette Wilson and her sisters Amy, Sophia, and Fanny
Lord Alvanley
Mr. Brummell

From William Wordsworth's (1770-1850) poetry, I've used excerpts from each of the following:

"She Dwelt among the Untrodden Ways"
"The Tables Turned"
"Lines written in Early Spring"
"She was a Phantom of Delight"
"Lines Composed a Few Miles above Tintern Abbey"
"Three Years She Grew"
"The Excursion"

Darnier sings a song called:

"London Town"

which is found in Pierce Egan's book, *Life in London*, dedicated to King George IV in 1821

# CONTENTS

# *Prologue*

"Look! There's a woman!" whispered a surprised male voice.

"What, some servant picking berries? Come on, man. I swear, you can't pass a female without going into transports."

"No, come and look—she's lying on the ground."

"Hmmm . . . she must be sleeping," said the other, fingering his jaw.

"Could be she's just had an assignation. Her shawl spread out in the grass, her fine clothes— You'd be amazed at the freedom of these country girls. Shhh, I'm going to investigate. There'll be little other diversion to be had while I'm here."

*"Leave her alone!"*

# Chapter 1

## The Strange Gift

Lady Briana knew, from a sudden, prickling feeling, that she was not alone. Raising her cheek from the comforting grass, she brushed hot tears away, petrified that someone should chance to see a lady like herself in this prone, tearful position.

With trepidation, she raised her bonnet brim a fraction, fully expecting to see the hem of her duenna's faded purple gown with its black looping trim. But what she saw beyond the woodbine could in no way be Anselma for a pair of gray leather boots were planted there.

She gasped in utter dismay. A man! And she, alone in the copse, far from anyone. *Just look*, said her conscience, *what comes of dodging your faithful Anselma. You have not even come out into Society; you know nothing about dealing with the masterful sex.*

With heart pounding, she willed herself to look higher. Pewter-colored pantaloons led to a waistcoat of apricot topped by a coat of deepest gray. Above a checked cravat, the man's narrow cleft chin gave frame to sculpted lips. A tall beaver perched on streaked wavy hair, and his almond-shaped eyes regarded her with the utmost interest.

"Is something amiss?" His clipped words fell softly as he searched the damp, startled face of the dusky beauty beneath the black hat brim. She raised herself quickly but gracefully to a sitting position on her shawl.

"Nothing significant, sir," she replied with a beautiful disregard for her sparkling tears. "I've just . . ." The lustrous eyes danced around for an idea. ". . . poked my eye into the grass."

"Ahh, provoking, to be sure." The gentleman's lips curved into a smile and he pulled a folded square from his pocket. "Perhaps this will soothe it, madam. Please— you would honor my handkerchief."

For a man in his mid-twenties and in this part of the world, he had considerable finesse, thought Briana. Even as she knew she should run away as fast as she could, something within her wouldn't allow her to do so. To ease her grief this day, she had been reading poetry, and what Wordsworth had written about his Lucy had hit home in Briana's heart:

> She dwelt among the untrodden ways
> Beside the springs of Dove,
> A maid whom there were none to praise
> And very few to love.

On top of everything else, the words had brought an upsurge of tears. Now Briana was romantic enough to let herself believe for a moment that this concerned, handsome gentleman had been bidden by her longing heart.

Between dabs at her lashes, she thanked him while, with her artistic eye, she memorized his face. His ash-colored brows rose and dropped in an intent expression, and his forehead was squared off at the temples, proclaiming his intelligence.

"Who are you?" she asked, trying to sound calm.

"Sir Reginald Channing."

"But do call him Rex," said a voice from the forest.

Briana whirled, unnerved at being startled by another stranger. From the mottled shadows behind her emerged a dark-haired, golden-skinned man loaded with fishing paraphernalia. His black boots were worn, his thighs muscular in close-fitting buckskins. Inky bracket-shaped brows marked his strong face, and his moustache gave him a look of the military. He cast Briana a cursory glance, propped his fishing rod against a moss-laden tree trunk, and dropped a heavy knapsack to the ground. His powerful shoulders set off a maroon waistcoat and white sleeves.

"Yes, certainly," continued Sir Reginald Channing, lowering himself gallantly onto one knee, "call me Rex, madam. All my friends do." As Briana gave him a tentative smile, he added, glancing at the fisherman, "Even some impertinent servants do."

Hands on hips, the recipient of this gibe returned the gleam in Rex's eye with a menacing squint. An undercurrent between the two left Briana uncomfortable as though they shared a joke at her expense. She could sit there no longer with the two of them speculating as if she were some blowsy damsel.

Scrambling to free her slippers from her flounces, she was suddenly seized by her slender waist and set upon her feet. She turned a disbelieving look on the bold servant who had hauled her up. Impulsive words would have issued from her if she had not spied the pained look that crossed his brow. "Is something the matter with *you?*" she inquired.

"If I would remember to stop lifting females, no matter how light they look, I would have no trouble at all," he said, wincing.

11

This drew a laugh from Rex. But Briana, knowing she could not be called petite, stiffened. She noted the fisherman's fingers working at his shoulder. "I am very sorry if I caused you such pain," she said. Not knowing whether to smile or glare, she chose to gift him with the gaze that had caused the Adam's apples of Shipston lads to bob. Her eyes were wide and superior, her cherry-colored lips parted over white teeth.

The tall servant seemed undisturbed by her poise. She judged him to be nearly thirty, which must account for it. "No need to be sorry," he told her. "It's my own fault. I . . . ah . . . got into a scrap."

Rex coughed to hide a grin.

"Were you victorious?" Briana inquired.

The hazel eyes glinted. "Yes."

"By the size of you, I'm not surprised. Who would have a chance? Well, excuse me, but I must be going."

The servant stepped more or less into her path and regarded her, his squinting black lashes shuttering his thoughts. Briana avoided that inscrutable look, noting instead that his jaw was dark with evidence that a razor had been dispensed with and that he had a handsome nose, not perfectly straight. "Pray tell us first," he said, "why Miss indulges in tears on such a glorious afternoon."

"I was not *indulging!*" What impertinence!

"Then you do it often?" he persisted, with the ghost of a grin.

"No!" said Briana. "As a matter of fact, I hardly ever— Why, what concern is it of yours, sir?"

"Touché," inserted Rex.

Briana cast him a grateful glance, stooped for her shawl, and flushed in shame that she had been betrayed into such schoolgirlish retorts to a servant, and in front of this peer.

The betrayer softly insisted, "But if we had not

12

interrupted you, tears would still be flowing down those pretty pink cheeks."

"They are not pink! That is, I am not in the habit of blushing." In her confusion Briana was afraid that, heaven forbid, she was blushing now.

Sternly Rex admonished, "Leave the young lady alone!" His beaver left his head in a sudden strengthening of the breeze, and he reached to catch it, missed, and had to sprint after it. In the same gust, Briana's hat blew down her back, allowing a cloud of dark tendrils to reveal her graceful neck.

"Forgive me," continued her tormentor, his voice gentle as he moved closer. "I should not be contradicting a young lady." As her bosom rose, he reached out and removed a snip of grass that remained pressed into her damp cheek.

"Darnier!" shouted Rex in sharp rebuke, running toward them.

Briana stood stunned by the casual but vital touch on her skin, especially that last caress at the corner of her mouth. How dare he!

"Darnier, upon my word, leave the young lady alone! Go tie me some more hooks!" The whiplash of Sir Reginald's voice caused Darnier to touch his forehead in ironic salute, and move to draw a coil of fishing line from his leather pouch. Under its flap Briana caught a glimpse of a fish, apparently the topmost of many.

"Are all those trout from the brook?" she asked curiously of Rex as she retied her hat ribbons.

"Two hours' work," quipped Darnier, turning round. "I'll give you half. Will that cheer you?" He shot Briana an inviting look. "In exchange for your name."

"Darnier," emphasized Rex, "the lady has not chosen to offer her name. Therefore, we should await her pleasure in that matter." He paused expectantly.

But Briana had spied the purple frock of her spinster

duenna crossing the lawn in the distance. "Lady Bri-a-na . . . !" her reedy voice carried on the wind.

"I see you are cheated," said Darnier, "for now I know you are Lady Briana Rosewynn, and I still have the fish."

"Keep them," she retorted. Eyeing Anselma nervously, she said, "Please make yourselves scarce, gentlemen, or I shall be in the basket."

"By all means, madam," said Rex. Briana, fearful of consequences, hid behind the trunk of the most spreading of the ancient elms while Darnier hunkered next the elderberry bush, still tying his hook.

Anselma's accents became sharp. *"Lady Briana!"* Briana's partners in stealth looked amused at her forbearance to answer the summons. They watched the spinster emerge from the brick pavilion trying to see against the afternoon sun, her eyes shaded by her bony hand, her bonnet resembling a dustbin with frills.

Briana's curiosity grew as she watched the dark-haired Darnier complete an intricate knot and tuck the hook into his bag. "Do you serve Sir Reginald?" she whispered.

"Not usually, but now for a time he's a guest at Brocco Park," came the low reply.

"You work for the duke of Brocco, then?"

Darnier smiled charmingly. "I am very dedicated to serving him. Do take these fish, my lady."

"Bring them to your cook for the duke's table," she whispered. "Does His Grace enjoy trout? He will likely require more than that."

"The duke has a definite preference for fresh-caught trout, but even he and his guest cannot put away sixteen. Here, half belongs to your ladyship, for I am a man of my word."

Briana capitulated shyly. "Since I have not allowed myself to poach on His Grace's brook . . ."

"An excellent reason to accept," he said, and seeing

Anselma's back turned, he reached quickly across the clearing and transferred the heavy string from his warm hand to Briana's cool ones.

"Thank His Grace for me," she said. "We heard he arrived last evening. One can only imagine how he feels realizing such a magnificent seat is all his." Knowing what much of it looked like for having decorated rooms there, Briana's eyes shone. "Do you like being one in his army of servants?"

Scrutinizing her, Darnier responded, "I begin to like it more and more."

Anselma rounded the clipped yew, the one shaped like a birdbath. Her bonnet was crooked and her temper in shreds. "Lady Briana, your *tea!*"

Rex lifted his hand and smiled farewell, for he was in a position to slip away. His parting look bore open admiration, which Briana found produced a sensation most pleasing.

Turning back, Darnier's eyes were fixed on her in an all-seeing way which made her feel vulnerable. "Thank you," she mouthed, summoning a smile in behalf of the string of fish she lifted.

*"Bon appétit,"* he said, his handsome mouth twisting into a half smile. Briana backed away through the branches at the bleating of her name near at hand. But there, behind that compelling Darnier, lay her new volume of Wordsworth. She would have to return for it. She could never chance her duenna's clapping eyes on the wildly attractive man lurking there. She raced on tiptoe to the far end of an overgrown hawthorn hedge and emerged at a walk near the pavilion, much to Anselma's bewilderment for she had just searched those environs.

"Lady Briana!" she exclaimed, closing in. "Come, come, tea is getting cold in the cup. Brrr, aren't you chilly? Where's your India scarf?"

"In my hand, Anselma. I don't need to wear it." To

avoid a spate of curiosity, Briana walked fast and carried the line of fish out of sight, covered by the dragging scarf.

"My, yes, we'll grow warm climbing to the house. Chalandra poured for you. Just feature, she is using your black-and-white tea set. Mrs. Milburn discovered it amongst the housewares you brought from Stotleigh Hall. She did not believe it came from Mr. Brummell as a thank-you for that dinner your parents gave for the Prince Regent, but I told her I saw the note myself that accompanied it. And only hear what happened: now they must needs use it! I am dreadful sorry I opened my lips."

Briana, accustomed to ignoring Anselma's tirades, mulled over the baronet and the Brocco servant. When her footsteps slowed, Anselma urged, "Lady Briana, do hasten! Your tea is getting cold, and I know you are the one who likes it scalding hot."

"I can't imagine why anyone would pour for me before I am in the room."

"Nor I. But your cousin Chalandra does not care to have tea alone, and I thought I could find you at your easel. And Mr. Winshire and his sister Charmaine came about buying some lambs from Mrs. Milburn. They asked for you, and I was at a loss. I had no idea you were *outside*. Why didn't you tell me? I would gladly have come with you, Lady Briana. You should not take such risks going out alone; now, in particular, since the duke of Brocco and his servants are likely to walk or ride by this place. You never want them to see you out totally alone. Your hat's down—here, let me help you. My land, your chignon has fallen completely out!"

Briana slid an exasperated glance over her chaperone's frizzled gray locks on her lined forehead, and put a stop to her hovering by jerking her own brim forward with her free hand. "I took my cat for a walk, Anselma. I wouldn't think of disturbing you just for that."

Anselma slammed the heavy black door into place when they passed into the dim back hall of the rambling Tudor house. "Exercising the cat. I still think the servants could do that for you. I hope you haven't caught cold; September days get nippy. Here, let me take your leghorn to your room. My, but you picked up grass and moss."

Briana relinquished her hat to the eager fingers, saying, "I can't come to tea in my dirt, so I'll duck into the kitchen first." Seducing her toward Wookey's domain was the aroma of nutmeg in bread-and-butter pudding.

Having hidden the fish by backing through the swinging door, Briana hefted them to a shelf in the larder. Smiling at the stout red-faced cook, she hurried to the washstand. "If you have pudding for me, Wookey, I have some trout for you."

His silence as he cut her a steaming piece of his specialty did not surprise her. A Cotsaller born, but an *emigré* eight miles east of his birthplace, he embodied the nature of thinking long and speaking only when vital. Briana felt a kinship of sorts with him, for he was an oddity: a man in a cook's apron, even as he had been in his army days. When he saw her settled on the stool she frequented during their chats, he asked ominously, "You puttin' me on the glad-'n-sorry, Lady Briany?"

She shook her head, savoring the hot raisins while a dimple played at the corner of her mouth. She knew how Wookey felt about buying fish or fowl: glad to have it, but sorry to have to pay for it. He was proud of the thrift he exercised with the kitchen accounts. "Then where'd m'lady get fish?" he asked in suspicion.

"From a fisherman, who else?" she returned, twinkling at him.

He eyed her from under orange brows, then clapped the rolling pin over the tart crust.

"It was no poacher, so don't stand there with a growl on your face. It was one of the new duke's servants who gave them to us."

Wookey's blue eyes came round, studying her. "Hmmm!" was all he said.

Having finished her treat, Briana sighed, "Heavenly, as usual. Now I won't starve at tea. You'll find the fish with the braids of onion and garlic, which is a hint." Her parting remark was, "Remember the lemon, the almonds, and your special sauce. It must be the best in Warwickshire."

She cast a look at the row of curved, scaled backs and round, staring eyes in the shadow of the larder. A strange but welcome gift. But how mortifying to be found weeping on the ground by Sir Reginald Channing, baronet, whose name she had read in London society columns; and even worse somehow, by that unorthodox servant, Darnier.

Wouldn't Mrs. Milburn fly into the boughs if she knew Briana had the jump on Chalandra in meeting a baronet.

Briana's arrival at the breakfast table earlier that day had seemed to put Mrs. Milburn out of temper, likely because of Briana's change of appearance. For, "This morning, no more mourning!" Lucy the maid had sung out, flinging apart Briana's bed curtains.

Briana had stretched cheerfully and directed Lucy to send the black, gray, and lavender frocks, pelisses, and shawls to the workhouse in Shipston-upon-Stour. Lucy had chattered and fastened on Briana's slim form a pink Circassian gown collared in French work, exclaiming how her ladyship's complexion glowed. To celebrate her freedom, they let Briana's freshly washed hair fall in a mane of loose curls. This metamorphosis uplifted her, but at the same time, made her restless to be otherwhere

18

than this depressing house especially when she felt herself increasingly the butt of Mrs. Milburn's refractory attitude.

"What was it your father liked to play at that Almack's club in London?" Mrs. Milburn inquired, pretending not to notice the pink dress.

"Faro was what he liked best." Briana met her relative's hard brown eyes over the *Morning Post*. "Why do you ask?"

"I was reading how some other earl's art treasures are up for auction because he lost forty thousand at Almack's—or was it White's?—I forget. Your father was a member of both clubs, was he not?"

"Why, yes."

"That's likely it, if you would but face these things," said Mrs. Milburn. "He lost your future there, laying some monstrous wager—"

"Don't make suppositions and turn them into facts, Mrs. Milburn," Briana interrupted, her eyes dangerous.

The older woman looked arch. "I didn't precisely call it a fact, but we all know that *some* vice wiped him clean." Her expression turned peevish. "How vexing you can't touch your dowry money; the Misses Leechby need payment," she said, lifting the bill next to her plate.

"I only ordered one gown from them, and I paid it in person," Briana stated. "That bill must be for Chalandra's gowns."

"Oh no, I don't believe *all* these gowns were hers."

They both knew they were. Briana decided against taking breakfast in an atmosphere which boded contention. She took a pair of plums from the bowl, the post package containing the new book of Wordsworth from the drawing room, and, with her small white cat picking her dainty way through the dry grass, she sneaked downhill to the unkempt boundary of Milburn Place where the elderberry bushes grew thickly toward the

19

quarry ground. There she read the whole book of picturesque verse, grew sentimental over having reached her eighteenth year with no hope of coming out in London, and then dwelt over-long on her shortage of money to leave her entrapment.

With elbows propped on her swirled scarf, she had finally given way to her bottled-up tears of frustration. If only her parents hadn't both departed for heaven so early! They had never planned to leave her on the doorstep of Milburn Place, but Mrs. Milburn, who Briana did not even know at the time, had come to fetch her after the funeral. A year and a month had crawled by, and how the kind Mrs. Milburn had changed!

A prayer for courage had winged upward from Briana's heart. How unnerving that, at her weakest moment, two strange men had strolled into her sanctuary!

# Chapter 2

## Jealousy at Milburn Place

Briana sped up the walnut staircase covered in ancient red carpet worked throughout with faded golden E's. Deer antlers in profusion cluttered the carved paneled walls and beams of the Elizabethan Hall.

The earl of Stotleigh, Briana's father, had given this house to his kinswoman, only to hear it renamed Milburn Place. When the countess of Stotleigh had asked her husband why he gave the manor to such a woman as Mrs. Milburn, he explained that the ten-acre sheep plot and house were too much trouble to bother with so far from his own estates in Devon, and should pacify Oonagh Milburn for his set-down over the title she had tried to wheedle out of him.

The house was falling to rack and ruin, but Mrs. Milburn had not spent a shilling on it since Phineas Milburn had died a decade ago, for how could she then afford gowns and fripperies for her one asset: Chalandra?

Entering her chamber, Briana applied a brush to her long wind-blown curls, lifted them to her crown, and thrust in long pins, then pulled dry bits of grass from the lace at her wrists. She marveled again at that cocky Darnier fellow picking grass from her face. She knew she should forget the presumptuous man. She would rather consider the hint of romantic promise in Sir Reginald's eyes.

"You decided to come to tea," said Chalandra a minute later, casting her cousin a reproachful look from under arching brown eyebrows.

"Anselma forced me," said Briana, settling into her chair before the array of Brummell's porcelain. "Come down from your high ropes, Chalandra. I just prefer to be outdoors when I read my Wordsworth."

Chalandra grimaced. She cared little for poetry since the romantic Lord Byron had left England and no chance remained for her ever to meet him.

Briana handed the tepid tea to the maid. "A steaming cup, please." While Effie pattered away shaking her head at such wastefulness, Briana had leisure to take in the startling sight of Chalandra's newest costume. Her puffed yellow sleeves were adorned with stiff mint green ruffs pointing upward at her shoulders, rivaling the gauze Betsie of the same color which grew from a three-inch ruffle on her bodice to a foot-high splay behind her head.

"You are noticing my ruffs," observed Chalandra. *"De rigueur*, aren't they?"

"Yes. Certainly not to be overlooked. You resemble a fairy on the verge of flight."

Chalandra, who would not be made a cake of, checked at this, so Briana gave her a friendly, inquiring smile. "Your mother isn't joining us?"

"She has a migraine."

"What about?"

"Likely the state of our finances," Chalandra replied dismally.

"She'll feel better when the sheep money comes in.

She sold eighty head at last Shipston market. After her debts, it will still give her something."

Chalandra wasn't interested in sheep or finances. "Mother says Betsies and sleeve ruffs shouldn't be worn by the plump."

"Then *she* should not order them," quipped Briana before she could stop herself.

Chalandra's laugh tinkled. "There would be teacups shattered if she heard you say that!"

"You'll tell her, I'm certain."

"Do you take me for a wool-head? Why would I bring her wrath down on me?" Chalandra rearranged yellow and white dahlias in the vase.

"*Exactement*," murmured Briana. "She would deny your next request for a gown with a *two*-foot Betsie."

Chalandra shot Briana a withering look, and chose the most perfect of the apricot tarts.

Sliding the other two off the plate, Briana said, "But not to worry your head, for in will come the Leechbys next week because you and your dear parent will have decided that you have nothing new to wear to the assembly," she said, accurately portraying the erratic behavior of Mrs. Milburn.

"I hope you don't mind, but I have your newest *Journal des Dames* in my room, and am having another gown copied by the Misses Leechby. *If* they can do it." Chalandra raised her dainty profile to scan the topiary beyond the torn lace curtains. She was showing off her elaborately piled coiffure—mint and yellow ribbons threaded through the heavy brown coils—and Briana wondered for the fortieth time how Chalandra's slim neck held it all up.

"Why would I mind?" Briana felt in need of no more frocks for this country life, for she was just dipping into the new wardrobe she had amassed a year ago before her parents died. Chalandra, however, thrived on show and

23

admiration so Briana said, "Your curls are very fetching today."

"Thank you. Lester and Charmaine liked them, also. They stared at my gown, though. I'm sure they've never seen anything like."

"Certainly not around here. It's much more lavish than what one normally sees in the country." Chalandra took this as her due, and Briana moved to a topic she half-feared to bring up. "I feel the need to question your flirtation with Lester Winshire, Cousin."

"You have no right to offer any opinions about it, Bri. He's *my* admirer."

"Chalandra, you know you have shamelessly strung him along like—like fish on a line—and you care nothing whatsoever about him!"

A sly smile flickered across Chalandra's thin lips. "Halt the inquisition, Bri."

"If I don't tell you what a shame it is to be snaring men and setting them loose wounded, who will?" Briana saw that her riposte hit the mark, for Chalandra's padded chest rose and words failed her.

In a kinder tone Briana added, "And all this correspondence your mother encourages you to keep with Oxford men; is it fair to them? You have each thinking he's the only one. I fear for you, Chalandra dear, for you are in danger of closing the clamps on your reputation." Briana felt relief at finally having made her cousin listen.

"You are just *jealous* of her!"

Their eyes riveted to the doorway from whence the accusing voice had come. Mrs. Milburn, swathed in an orange and blue paisley shawl sporting seven-inch black tassles, advanced like a cold wind into the room. Either her migraine was excruciating or she had recovered with new torment for her titled relation.

"My daughter has a *fine* reputation, and she is sought-after! All men take to Chalandra's beauty and wit, and you and I both know it. That is nothing but envy showing in you!" Oonagh Milburn's brown-gray curls quivered with the effort taken by this vehement speech.

"I beg your pardon?" Briana shot back incredulously. "Is that what you believe, that I harbor jealousy? Mrs. Milburn, with all due respect, you are mistaken."

"I'm *not* mistaken!" shouted Mrs. Milburn. "What else is that kind of talk? Poor Chalandra, because she has so much charm and daintiness—and is so petite—you can't endure it!"

Another poke at Briana's five feet eight inches. As if standing or sitting next to five-foot Chalandra could ever let her forget. Briana struggled to hold her tongue. With an appearance of regal calm, she slowly stirred her tea.

Believing her darts had not pierced after all, Oonagh Milburn's chins lifted. "I will not countenance your speaking to my daughter in the malicious way you were when I walked in—do you mark me? This is our house, and we do not have to keep you here. You have no right to cause upset to Chalandra's happiness. Or to my health, for that matter."

"Oh, my!" expelled Briana, rising to her feet. She gripped the carved chair back and said with admirable control, "If it's trouble you wish to avoid, Mrs. Milburn, you ought to consider what is being done to Lester Winshire, Newton James, and how many others? I was telling Chalandra what I think about deceptive attitudes; about playing games with foolish, honest men."

Mrs. Milburn turned livid and jerked instantly to her feet from the sofa into which she had plunked. "Deceptive! Oho—you are at it again! *So* envious because Chalandra has all the men courting *her!*"

Her daughter fiddled nervously with the curls at her nape, a smile pulling her mouth which she tardily bent to hide. "Mother," she drawled reprovingly. "Give her a

25

chance. She doesn't even try."

Briana shot her cousin a disgusted look, and pushed the chair scrapingly over the floor. "Mrs. Milburn," she said, turning, "I feel it is deplorable ethics—you, as a mother, teaching your daughter to *collect suitors*. What do you plan to *do* with all of them?" Turning in an angry swish of skirts, she strode across the hall, leaving a stunned silence behind.

But silence never lasted in a room inhabited by a riled Mrs. Milburn. Briana barely reached the kitchen when the flow of bitter invectives was launched. She slipped through the door before she was forced to hear particulars.

Wookey looked up from the fish bodies he was decapitating. Briana's beautiful blue eyes blazed, her brows formed a dark line, and she was shaking.

"The chimney smokes, eh, Lady Briany?"

Attempting to squelch her impotent anger, Briana brushed by the two kitchen maids peeling potatoes, carrots, and turnips. Their caps remained properly lowered while their eyes lifted sidewise in curiosity.

Briana loosened her fists with a will. "Wookey," she sighed, averting her gaze from the bloodied fish, "I am out of sorts. Where did you put my pudding?"

"Sally, git it out'n the larder, skawt," he shooed away the carrot peeler. "What be this mugglement, now?" he asked gruffly of Briana in his kindest manner.

"Injustice, Wookey," she whispered, turning her back on the maids as tears threatened to wet her eyes. The mongrel trotting in his revolving cage high in the wall looked down at her with eyes of pity.

Briana gave a short laugh. "My advice doesn't change a thing. She deliberately misunderstands me and rages on. They just don't care what they do to people."

Wookey wiped his hands on his apron and leaned near. "A fly-by-night, is Missis," he explained, "tryin' to git every man to 'ang 'is 'at, an' yet not 'ang it, know what I mean? Waitin' to pounce on the biggest purse."

He drew her away from the maids who had quieted their chopping and the pot boy whose brush had ceased altogether. "Mr. Milburn was under petticoat government, an' young miss 'as no chance o' bein' upstandin' like you, Lady Briany. Ain't 'ad the breedin' neither," Wookey added as the clincher.

Briana leaned her willowy frame against the cupboard door and said, "Perhaps you're right."

"Mr. Milburn, I knew 'e made a mistake when I sees 'un like a fool in a fit two days after meetin' missis, her all batty eyes and talkin' sudden of makin' to Gretna Green for a marriage in the smithy." Wookey shook his head with foreboding. "When a man ties a knot with 'is tongue that 'e can't untie with 'is 'ands on such short acquaintance, 'e's bound to be a mumblin' like a dumbledore in a pitcher afore long. A reminder to you, Lady Briany, to do unlikewise."

"Yes, Wookey," she said, a grateful smile welling up past the lump in her throat. "What would I do without you to pluck me up?"

He ignored that entirely and cut her an extra-generous helping of the pudding. "Sally, fetch Lady Briany cup o' tay. Them wimmin couldna let 'er finish in there."

Seating herself in the hearth corner, Briana watched the flames. They leapt high when juices fell hissing from the roasting ham on the spit, turned by the running dog. That is what she does, thought Briana, she hisses more and more every day. It wasn't enough for Mrs. Milburn to vaunt Chalandra's merits to the skies for anyone who would listen or to clothe her in replicas of fashion plates; now she had to have Briana jealous of her.

And those gullible men. Were they such corkbrains that they could not see past Chalandra's inviting smiles and mysterious brown eyes to her lack of heart? Jealous!

Mrs. Milburn judges me by her own emotions. Should I perhaps envy Chalandra for having a parent when I do not?

The earl and countess of Stotleigh, Briana's beloved parents, had contracted the highly contagious cholera, and as hard as Briana had prayed from the safety of their neighbor's home, they had succumbed within two days of one another. Now the sorrow had diminished, but Briana was treated as someone out of her realm. The utmost respect was paid her in Shipston despite the fact she resided with poor relations, and it seemed that her every intake of breath was discussed—interpreted by sharp-eyed gossips as nostalgia for her former life. Speculation abounded over whether such an extraordinary creature as Lady Briana Rosewynn would ever find a mate in this life.

Briana leaned back, thinking. Should she leave Milburn Place? She doubted that she had enough money to pay turnpike charges for her own traveling chariot. It would be cheaper to take the "Tantivy" or the "Courier" stages from Shipston. She would have to take Anselma with her. That was small comfort. The spinster had taken on the role of Lady Stotleigh's companion and Briana's chaperone after arriving from Ireland unannounced three years ago, claiming a distant kinship. No matter how irksome Briana found her, she could never desert the poor woman with a clean conscience, for the countess had put up with her uncomplainingly, and even had had Anselma teach them the crocheting of lace which was popular in Monaghan.

Briana wondered where in England she could go. Her childhood home in Devon had been sold by her father on his deathbed. He had not enough money left for Briana to keep it for another year, for he had paid all his accounts and made it known there was very little aside from her dowry. In his last note he wrote incoherently that he had lost a piece of paper which might have given her another house to live in. He had been so sorry.

In her misery at losing them, Briana had raged that she didn't care. Now she cared a great deal. She suspected Mrs. Milburn had taken her in with hopes of monetary gain, but there her relative's aspirations had been dashed.

Briana thought of her sixteenth year when her mother, with no satisfying explanation, took Briana to Bath instead of London for the winter. The earl took his place in the House of Lords, as usual, and they did not see him until the season was over in June. Briana was still perplexed by that separation, and could not imagine how her father depleted his whole fortune that year.

The earl of Stotleigh's affairs, and the uncertainties thereof, were being processed by his solicitors in London. Mr. Runton gave no clue to the reason for the delay, but assured Briana it would all be worked out. In the eleven months since he had spoken the words, she had had two letters from him which requested her continued patience in the intricacies of their legal investigations.

"Is Lady Briana in here?" The voice of Anselma came sharply over the supper preparations. "Oh, there you are," Anselma prattled, setting her sights on Briana. "Chalandra says you left in the midst of tea. Why, what is the matter?"

Wookey stepped into her path. Briana was startled to hear him punctuate gruffly, "Lady Briany's mumchancin' in 'er corner, wantin' to be alone."

"Alone! How can she be alone in all this commotion? You make no sense. Furthermore, a lady should not frequent a kitchen. Especially, Mr. Wookey, when this kitchen is presided over by a man. It is my duty to remind her of the fact. Please move aside."

Wookey did not budge. "Step a foot forrard, twunt do you no good."

Trying to sound playful, Anselma warned, "I shall go around."

Wookey leaned forward. "Twunt 'ave 'er flommoxed by the likes o' you!"

The whole staff was staring. Briana felt like laughing.

Anselma turned on her heel. Ramrod stiff, she marched back to do just what she had said. Before the spinster reached the far end of the table, Briana took action at Wookey's peremptory motions toward the kitchen door. She ran over the leaf-strewn bricks of the herb garden and through the squeaking gate on the far side.

Fiddle on conventions and chaperones! As Wookey knew, she needed a reprieve from the women of Milburn Place.

# Chapter 3

## The Book of Wordsworth

Shadows slanted long in the evening chill as Briana ran to the grove of oaks fanned out in silhouette. A rook cawed at her intrusion and rose with flapping wings to a lofty perch. The breeze had blown away toward the Cotswolds, leaving Milburn Place in the hush of sunset.

She reached under the elderberry bushes, but her red volume of Wordsworth was nowhere to be found. Her heart sank at losing the new book she had ordered for the Shipston Reading Society, for if she didn't find it, she would be obliged to forfeit ten shillings sixpence, and she had looked forward to presenting the Wordsworth as her year's contribution.

Her agitated search led her peering behind trees near the lane which led to Brocco Park. A rhythmic crunch of horse's hoofs on new gravel sent her dashing behind a twisted oak. At the same time, Anselma's irate call of "Lady Bri-a-na!" came echoing clearly over the evening stillness.

The horse approached at a walk, halting at Anselma's second call. Briana jerked her pink flounce out of the

31

patch of fading light just before the chestnut gelding's nose appeared. She saw a bottle green coat and Darnier's wavy hair black above his forehead, his features in partial shadows. If statues could look as if they needed a shave from cheekbone to jaw, then Darnier resembled a sculpted museum piece. A conqueror, Briana decided, or Atlas with the heavens slipped from his injured shoulders.

Anselma broke twigs with her sturdy boots as she ventured across the shallow ditch to peer up and down the lane. At the sight of her, the gelding gave an angry whicker. She flung up her hands and screamed, "Stay away, st-stay away! I do not like horses, I never have, no never. They scare me, they do!"

Poor Anselma, thought Briana; she could truthfully make the same speech about men.

Darnier's voice carried an undercurrent of mirth. "Take no fear, my good woman, I have my horse under control."

Anselma regarded him rigidly, her mouth in nervous spasms, her fingers clutching her gown as she prepared for hasty retreat.

"I believe I heard someone calling out. Was it you, Mrs.—?" He looked at her questioningly. His horse, the whites of his eyes enlarging, gave a sudden snort through his nostrils.

Anselma turned with a shriek, and bolted. As she tottered up the hill, Darnier was heard to chuckle regretfully, "Whatever possessed you, Hougoumont?"

He dismounted with deliberation and threw the reins over a low branch. From the breast pocket of his coat he withdrew a slim volume bound in red. It looked like Briana's Wordsworth. She put her hand on her heart in relief.

He hunted for a certain page and stood there reading, a ghost of a smile hovering on his lips. He tucked the open book beneath his elbow, and with eyes squinting, scanned the towering oaks, walking until he stood beneath a yellowing elm. Plucking a leaf, he twirled it between his fingers while he contemplated something on the page before him. Briana could not see what his next actions accomplished, as his back was turned, but the gold binding flashed as he closed the book.

Then he walked onto Milburn grounds. She tried to see where he went but could not, so she waited, wondering how long she was trapped in her crouching position. The dampening earth was making her shiver.

The hack shook his mane, bridle clinking. Darnier came into view again before Briana heard his footfall. He turned the animal around and swung slowly into the saddle. Scanning the park and yet missing her behind the tree, he clicked his tongue. Briana watched the silhouette of horse and man vault up the hill through the leafy archway leading to the twinkling lights and the eight hundred manicured acres of Brocco Park.

Curiosity burned within her. She sped to the oak grove in deep dusk and burst around the tree trunk to stare at the ground. She saw nothing, but when she reached beneath the elderberry bush, she felt the pile of oak leaves and beneath it, a corner of her book.

The leather was warm. When she balanced the book on its spine, it opened to the page where lay the yellow elm leaf. She was surprised to see a small rectangle of paper beneath. Her heart began to thud unaccountably as she unfolded the sheet. Embossed at the top was the Brocco crest. Slashed in sabrelike script were the words:

Your ladyship:
The duke of Brocco wishes to express his gratitude for the changes effected in his private suite. He feels your ladyship has shown superior taste.

33

His Grace asks you to approach the tree which bears this leaf tomorrow afternoon at four o'clock to accept a token of appreciation from him.

Darnier, for Brocco

Briana put a hand to her temple and smiled in happy wonder at the words. She had received a sum of money before she began her decorating for the absent duke, and had turned that money over to Mrs. Milburn to more than pay for her year's keep. The remainder was promised Briana upon the duke's inspection. Perhaps that was it—the remainder of her pay. It would be welcome now indeed.

Four months after the eleventh duke had died, his heir and successor had stopped at Brocco Park for a night, and the next morning had ordered his rooms redone. The late duke's housekeeper had suggested Lady Briana Rosewynn for the task of redecorating. The Brocco housekeeper knew all about Lady Briana's artistic abilities thanks to Anselma, who had been the provider of such details at their occasional teas together.

The rooms Briana had refurbished at Stotleigh Hall with her mother had given Briana plenty of experience. The Brocco project became an outlet on which to focus when Mrs. Milburn began to show her true nature. It had been great fun to spend someone else's money and to order whatever items would creatively enhance the majestic rooms.

It was said in Shipston that the twelfth duke, the new unknown, moved about by means of a Bath chair, a result of an injury to his legs while fighting with Wellington at Waterloo last year. He was touted as a hero, sight unseen and rumors unverified. The Milburn groom reported that the duke's servants just arrived were a close-mouthed lot, and nothing was learned from sharing a mug at the Black Horse with one of them.

Whether the duke had married was uncertain; most thought not. He was said to be going on forty, according to Mrs. Brewer, Shipston's most gifted gossip. Briana sighed in glad relief. Whatever he was, he liked his rooms.

She turned her steps toward the gabled half-timbered manor and heard bleats and bells and the bark of the sheep dog as the flock was chased into the sheepcote for the night. Slipping into the back hall, fragrant with the smell of cooking ham, Briana aimed to avoid the drawing room and whisk herself up the stairs without being seen.

Chalandra emerged from the music room having crashed a final chord on the spinet. "Where have you been, Bri? Anselma's turning the house upside down looking for you."

"Retrieving my dear Wordsworth. I could hardly leave him to mildew out on the lawn, could I?" Briana descended two steps and searched Chalandra's brown eyes. "Is your mother still upset?"

"She is always upset," expelled Chalandra below her breath.

Briana touched her cousin's hand on the newel post. "I'm sorry there has to be such war in this house. But she cannot go on accusing me."

"She can," attested Chalandra, "but you certainly do not have to take it. You held your own rather splendidly; she was quite miffed. Shall we go to your room?"

"Is it still mine?"

"In spite of her talk, I hardly think Mother would throw you out."

"I imagine I should be relieved to hear you say so. What concerns me more at the moment is whether you have taken a pet at what I said." Briana searched her cousin's narrow, pretty face.

"No, not at all," said Chalandra airily. "I expect you're right."

Briana looked her amazement.

"Granted, Bri, you seem to see us better than we do ourselves. It was quite shocking to realize it. After all is said and done," Chalandra sighed, "it's impossible to find husband material from these country yokels."

Briana's suspicions rose at this turnabout. She entered the room without comment, and set Wordsworth on the rickety escritoire.

Chalandra dropped into the patchy pink armchair. Her thoughts were revealed with the words: "I wonder what this new duke of Brocco looks like."

"I believe we're all wondering that."

Chalandra rose suddenly, surveyed herself in the glass, and rustled to the door. "I can't sit here chatting; I must have my hair redone."

"Whatever for? It looks neat as can be."

"I have an idea for a certain piece of lace if Frances can only thread it through right this time. Ta ta. Dinner's been moved to quarter of eight."

"Why such a fashionable hour? Is the duke coming?" Briana called after her. Why else would Chalandra improve upon a perfect coiffure? Not for an ordinary dinner between the three of them. Chalandra offered no answer, though she must have heard.

Briana looked into the mirror in alarm. An hour to ready herself. Was it possible that the new duke of Brocco would come to Milburn? The old duke never had.

Loose pins hung from Briana's chignon and she looked like a hoyden. Pulling the bell rope for Lucy, Briana snatched up her book, perusing the note once more. Mr. Darnier must be His Grace's secretary, and well-educated judging by the letter he had penned.

It suddenly occurred to her to look in the book itself which he had been reading. The leaf still marked the page. Three of Wordsworth's poems were printed there. "The Tables Turned" was the first, and it began:

> Up! up! my friend, and quit your books;
> Or surely you'll grow double.
> Up! up! my friend, and clear your looks;
> Why all this toil and trouble?

"Indeed!" huffed Briana, her eyes lighting. No doubt she had looked ghastly weeping, and with the impressions of grass blades on her skin. This Darnier fellow had arrogance indeed to remind her of it in the very poetry she had been reading.

Briana ran her eyes over the first stanza of the next poem. It was "Lines Written in Early Spring":

> I heard a thousand blended notes,
> While in a grove I sate reclined,
> In that sweet mood when pleasant thoughts
> Bring sad thoughts to the mind.

Recline in a grove she had done, listening to the nature sounds with half an ear, but pleasant thoughts had not occurred to her so this poem did not fit. Did he mock her? The third poem—oh my!—was:

> She was a phantom of delight
> When first she gleamed upon my sight;
> A lovely apparition, sent
> To be a moment's ornament;
> Her eyes as stars of twilight fair;
> Like twilight's, too, her dusky hair;
> But all things else about her drawn
> From May-time and the cheerful dawn;
> A dancing shape, an image gay,
> To haunt, to startle, and way-lay.

Briana clapped the book shut. She knew that the smirking Darnier would never have meant her to think this poem relevant—would he? What a taunting man he was; hadn't she seen his lips curve?

Her maid scratched on the door. "You must perform miracles, Lucy," Briana said, suddenly flushed. "I'll wear the white crepe round dress with the ruched hem, and my locks need more curl."

"Yes, my lady." Unhooking Briana's frock, Lucy said, "I heard the duke cannot come."

"The duke of Brocco? Was he truly invited for tonight, then?" Mrs. Milburn must be mad.

"That he was, your ladyship. My brother took the message there and back himself."

So Mrs. Milburn had not wasted a day, but had instantly encroached on a peer of the realm with an invitation. Briana knew she should be ashamed of the gladness she felt that His Grace had declined. His acceptance would have been an intolerably large plume in Mrs. Milburn's turban.

Mrs. Brewer, who with her silent husband had been invited at the last minute, expressed this thought in more tactful terms at table. "Why, Oonagh, don't you think you are overstepping? I declare, he has just arrived, after all, and I believe you should observe conventions and wait until he pays you a call. One cannot invite a duke to one's house as one does the parson."

Mrs. Milburn replied with a sharp laugh, "I'm certainly not afraid of asking the duke of Brocco here. I'll do so again in a few days' time when he has had a chance to settle in. One must be neighborly, and who else will His Grace have but me?"

Briana uttered a soft groan, which Mrs. Brewer heard. Their eyes met. Likely they had the same thought: the duke must be thrown together with Chalandra, by fair means or foul.

# Chapter 4

## "We Live by Admiration, Hope, and Love"

The next day Chalandra said she must go to Shipston to pick up the gloves she had ordered, and asked if she could use Briana's landau, the weather turning fair.

"Fine with me," said Briana. "I'll come with you and call for the post."

Anselma and Frances had to accompany them as usual, sitting backwards and enduring the bright sunshine. Anselma related with feeling how risky it was for females to venture out their doors in this day and age. "There are men and wild horses on the loose in this very county!"

Briana was hard put not to laugh, and pulled her parasol across her face.

Chalandra said, "I am sure that is true. How unwise to venture out at all," then gave Briana a roll of her eyes behind the light umbrella.

"But you see, Anselma," said Briana, emerging with a straight face, "we are going out of the county to Worcestershire, so we should have nothing to fear."

The prospect was panoramic as they rounded the bend, and Wolford, the coachman, hopped down to set the brake for the descent. Briana breathed the crisp air and took in the view of Stow-on-the-Wold in the southwest, Bourton Hill, and honey-colored Broadway Tower standing sentinel in the west. Fields harvested or plowed lay between groves of green, and flocks of sheep dotted the meadows. Ahead was the shadowed beauty of Ilmington Hill, and Brailes Hill with its ruler-straight line of trees. Briana, though missing at times the heathered moors and rocky outcrops of Devon, had become particularly fond of this view.

The Stour Brook glistened in the sun as they passed, and she pictured Sir Reginald and that Darnier character fishing there. Brocco's battlements rose pale gold and regal through the oaks. What could she possibly say to His Grace this afternoon?

The turnpike teemed with gigs, farm wagons, and passenger coaches, and the two brunettes beneath the parasols received more than common notice, a situation in which Chalandra reveled. After the landau passed through the tollgate, she directed Wolford to halt in Church Street where she and Frances alighted at the glover's shop. "I'll meet you at the George, Bri, where Wolford can get us each a glass of cordial," declared Chalandra daringly. She was aware that passersby and shopkeepers were looking at Lady Briana and, of course, her own ornamental person.

"I'll meet you at the *tea house*, Chalandra," corrected Briana, rolling her eyes. Her cousin would try anything for attention.

Wolford, watching Chalandra flounce into the shop with her maid in tow, muttered, "Pig's eyes ain't always pork."

Briana laughed.

40

Wolford jauntily tooled the team past Shipston Church with its square embattled tower from which melodious change-ringing filled the air. As they halted inside the George's arched inn-yard gate, around the corner from Custard Lane came a ringing of rapid hoofs on the stone paving. It materialized into Sir Reginald Channing on a spirited brown hunter.

Anselma gasped and uttered, "What did I tell you? Wild men on wild horses everywhere!"

Briana choked back a giggle.

"Lady Briana Rosewynn! How providently met!" Rex's eyes glowed as he dismounted and led his splendid horse toward them.

Anselma demanded, "Lady Briana, how do you know that man?"

Resisting the stiff fingers on her arm, Briana called, "Good day, Sir Reginald. Are you here alone?"

"Yes, the duke is closeted over accounts, and I was in need of more stimulation than the inside of a library could provide. He set me free until this afternoon."

"Do you plan to stay long at Brocco?"

Relinquishing his horse to an ostler from the inn, Rex replied, "As long as His Grace requires my assistance." His smile flashed down at her, and he explained, "Brocco came into this dukedom at least twenty years before he expected to. What I mean is, the late duke was only fifty-three when he died. Our new duke expected his father to inherit, but his father, a London banker, died six months ago in a phaeton accident. So, naturally, our new duke feels he has a few matters on which to educate himself."

Rex drew his crop between his gloves and added, "At the risk of boring you, Lady Briana, I'll refrain from going into management of estates and tenants with you. It's quite enough to expound on that with him. May I say instead that your ladyship vastly improves the scenery of

41

these rural climes?" He took in her white spenceret over an ice yellow muslin gown, and smiled into her dark blue eyes beneath the beribboned French hat.

"You do not appreciate our lovely town?" she asked in mock hurt.

He turned to survey the central square of Heigh Street. Half-timbererd edifices with projecting upper stories snuggled with steep-roofed shops of honey Cotswold stone or gray-blue lias. Diamond panes from mullioned windows reflected the sun. Rex, squinting, revolved on his heel, dutifully surveying the brick facade of the George and the high bow window next door. Briana made a startlingly beautiful portrait at its base.

"I might stand here all day and admire Shipston's architectural merits were there no tenderer subject for my eyes," murmured Rex.

Anselma had keen ears even through the peal of the bells. "Lady Briana, we must go to the post office!" Commotion from the inn yard drowned out her words.

"Oh no, a bustling coaching center," observed Rex with drollery as a yard of tin gave a blast and the "Tantivy" came rumbling out of the George's inn yard, filled to bursting with passengers inside and out. Offering his arm to Briana, he said, "Let us escape this melee and go inside."

"Pardon me for speaking up, sir," said Anselma, bristling, "but my lady does *not* take refreshment in public rooms with gentlemen."

"Why, certainly not," said Rex, looking askance. "I am engaging a private parlor."

"Sir, I do not find that proper!"

"What would meet with your good judgment, then?"

Anselma clearly wanted to send him on his way but lacked the courage to do so. Her mouth worked nervously.

Briana suggested, "Since we are taking space in the inn yard, why don't we have Wolford move the landau here into Heigh Street, and we can take our refreshment sitting in it? After all, it's a perfect day, and autumn will soon be upon us."

"What a plan," commended Rex.

Anselma stood bereft of words, so Briana told her to see it done and then to wait in the landau. "We will only walk to Butchers Row for my post."

With an inviting lift of his eyebrows, Rex offered his arm. Briana found him a striking escort in his deep blue riding coat. The tassels on his Hessians danced as he and Briana strolled through the Market House arches where men and a few industrious women were setting up stalls for tomorrow's market. Now it would be all over Shipston that Lady Briana had found a gentleman of the nobility. Briana, for once, did not mind their curiosity, for at Rex's side she felt impervious to the stares as she never had when appearing in the streets with Chalandra or Anselma.

Briana's heart leapt as the postmistress handed her a letter from Mr. Runton, her solicitor. "Do you mind, Sir Reginald? I have waited long for this," she said, her tone conveying her urgency.

"Please, call me Rex. And read your letter, by all means."

Breaking the red seal, she leaned in the doorway and read:

My lady,

On behalf of the firm of Runton, Colier, and Smythe, I am happy to report that the late earl of Stotleigh's affairs are now settled. All particulars will be unfolded to you in person; however, I believe it will please you to know that you are in

43

possession of a house in Berkeley Square which may be inhabited by you at any time. Should you wish to inspect it, send me word, and I will have a skeleton staff hired for your arrival.

With your assent by return post, I will send you a note for two hundred pounds, on any bank you name, for your journey to London.

I remain your respectful servant,
Sidney Runton, Solicitor

Briana stared at the spidery writing. *She* had a house in London? Impossible. Her father hadn't even succeeded in hiring a lodging in ultra-fashionable Berkeley Square. Mr. Runton must be mistaken.

She looked at Rex quizzically, trying to figure it out. "It sounds as though I have money as well. Isn't two hundred pounds a monstrous sum for a mere trip to London?"

"I would say so, even staying at the best inns, yes."

Her spirits began to soar. Was it possible it was true? That she could be free of Milburn Place? And, hope of all hopes, free of Mrs. Milburn?

"It must be good news."

"Yes!" Briana flashed a smile. "I've been summoned to London to inspect my house. I never knew I had one there, you see."

"Ah, how very providential." His brows lifted pleasantly. "When do you go?"

"I don't know how soon I can leave, but you have no idea what a relief this will be. It is the most lowering thing to live with relations." Whereupon he asked her if she would mind expounding, and she told him briefly of her parents' death and the succeeding course of her life.

"Then I congratulate you, Briana! Things are looking up, are they not?"

"They are, but I dare not weigh the wool before it's off the sheep."

"I'm with you there. Likely the least said about your affairs to these relations of yours, the better, *n'est-ce pas?*"

"That is wisdom indeed." As they strolled along, Briana glowed with breathless good spirits. Chalandra could be seen fanning herself in the east arch of the Market House, doubtless hoping for male eyes to admire her in the pink promenade dress with its ladders of pea green bows. Briana knew that Rex couldn't have missed seeing the fetching sight, but he did not make the mistake of looking again. He guided Briana through the cool shade and out to where Anselma sat propping Briana's parasol in the landau, and Molly from the George stood waiting with a tray of carafe and glasses, fruits and Warwickshire scones.

Rex handed Briana to her seat. Molly served them from a porcelain tray, pouring into crystal goblets sweet ratafia for Lady Briana and Anselma, and a long glass tankard of local elderberry wine for Rex.

Briana, from the corner of her eye, watched Chalandra dispense with her maid, pat her curls in a window, and make her way toward the landau.

Rex lifted his tankard to Briana. "Soon it will be all the crack to take refreshment in one's carriage *à la Lady Briana.*"

Chalandra looked positively bursting to know where Briana had acquired a male escort. "Briana, who is our guest?" was the way she put it, twirling her green parasol. Her eyes fluttered up and down Rex with his long legs crossed and the brim of his beaver shading his eyes.

He shot an inquiring look at Briana, then lithely jumped down.

"Rex, this is Miss Milburn, my cousin. Chalandra, Sir

Reginald Channing. He is staying with the duke."

These words had a marked effect on Chalandra. Holding too long to his hand, she parted her lips in a beguiling smile. "Why, that's but a stone's throw from us, Sir Reginald. My, aren't we honored, Bri, to have him here to improve our social life!"

Rex gave a short laugh and replied, "I had hoped to escape the social scene until I'm forced back to town."

"Where do you call home?" Chalandra asked as he settled less comfortably into the seat beside her.

"London during the Season, Berkshire otherwise."

Chalandra leaned toward him, pressing his arm. "You know, you are just the man to tell us about the duke." With a little laugh, she declared, "We have taken to calling him 'His Grace the Invisible' because he just has not been seen."

We have? thought Briana.

Chalandra chattered on. "He even declined my mother's invitation. Tell us, Sir Reginald, what is he like?"

Briana sighed, feeling it highly inappropriate for Chalandra to be asking such things of the man.

Rex crossed one knee over the other, accidentally lifting Briana's flounce, so he leaned forward and charmingly straightened it for her before he answered. Chalandra watched enviously. Anselma was positively rigid.

"I would say Brocco is a very intense person," he said. "He shakes the hand of the Lord Chancellor in a month's time, and then he sits in the House of Lords. He studies and corresponds until I fear he'll wear his eyes out." Rex turned to Briana. "But he's got himself a secretary, which helps a great deal."

Briana nodded, thinking of Darnier and his well-executed letter.

46

"But what does the duke look like?" asked Chalandra.

"The ugliest man I ever saw," said Rex.

"A fine thing to say about a friend of yours," Chalandra crowed, wide-eyed with speculation.

Rex chuckled. "Sadly, 'tis true."

Briana studied him, wondering.

This conversation ceased as a harried-looking Frances approached with packages in her arms. Rex handed his empty tankard to the dimpling Molly from the inn. "It's been a pleasure, Lady Briana," and turning, he added, "Miss Milburn."

"You must call me Chalandra," purred that one, gifting him with her most flirtatious pose, shoulder lifted.

Wolford snorted and pointed the horses homeward. Chalandra waved at Rex. "My, what a specimen!" she expelled. "Where on the planet did you find *him*, Bri?"

Anselma and Frances hung on her answer.

"I . . . I've known him from before," Briana decided it most expedient to say.

Back at Milburn Place, Chalandra followed Briana to her chamber, dropped onto the bed, and said, "I saw Newton James in town. He wasn't too elated about the duke's arrival at Brocco."

"Why should he be, anyway?"

"He fears rivalry. Isn't that amusing? And I'll just lay a wager that Sir Reginald does, too, telling us that the duke is ugly."

Briana gave her a slanted look. "Perhaps. But regarding Mr. James, I saw you take him to the armor gallery after supper last Thursday. Satisfy me on this point: why did you go without a candle?"

"I doubt you'd understand even if I did tell you."

"Give my brain a chance," said Briana dryly.

"Well, first I showed him the épaulières and the cuirasses."

"Without light?"

Chalandra laughed, grasped one knee, and studied the chintz tester. "The moon came through the windows a little," she said slyly. "I let him hold my hand, then my waist . . . and then we kissed."

Briana's lashes flicked up. "You what?"

"Kissed! Like this, Briana." Chalandra stood up, embraced the bedpost, and with mouth pouted, rolled her head about on her little neck, made an exaggeratedly long smack on the old wood, and collapsed back on the counterpane with a trilling laugh.

"You didn't!" expelled Briana, thinking she probably did.

"Why not? He wanted it so."

"You mean *you* wanted it so."

Chalandra was full of her triumph. "He's fascinated with me."

"Fascinated to think he's found a woman of easy virtue! Is this what you've done with Lester Winshire and William Westleigh and—"

The superior look on Chalandra's face told much. "All men want to kiss women, don't you know that? Even Sir Reginald Channing does."

Briana eyed her coolly. "Well, I'm appalled that you give them all that option."

"Oh come, Bri—don't you find life utterly boring? If I couldn't kiss men and listen to their compliments, I'd just die."

"Yes," said Briana consideringly, "I've found life quite tedious of late, but that would never induce me to—" She broke off, recalling her encounter with Rex and Darnier, and the way that bold Darnier had touched her cheek.

"You really should try it sometime," suggested Chalandra, watching her. "But Bri, don't you find men from our church insipid? All they do is bow gravely, or venture tight little smiles. I find worldly men *much* more interesting."

"Obviously. Newton is certainly a rake, everyone knows that. You're taking your chances with that one."

"*Exactement.* Every chance I have, I take." Chalandra tittered gaily and left the room.

There is one, thought Briana, who daily needs my prayers.

# Chapter 5
## The Rendezvous

Briana's artistic script flowed rapidly across the paper as she wrote asking Mr. Runton to explain what he could by post, and to send the money to her bank in Shipston if she indeed had money.

Through the door Anselma called, "Do you plan to paint this afternoon, Lady Briana?"

"No, but I'm going outdoors." Too late Briana realized her mistake in revealing her plans.

"Splendid. I'll get my shawl." Anselma soon came into the room, drawing on olive suede gloves and a self-crocheted shawl. "My word, you've changed your yellow for rose red! I suppose, though, that that is a better color for walking, and I see you've got your half-boots on. Sensible. Lady Briana will want that chip-straw bonnet," she directed to Lucy, pointing.

Briana shook her head at Lucy in the mirror. "I'll have the dark red leghorn with the turned-up brim."

"Not the new one with the plumes and cherries!" Anselma exclaimed. "The only one you've bought since you came here?"

"Yes, it goes well with this spencer."

Anselma looked startled. "But, Lady Briana, isn't that for going to church and for paying calls? We are only taking a walk, for mercy sakes."

"Anselma, please refrain from crossing my wishes. Lucy, give me what I ask for."

Anselma said hollowly, "Lady Briana, I merely thought—"

"Yes, I know your thought was for preserving my good things, Anselma dear, but since there are few occasions on which to wear fashionable hats, let me at least enjoy wearing them on fine days."

Silence fell while Briana tied the black satin ribbons into a large bow at the side of her chin. Anselma was doubtless thinking her out-of-reason frivolous. Briana scoured her mind for a way to be rid of her duenna so she could meet the duke at four o'clock. Only a quarter-hour remained before she must appear beneath the elm tree.

Her last glance in the mirror gave her confidence, for the cherry red brought out her cheekbones and lips, and the black lace accentuated her dark-lashed eyes. It had been long months since she had cared about beauty.

When Anselma tiptoed off to change her bonnet for her better one, Briana asked Lucy if there were any walnuts on the ground.

"Yes, my lady, the first have started to drop."

"Bring a basket, please, Anselma," Briana directed as they descended the staircase.

Anselma asked blankly, "What for?"

Briana merely stole out the front door when Mrs. Milburn was safely in conference with her steward. With the duenna in her wake, Briana led the way uphill and down into the vale where the old walnut tree spread its

51

gray gnarled limbs to lift a canopy of yellow-green leaves.

"I have a craving for walnuts," Briana explained. Taking the basket, she stooped in her finery and started picking nuts from the ground and tossing them into the basket.

Anselma's face bore a shocked frown as she considered the walnuts strewn amongst the grass and leaves. "Let me pick some for you, Lady Briana," she said, forcing more enthusiasm into her voice than she obviously felt, "for you will spoil your gown if your hem hits those hulls. They stain anything they touch."

"Do they?" Briana jumped up in alarm. "I daresay you're right. Are you sure you don't mind? Is that your oldest frock? Good. And being brown, it won't show a thing."

When Anselma had revealed that it was a decade old and not to worry overmuch about it, she squatted, and with quick movements, took over the task.

As if inspired, Briana said, "I'll go check if we have any blackberries left. The maids can make jam. I may have to fetch another basket, but I'll come back to see how you're doing. Thank you for being so kind as to pick those walnuts for me. Let's hope there are enough for Wookey to pickle some," she concluded, and made good her escape.

Her heart began to thud in her bosom as she neared the lane where the odd elm stood. Doubtless coming here alone was improper, but it was unthinkable to have Anselma along putting such a different mood into the meeting with His Grace.

Beneath a leafy branch shadowed by the majestic lane of oaks, Briana could see a brown coat and white cravat. With his shoulders leaning against the elm, arms folded, a dark-haired man watched her approach. Oh, no, it was Darnier all alone.

"Mr. Darnier," she said, looking about. "Good afternoon."

"Good afternoon, your ladyship." Darnier bowed and Briana's heart lurched. "Is something wrong?"

"Where is . . . the duke?"

Darnier replaced his hat at an angle, his eyes bearing a glint of amusement. "Your ladyship expected to see His Grace here?"

Briana felt stupid and presumptuous. She tried to conceal this by saying, "I came to pay my respects to the duke of Brocco, as I took to believe from your letter, Mr. Darnier."

"I shall relay your sentiments to him, your ladyship," he returned just as formally. It sounded like mockery to Briana.

Observing her perplexity, he grinned. "I'm sorry that you perceived the message differently than it was intended. The duke prefers anonymity from the populace at the moment, but he wanted you to have this." He produced, from up in the tree, a large flat box of wine-colored leather embossed with a golden border.

Briana received it with widened eyes.

"And this," continued Darnier, extracting a purse from his breast pocket, "is the second payment for your services."

"Thank you kindly, but what *is* this?" she asked, looking at the case.

"Open it. His Grace will wish to know how you received it."

Briana looked directly into Darnier's watchful eyes and said, "By the way, the trout were delicious."

His smile was vastly refreshing, a flash of excellent white teeth. "Good," he said, and raised the cover of the box for her. Inside she saw an assortment of papers for sketching and painting, fastened at the top with a gold

53

clasp. In a separate compartment were tools: pens, ink, pencils, brushes, charcoal, and a set of water colors.

"How ingenious! This is a wonderful thing to carry out of the house." Suddenly doubtful, Briana said, "But how can I accept it?"

"How can you not?" Darnier countered.

"Ah yes, the duke would take offense if I returned it. Then I must send him a note of thanks."

"You have everything to do so here." Darnier indicated the case.

"Yes, it's a good idea to do it immediately," agreed Briana. "Would you mind uncorking this ink bottle, Mr. Darnier?"

"You may leave off the Mister," he said as he opened the bottle. "In this occupation of mine, I have no title." He supported the clipboard so she could write.

When Briana steadied the box to begin, his hand felt warm and vital, and she flushed at having touched him. That was one reason her concentration suffered in writing the missive. As she dipped her pen into the bottle he held, she was excruciatingly aware that he examined her from the black plumes arcing forward on her hat to the black lace dipping at her bodice. Why hadn't she fastened up her spencer! Signing her name, she stepped back feeling rather heated.

"I shall convey this at once to His Grace," Darnier assured her, holding it in the breeze to dry. He carefully folded it and tucked it into his breast pocket.

Grabbing at the shreds of her self-assurance, Briana took a few steps with him up the shady lane. "May I ask you something, Darnier?"

"Please do."

"Does His Grace really move about in a Bath chair?"

"He used to after the war, but he's not had to be so confined for the last few months. Weeks of climbing the

54

mountain slopes in Switzerland built up his strength. He can do most everything now."

"That's fortunate."

"Yes."

"Why did you devise such an odd rendezvous, Darnier? An elm leaf." Her thoughts flew to the poems he had marked, but nothing would induce her to mention *those*.

"The duke is a secretive man," said Darnier with a scheming look, "and knowing his wont to be—shall we say—quite an eccentric, I devised this method as one which would amuse him, which it did. He has very little to gladden his heart. The fact that you make a career of eluding your duenna also tickled his fancy. He used to hide from his tutor, you see."

Briana met Darnier's deep eyes with interest, trying to envision the strange duke.

"Lady Briana . . ."

Her attention was fixed on the sun-bronzed planes of his face, and she was caught wondering how one acquired such a picturesque secretary. She supposed it was not so difficult if one were a duke.

"Yes?" she prompted.

"Would you consider decorating the suite of rooms next to the duke's?"

"I . . . please explain."

"Since there is no duchess, the duke desires you to furnish them with a decor which, in your feminine opinion, seems fitting."

"Fitting for a future duchess?"

"Yes. He hopes you would find this work more to your liking."

Briana felt excited at the prospect. "Is His Grace betrothed?"

"Not yet, but he's thinking a wife would be an asset

when he takes his seat in the House, and an heir would certainly be desirable."

"I see." Briana knew that she would relish the project. As she opened her mouth to respond, she stopped in her tracks. "But I'm going to London, Darnier."

"When?"

"As soon as I hear from my solicitor."

"Hmm." He rubbed his jaw which she noted had been shaved today, but still retained a hint of a shadow.

"I cannot see disappointing His Grace," she regretted. "He has been so generous."

Darnier seemed to be turning this over as he watched a squirrel leap from one branch to another, cheeks puffed with wild hazelnuts.

Briana brightened. "Darnier, what if—" She slipped away so that a branch of the young tree separated them. Thinking was becoming difficult with this attractive man observing her every move. "What if I were to come to Brocco Park, decide what is needed, and take all the measurements? Then when I go to London I could buy everything in person. I believe that could work out more advantageously than sending away for samples."

Darnier laid his arms on the limb. "It sounds feasible to me," he said. "When can you begin?"

Briana was mesmerized by the autumn colors in his eyes: rust, brown, and green, with flecks of amber. She managed to say, "Today, if this plan finds favor with His Grace."

"I'll ask him, Lady Briana. Shall I send a message over as soon as I have his approval?"

An ant had traveled from the tree to Briana's neck, and as it ran ticklingly down to her bodice, she, with arms full, gave a mortified gasp.

Darnier's hand shot out and his deft fingers captured the ant from her soft curve.

Color flamed in her cheeks. The touch of his fingers had sent a delicious melting feeling through her bones. "Was it an ant?" she asked, not knowing what on earth to do about it. How screechingly improper this man was!

"Forgive me," he said in his deep voice.

"No, I—I should thank you, I—"

"You are welcome, Lady Briana." With a handsome grin, he added, "Whenever I can prevent you any . . . discomfort . . . I shall be happy to oblige your ladyship."

Exasperated, Briana turned away from the sparkle in his eyes, thankful for wide hat brims.

"Unless that is a mirage," he remarked, "your chaperone cometh." The top of Anselma's bonnet appeared in the distance. "If you slip toward the house in that direction, I'll endeavor to throw her off your scent by attacking from the lane. Adieu for now, Lady Briana. I shall be . . . in touch."

With a look full of meaning, he was off. Briana heard him whistling through his teeth as he headed for his prey.

Clutching her leather box, she made a dash behind the border hedge and succeeded in gaining the kitchen garden door, unable to shake off her confusion. So this was why Anselma kept such tight hold on Briana's leading strings! Things of an improper nature did occur between "wild" men and young ladies.

She latched the door to her chamber and dropped her armful onto the bed. The purse contained twice the amount she received in the beginning: a hundred pounds. Had the duke forgotten he had already paid her half? Was the man senile?

Briana rushed back to meet Anselma coming through the yew grove. Agitation was written all over her wrinkled face.

"Lady Briana, I had *such* a fright! That same man was in the lane, whistling madly! He even spoke to me and

57

came to look at these walnuts. I have never seen such a brash, forward creature! But you don't know about him, do you? Thank heaven for that! He scared me witless yesterday with his horse. I was so afraid he would see you somewhere by yourself. But you were in the house, I see. Thank the lucky stars! There weren't very many walnuts, but here they are. I really do think the servants should pick the rest that fall, not that I mind doing it for you, Lady Briana, especially knowing you are longing for the taste of them, but—"

"Thanks forever, Anselma dear," said Briana, weak with the urge to laugh.

# Chapter 6

## The Duke's Rebuff

"Go find out who that was," Mrs. Milburn directed Effie. From the tea table they had all heard the bell, then the front door closing.

When Effie shuffled back with a wealth of yellow roses cradled in her arms, all three women exclaimed in delight. With brown eyes snapping in pleasure, Mrs. Milburn declared, "For my daughter, no doubt."

Effie dumped them on the table. "Nay, for Lady Briana."

Mrs. Milburn's smile froze.

"Who on earth could they be from?" demanded Chalandra, lifting a card tied with lace to the stems. "Oops, pardon me. Well Bri, are you ever going to open it?"

Briana did not want to do so with three pairs of hostile eyes observing her, and almost wished Anselma in the room. Briana's title was written in a masculine sweep. The note, which she soon relinquished to Chalandra's eager fingers, said:

Dear Lady Briana,

Thank you for your kindness in Shipston. Here's hoping you're still wearing that yellow gown.

Rex

"What did you do for him in Shipston?" asked Chalandra, eyeing her curiously.

"Nothing!" protested Briana. "You were there." Her heart beat faster knowing that Rex admired her to the point of sending flowers. Explaining haltingly to a resistant Mrs. Milburn how Sir Reginald Channing was staying with the duke, Briana soon gave it up for it was obvious Chalandra had already told her version of the outing, which did not concur with the arrival of roses for Briana.

She excused herself, and took her note and flowers to the kitchen. There Wookey brought her a vase, poured in hot water from the tea kettle, and trimmed the thorny stems. As he handed them to her for arranging, he perused Rex's note lying on the table. "Got yerself a spark?" he teased. "'Bout time, I'd say."

"Oh hush," smiled Briana, inhaling fragrance from a half-dozen roses.

"There'll be no peace from them wimmin now, mark my words. Put on yer best armor, Lady Briany."

"What's that?"

"Keep yer head clear and your tongue in it, and see yer spark behind their backs."

The note from Darnier arrived by messenger the next morning, asking Lady Briana to come at her earliest convenience to Brocco Park to begin her decorating project. She chose a morning dress of turquoise batiste with triple-puffed sleeves. Lucy was tying white slipper ribbons around Briana's ankles when Anselma burst in to report that Mrs. Milburn and Chalandra were off to Shipston, for this was market day. Anselma thought it outrageous that they had not asked Briana to go along. "Especially since they took *your* landau."

But when Anselma heard where Briana was going, she was instantly in transports. "The Duchess's rooms! You are going to decorate the future Duchess's rooms? My heavens!" And she rushed to don her best lavender floral for the occasion.

The two women soon alighted from Briana's town chariot into the mist which rose visibly along the mansion walls as sunshine swirled through. The rays glinted on the oriel windows and warmed the honeyed stone facade to the third story where battlemented walks ranged along its front and domes graced each of the six towers. A fountain played in the center of the oval driveway, its splashing providing a backdrop for the calling of swifts as they darted down to tease at their reflections in the sparkling water.

The porter, new since Briana had been there, was a small, white-haired individual who silently ushered them to a reception salon off the great hall. In comical contrast, a large black-haired butler wheeled in a brass cart of various refreshments, and in a booming voice, offered his wares. Briana graciously declined, having just come from the breakfast table.

Briana started when Darnier appeared in the doorway, looking rakish in shirt sleeves and open waistcoat. "You rise early, Lady Briana," he said with a respectful bow of the head. To Anselma cowering behind her, he said, holding out his hand, "How glad I am that there is no horse between us this time, Mrs.—"

Anselma's open mouth clopped shut.

Briana said, with laughing censure in her eyes, "Darnier, this is Miss Anselma Snivelton. Anselma, Mr. Darnier, the duke's secretary . . . ?" She lifted her brow at him for verification.

He nodded at Briana, and expressed his great pleasure at being introduced to Miss Snivelton at last. Anselma sputtered something as she withdrew her hand, and the tiny network of red veins in her cheeks grew quite pronounced.

Offering Briana his arm, Darnier led her up the white marble staircase. She knew Anselma was having conniptions, but Briana felt it most appropriate for him to aid her up that long, oval staircase lest she trip upon her petticoat. She felt the strong arm beneath her fingers, and dared not look at him because she liked the feeling well. He made her feel utterly feminine, and yes—special.

Upon reaching the gallery she asked, "Is His Grace at home today?"

"Yes, my lady."

Briana withdrew an enamel box from her reticule. "May I send in my card and request a short visit? I would like to thank him personally for everything."

"By all means," said Darnier.

Briana took a calling card from the box, bent the upper left corner, and handed it to him. He advised her to be seated on the Louis Quatorze divan, and he entered the antechamber of the rooms Briana had redecorated.

Briana knew she had asserted herself rather boldly, not actually being invited by the duke for a visit. But she wanted in the worst way to see him, to find out what kind of man it was who sent her gifts sight unseen and overpaid her. If Anselma doubted Briana's wisdom in such a request, the thought of actually clapping eyes on this new duke must have been the deciding factor in keeping her tongue still.

The door had not clicked shut behind Darnier, so Briana and Anselma, in the silence of the spacious gallery, heard his deep tones but not his words as he explained her request.

"*Keep her out of here!*" came a roar from the inner chamber.

Anselma jerked bolt upright. Briana quailed and met Anselma's lashless eyes in astonishment.

Footsteps sounded, and Briana saw Rex's wavy head rising round the staircase. He was just in time to hear, "Are you touched in the upper works?" bellowing from the room.

Rex halted as if struck. He stared with comical dismay at the door.

"My word!" quavered Anselma, on the verge of running for life and limb.

Briana snatched her back. From within, Darnier's voice sounded calm but indistinct. Crystal clear came the rasping rejoinder. "Darnier, I want no woman looking at me! I'm a wreck and you know it! Keep her away, lock my door. Let her get on with her work."

Rex whistled.

Darnier reappeared, looking sheepish. "I am very sorry," he said, "but His Grace cannot see you today. He's . . . rather out of charity with himself."

"I regret to hear it," was all Briana could put into words. How could Darnier remain so pleasant working for such an ogre?

"I must apologize in his behalf, Lady Briana. Doubtless you heard a few inappropriate words," Darnier said, turning the key in the lock as directed.

Anselma looked positively alarmed when Briana accepted his invitation to overlook the rooms she was to decorate. "Gracious me!" she whispered. "It's right next door to *his!*"

"That's usually where a duchess has her rooms, Anselma, next to the duke's."

Darnier smirked at this exchange.

Briana said, "It's my impression he doesn't wish to see

63

us, Anselma, so there's no need to go into hysterics."

Passing through the antechambers with their Holland covers layered in dust, Briana turned the knob to the bedchamber. She fingered the frayed velvet draperies and commented that the room needed lightening up. Darnier drew the drapes wide at that, asking if it improved matters, but Briana pensively watched him. "Forgive my blatant curiosity, but why did he call himself a *wreck?*"

Rex shifted, fixing his eyes on Darnier.

The Brocco secretary fingered his dark jaw, apparently searching for the right words. Anselma inched her way into the room, examining with pretended interest each picture on the wall.

"The present duke, you see," said Rex before Darnier could speak, "was one of the defenders of the Hougoumont. That was the fortress, you recall, of which Wellington said 'The success of the battle of Waterloo depended on the closing of the gates of Hougoumont.'"

At Briana's look of recognition, Darnier picked up the story. "In that skirmish with the French, he—the present duke—was slashed in the leg and upper body—"

"Lord have mercy!" gasped Anselma.

Darnier's eyes lingered warily on her while she composed herself. "The Lord did have mercy. The duke is still alive after being injured by Boney's troops storming through the door; that is, before he and four others managed to close it. Now he wishes to remain unseen, especially by the fair sex."

"Oh, my sympathies are with him!" breathed Briana, quite affected. "Then His Grace is, in truth, a hero of our nation! He should be recognized."

"He wants none of that," said Darnier as he pulled a wing chair to the window where the light was good. He gestured her to sit. "I hope you won't take offense, Lady Briana, for his temper was nothing personal against you.

Heaven forbid. He is highly pleased with your work and your willingness."

"Oh yes," affirmed Rex, "I know that to be true. Still, Brocco is not a man you would wish to meet, for he's a bungling ox with the ladies."

Briana's surprise at another such disparaging statement seemed to be equaled by Darnier's. He regarded the mirthful Sir Reginald askance, then turned to say to Briana, "Your ladyship's trip to London poses no problem with His Grace since you offered to take your sketches with you." Anselma goggled visibly at the reference to London.

"That relieves my mind," Briana said. How unnerving this hiding duke was, but she would do her best for him nonetheless.

With sure pencil strokes, she sketched the curtained four-poster bed, the twin armoires, the bookcases, and the Cotswold stone fireplace. Then she drew the chairs, tables, vanity, and shaded in the oriel window seat.

Rex came to watch over her shoulder. "Will you look at this representation? The lady possesses talent."

Darnier opened a bookcase full of old books and offered a few to Anselma for her perusal. "Yes, we've seen her work in the duke's chambers," he said.

Briana had a need to thank Rex for his roses, but she suspected she'd have no moments alone with him, so she lifted her paper and wrote on the page beneath: "Your gift is lovely and fragrant. Thank you." She penciled in a spray of roses and turned the page toward Rex.

It brought an attractive curve to his lips. He touched Briana's curl, winked, and strolled toward the door before Anselma looked up from her book of sermons. Darnier, handing the pleased spinster another volume, witnessed all.

Briana bent over her work after that. What was he thinking she had written to Rex? Why was she sensitive over Darnier's opinion, anyway?

Rex poked his head back in, saying, "I'll order tea laid for Lady Briana. You can show her to that round breakfast room with the tall French doors. Don't let her suffer much longer on this task, Darnier."

Darnier eyed him without humor. "Yes, sir." When he saw Briana take out her measuring tape, he took the other end. "What would you measure, your ladyship?"

She could hardly face him, for he doubtless thought she had suggested a tea for herself and Rex on that paper. "The length and width of the bed hangings, please."

That done, Darnier helped her size the bed. In the shadow of half-closed bed curtains where Anselma could not see them, he tugged the tape from Briana's fingers. He looked her up and down, gently chiding, "My fair lady, you take this work so seriously."

"Why should I not?" she asked, finding his shadowed face too attractive for her own serenity. "The duke wants me to get on with it, and I am sure he expects it done to perfection."

"As I am sure it will be." He read her the width. "What kind of decor do you foresee for this dilapidated room?"

"I visualize a color scheme of white lace for the bed and window curtains, but I may dye it all in tea to age it. I believe that would give the future duchess's room more élan than vulgar newness, don't you?" Her dimple appeared.

"Yes, but you forget that white is more bridal. You could dye it all later when the duchess grows old. What else?"

With lips curving, Briana said, "Touches of rosebud pink and French blue with a mint or sea green would be nice for sashes, chair cushions, and so forth. It'll be an Italian-flavored room, light and inviting, with lace bolsters beneath yards and yards of wispy bed curtains."

"Sounds sumptuous," declared Rex, strolling in.

66

"Sounds heavenly," amended Darnier.

"Instead of wall covering," Briana continued, "I'd like to have vines and flowers painted as stringcourse borders on the champagne plaster walls I'm envisioning. The stringcourse could go round that oval mirror and continue down and out over the fireplace to make that a focal point; what do you think?" she put to Darnier.

He peered behind him as though it were materializing on the wall. "Superb. Will you paint the stringcourse yourself?"

"I can." She thought, I'll come back from London to do it if I have to.

"Please do, your ladyship, if it's not too much trouble. I doubt His Grace would trust anyone else."

"Thank you."

He excused himself and left the room.

"What an accomplished lady," said Rex, moving near to view her drawings. Anselma, eyeing this maneuver, wedged herself between them and exclaimed at the transfigured room represented on paper. Rex added, "Again, you could be all the rage in London if the ton found out about your talents. Better keep them well under wraps unless you want to make a habit of this."

Briana smiled and confessed, "I grow impatient to ransack the shops of London and put this all together."

Darnier walked in. "Here is the money to do just that." He dropped a bag onto her lap. To Rex he said evenly, "I believe tea is served."

Rex tossed him the measuring tape he had been spinning around. "Thanks. Finish up her measuring, will you?"

"Certainly. What else do you require, your ladyship?"

"Only the size of the fireplace for a new screen. I'm grateful for your help." Oddly, she felt a twinge of guilt in leaving the Brocco secretary to do her work. And his formality all of a sudden bothered her.

The round turret room was on the ground floor, allowing for a charming view of the courtyard garden through French windows heightened by arched panes and perpendicular tracery. Two maids in gray and white lit tapers in the candelabrum while a heavy tread produced the butler bearing a tray with steaming teapot.

Briana took appreciative note of the lilac-patterned china and flaky Banbury cakes smelling warmly of spice and currants. The talk went well. Rex relaxed his arm over the chair back and said, "Before I forget, Briana, will you give me the address of your London house?"

"Berkeley Square," she told him, seeing Anselma drop a full spoon of sugar into her tea in her astonishment. "I don't have the number yet."

"I, too, shall be in London soon. May I call on you?"

Anselma cleared her throat in warning.

"I would be honored," Briana replied. Her future was looking more promising every moment if her duenna would but realize it.

The large butler materialized. "Excuse me, Sir Reginald."

"What is it, Trump?"

"The duke wants to see you in his study. He has tenants coming at eleven o'clock to pay their rents and requires your advice on the quarterly system you recommended."

Rex glued his eyes on the butler's. When this request was concluded, he passed a hand over his brow and shook his head. "Tell His Grace," said Rex unsteadily, "that I come at once."

To Briana he said, "This is unfortunate, but the duke may be a trifle *displeased* if not instantly obeyed."

"Yes, by all means, go at once."

"Yes, sir, do go!" Anselma urged, looking fearful.

Rex lifted Briana's hand, saying, "I shall see you soon."

As his footsteps echoed down the gleaming south corridor, Anselma whispered, "Lady Briana, we had best take our leave now. Make haste!"

Briana rose and snitched a sugared bonbon and joined her nervous chaperone in the corridor. They made their way to the great hall. There they saw Darnier coming down the staircase. "Finished with tea already?" he called.

"Yes. You see, Sir Reginald was wanted by His Grace."

"Ah. Here are your sketches." He presented her leather case.

She had only made one sketch of the room. By the plural form he used, Darnier must have seen the one to Rex. In a way it was a relief, for it was only a thank-you and not anything unbecoming.

Anselma demanded as soon as their coachman pointed the team home, "Lady Briana, what did that Sir Reginald Channing mean when he talked of your trip to *London?*"

"We are going at some unknown date in the future."

"*We* are going to London? My word! Whatever for?"

"I have a letter from Mr. Runton. He wants to see me on a matter of importance. I wish you will not bandy it about, for I know nothing of certainties until I hear from him again."

"Of course not, Lady Briana. Do you think I would talk about your private business to any other soul?"

But talk she did, and not only about the ogre of a duke who lived in that mansion. In an argument with Chalandra's maid, Anselma reportedly said, "You should not behave so selfishly, Frances. You may have the chair in the garden every day while I'm in London."

This produced incredulous inquiries from Frances whereupon Anselma was gulled into saying she was not a falsifier. The very day Briana received a reply from Mr. Runton, accompanied by the two-hundred-pound banknote, the rumor had reached Chalandra's ears.

That young lady alighted at the supper table in a cloud of cheap tangerine gauze and, with brown eyes unusually aglow, declared, "Mother, we must hear if Briana really *is* going to London."

Reprehension crossed Mrs. Milburn's face. "London! What kind of talk is that?"

Briana calmly accepted a lamb patty and creamed peas from Effie. "Yes, I will be making a trip to hear the settlement of my father's affairs."

Mrs. Milburn and her daughter exchanged speculative looks. "When do you believe you are going?" questioned Mrs. Milburn, pinning her eyes on Briana.

"Do not fear footing any expense on my behalf," Briana said lightly. "I've been advanced enough for the trip. In a day or two I should be on my way. And out of yours."

This did not appear to gladden Mrs. Milburn as it ought. Briana deduced that the displeasure stemmed from the sound of money in her coffers.

Chalandra fought to contain her elation. Raising a sidewise pleading look to her mother, she sweetly said, "I should like to go with her, Mother. You have no objections, surely, for I am *dying* of rustication here."

This was inspiration indeed. As Briana felt a wave of panic, Mrs. Milburn perked up. She half-smiled as she said carefully, "Chalandra, dear heart, why would I object to your going if your cousin says she is going? Since the duke of Brocco has consistently refused our invitations, there will be no society here. Briana will be relieved to have company on the way, especially in London. Isn't that so, Briana?"

"Thank you, but there is no need to fuss over me. Anselma will be bearing me company."

"Where do you think you will stay in the city? Have you thought of that?"

"Mr. Runton has made arrangements for me."

"Let me see his letter," said Mrs. Milburn. "I must make sure that this is legitimate. After all, you are in my care, and I can't allow you to go rambling off into the unknown."

Briana knew that if Chalandra were coming with her, the truth about her house would soon be out. With a sigh, she withdrew the letter from her bodice. Chalandra perched on the edge of her chair. Objecting to Mrs. Milburn's reading that there was more money awaiting her, Briana pretended to read the entire letter, leaving that out. It informed her that the house in Berkeley Square was ready for her arrival.

Mrs. Milburn's wheels were turning in the clockwork of her greed. "A house, you say. It must be *somewhat* presentable if it's in—where was it?—Berkeley Square. You know . . ." she said, pretending to consider, "this wouldn't be a bad time to introduce you to some society, Briana, now that you've put off mourning. I believe I could get Lady Wipplingote to show us about in London." She lifted her eyebrows significantly at Chalandra, and that miss looked overjoyed.

How can she be so high-handed with my affairs! raged Briana inwardly. Lady Wipplingote, indeed. They all knew she was Mrs. Wipplingote, she of the vulgar letters from London, an old school chum of Mrs. Milburn's.

Talk and plans continued which Briana had to endure with depressing resignation throughout the meal. When the plum pudding and tea were consumed, she stood up. "Excuse me, Mrs. Milburn, Chalandra. Since I go to Brocco Park for another measurement in the morning, I must get to bed." With her resentment welling up, she could not stay another moment and remain polite.

As she left, a quip from Mrs. Milburn caught her ear, calculated to do so. "After all, she owes us a stay in her London house. Look how long we've let her stay here."

Breathlessly, Chalandra caught up with Briana on the

71

stairs. "I wish to come with you to Brocco Park tomorrow to see what you're working on."

"You mean that you want to inspect Sir Reginald Channing some more," taunted Briana.

"Oh, is he still there?" Chalandra contrived to look innocent. "Really, Bri, do you have the time to be decorating someone's house when we must leave for London?"

"I certainly must take the time to finish my project since I have committed to it. I'll leave as soon as I feel I can do the correct buying in town."

"I will help you," Chalandra decided.

Briana neither wanted nor needed her help, but that was small pence compared with the prospect of being saddled now with the Milburns in London. Briana's soaring hope of freedom had taken a swift dive.

# Chapter 7

## Unladylike Longings

Chalandra fluttered her fan as she and Briana watched Darnier descend the dramatic staircase. At first sight of his arresting form, Chalandra's eyes grew huge and she whispered, "Well, bless my mittens! Is *this* the duke?"

"The duke's secretary," corrected Briana behind her glove.

This instantly transformed Chalandra's behavior. She turned away, fanning, to peruse the late duke of Brocco painted by Romney.

"Good afternoon, ladies."

Briana, with a smile of greeting, looked into his dark-lashed eyes and felt another bump of her heart. There was something mysterious about him, and that intrigued her each time she met him. "Chalandra," she said, "meet Mr. Darnier, secretary to the duke of Brocco. Darnier, this is Miss Milburn, my cousin."

Chalandra appalled Briana by barely turning her head in acknowledgment. As usual, her charm did not extend to mere servants.

Briana turned apologetically to Darnier. A wisp of a

smile moved his lips. She said, "I've decided to measure the doors between the antechambers for stained-glass windows. It's the last bit of information I need."

"You'd do well to install one in the connecting door to the duke's room, then. I am quite sure His Grace would like that. May I escort you, Lady Briana?"

Remembering how she had felt the last time she touched him, she hesitated, then said, "Yes," tacking on, "please."

"Where is Sir Reginald Channing at the moment?" inquired Chalandra.

"He has gone out riding. Was he expecting you, Miss Milburn?"

"Why, no. I did think, however, that we should return his visit."

What visit? thought Briana. The one in my landau in Shipston?

"How is the duke?" Briana asked Darnier as they rounded the airy staircase streaming with light from the central tower.

"Extremely well at the moment. He has had few better days."

"Does that mean I can venture sending in my card again?"

"You're persistent, my lady," Darnier laughed. "I'll gladly make another attempt in your behalf. Who knows when you will meet otherwise?"

"Yes, and what a shame not to. Only from my viewpoint, however."

Chalandra gained the domed gallery first, pausing there on display while she looked at the painted murals rising to the heights. "Whom might you never meet again?" she wanted to know.

"Miss Milburn, we were discussing the possibility of the duke seeing Lady Briana and yourself for a few minutes. Would you find that agreeable?"

Chalandra deliberated, head on one side, and then condescended to say, "I suppose so."

Briana could have slapped her for such impertinence. Instead, she headed for the duchess's rooms.

Darnier said, "You'll be more comfortable within, Miss Milburn," and gestured politely for her to follow Briana.

She looked coldly through him, but did as he wished. Brushing past Briana, Chalandra was suddenly in a hurry. "Is there a pier glass in here?" she worried. She rushed to the great gilded glass above the mantelpiece and wound her temple curls around her finger one by one. "Is my flounce straight in back? It's not folded up anywhere?"

"It's fine," said Briana dryly. "You look perfect, except for your disagreeable behavior showing on your face."

"What do you mean?"

"I mean Mr. Darnier. Didn't you treat him abominably?"

Chalandra waved that aside. "Will you retie my sash? It's loosened on the ride over."

As Briana tied it with exasperated jerks, Chalandra said, "Who cares about some secretary, anyway? He must be used to aristocrats."

"You are not an aristocrat and they do not act like you just did."

As Briana left Chalandra to her primping and sat down at a table to organize her papers, an odd feeling came upon her, like that of being watched.

When she had decorated the duke's chambers, she had discovered something in the mirror frame over the cravat cupboard. Perched above carved mahogany leaves and flowers, the gleaming round eye of the cuckoo had revealed a view into the next room, this one. Briana had been scandalized, wondering if past duchesses had known their husbands could leer at them in all freedom while they were dressing and undressing. Briana knew that someone's eye looked through the cuckoo's even now.

"How long must we wait?" Chalandra said petulantly, turning this way and that before the glass while Briana measured the door panels. At Briana's admonition to be patient, Chalandra went to the open window to look out.

Briana, completing her task, joined her cousin at the window to gaze at the avenue of dark oaks which stretched on to infinity, or so it seemed.

A man's voice broke the silence from another open window of the house. "No, I will not see them! What would I say to schoolroom chits? What I want, Darnier, is wife material. A fine woman who knows how to go about pleasing a man. Green little fillies eighteen years old know nothing whatever on the subject. Bah!" There was a sound of derision.

The whites of Chalandra's eyes grew enormous. "Did you hear that?" she squeaked. "Was *that* the duke of Brocco?"

At Briana's rueful nod, Chalandra expostulated in helpless fury, "He thinks we're green little chits!"

"Aren't we?" Briana gave way to helpless laughter which only served to increase Chalandra's outrage. She dramatically slammed the window shut, only too glad to follow Briana out of the chamber.

Darnier was standing at the gallery rail. Chalandra instantly attacked him. "We heard your duke shouting about us! It was the most offensive thing I have ever heard! Why, pray tell, should Lady Briana decorate for such an arrogant man, duke or no duke?"

"Chalandra!" cried Briana. "We must not mind the duke of Brocco. He has a right to his own opinions."

Her cousin looked more offended than ever. "How can he judge without seeing us, anyway?"

Darnier watched this heated interchange with twitching lips. Briana stared hard at him until he met her eye. The rogue knew about the peephole!

"How, may I ask, Mr. Secretary," Chalandra went on, "is His Grace going to find a wife to please him since he won't deign to come out and meet the most eligible lady," here she indicated Briana, "in the neighborhood?"

Darnier shook his head gravely. "A perplexing situation, is it not, Miss Milburn?"

Chalandra hooded her eyes and swooped down the staircase, her flounces fluffing with every angry step.

Darnier said quietly to Briana, "Perhaps I should suggest the duke hold a soirée in the duchess's chamber so he may look prospectives over."

At Briana's laugh, Chalandra shot an indignant look over her ruff. And as soon as Darnier had bid them both farewell at the carriage, she let loose. "My! You certainly have taken to hobnobbing with servants, Briana. You should never giggle at their uncultured quips. One would think the *lady* you are supposed to be would surface at least in front of a duke's employees!"

"Was I to take my cue from your manners, then?"

Chalandra slid her a cold look. "I'm not talking to you anymore if you insist on acting so ill-bred!"

Briana desisted from continuing the conversation, diverting as it was, so they rolled home in stilted silence. When they reached their doorstep, Chalandra had recovered her thoughts of London and the necessity of humoring Briana who was making it all possible. "Pardon me, Bri, but I cannot tolerate unjust dukes or servants who do not show proper respect."

"Yes, I know you have strict values on respect."

"That duke! Ohhh! He makes me want to strangle something! How does he know we cannot please men?"

"So that's what piques you the most, is it?"

"He called us schoolroom chits and green fillies! How on earth does *he* know? I'd like to show him!"

"Show him what? That you can please him?" Briana saw Wolford's shoulders shaking.

Chalandra jumped down from the landau with emphasis. "When can we leave this insipid countryside? Can I set Frances packing?"

"May as well. We leave the day after tomorrow if our clothes can be ready."

"They will be! I'll call the servants myself and make sure they stir their stumps."

Since Briana had to cash her note at the bank, next morning she donned a riding habit of dark blue merino and sent for the groom. They trotted through the misty morning down a bridleway which threaded through a corner of the Brocco estate. As her horse descended the slope, there came a sound of men's voices and a drumming of hooves from behind. Darnier appeared on a chestnut with black mane flying, and in his dust, Sir Reginald on his brown hunter.

"Lady Briana!" shouted Rex, clattering up.

"Yes?" she turned in her saddle and smiled at him from under her plume.

"Just wanted to say that I wish you an enjoyable sojourn to the metropolis," said Rex, his horse's shoes clicking on stones as he trotted by her side, easing the groom out.

"Thank you, so do I wish it." After a pause, she said heavily, "My Milburn relations go with me."

"Lord have mercy," groaned Darnier from her other side, his moustache twitching.

Banter flourished until Briana laid her horse out for a gallop, partly to hurry her preparations but mostly because she found Darnier's magnetic eyes sliding over her, and that brought to mind the crawling ant incident.

When they drew rein in front of the bank in Shipston, Rex assisted her from the saddle, saying, "Dark blue renders you most striking, Briana."

"Thank you, but please don't scour the town for dark blue roses."

He was laughing handsomely when the three of them entered the bank. Her note cashed, Briana told her banker, Mr. Clark, that she was off to London. He wished her good fortune, and ventured to say he hoped they would see her again soon.

On the ride home, ludicrous as the thought was, the baronet and the duke's secretary seemed to be in competition for her attentions. Musing over this, Briana set her mare caracoling across the dusty lane, and Darnier, in keeping with her carefree turns, wove around her, sometimes letting her pass in front of him, at others spurring his gelding to vault across her path. Briana then noticed Rex had pulled up at a stile a ways back and had the groom checking his horse's shoes.

"Tell me, your ladyship," Darnier said, blocking her from going to Rex, "would it be revealing too much to answer the question uppermost in my mind?"

"Let me hear this mysterious question," she returned, half fearful what it might be.

With a frank look he asked, "What do you, Lady Briana, really wish for in this life?"

Briana's pupils widened. "What a question *that* is." She hesitated but a moment, a wistful smile touching her lips. "To have some freedom," she said earnestly, "to be able to see something of the real world—the men's world. I detest being sheltered from it all by chaperones and propriety night and day. Now I've shocked you, Darnier."

"That's what you wish?" A thoughtful smile dawned in his deep hazel eyes.

"That is my outrageous wish."

"With that kind of a longing, you had best be careful in London."

"Must I? How tiresome."

"I did not say to avoid adventure, Lady Briana, but just be careful with whom you have it."

Rex trotted up and resumed his place at Briana's side, regaling her with light-hearted conversation about the last London Season until they came to the shining lake at Brocco.

"Here is our parting of the ways," Briana said softly, looking at the clear reflection of the mansion in the water.

"I shall see you in London," said Rex.

Briana held out her hand, smiling. He turned it over, moved her glove down with his thumb, and raised the inside of her wrist to his lips.

Through her surprise, Briana said, "It's been a pleasure, Rex. Until we meet in London. Thank you, Darnier," she turned to that one, suddenly feeling an empty spot in her heart. "*Au revoir.*"

"To you, my lady," he returned, removing his hat. "I must not forget to give you the duke's best wishes. God go with you." He turned his horse around, looked over his shoulder at her, and went trotting off with the gaily waving Rex.

Taking a last, comprehensive look at the back of Darnier, from the set of his fine shoulders to the gentle way he held his reins, Briana wondered if she would ever see his wind-ruffled dark head again.

As she rode on home, she experienced an absurd pang of regret that she was leaving in the morning for London.

# Chapter 8

## The Scandalous House

Briana's incredulity finally found words. "What you are saying is that my father had a *mistress? My father?*"

Sidney Runton nodded, not meeting her eyes. "Obviously so. The house was bought for her use, but I suspected for months that it was not hers to keep. Grateful I am that this document turned up."

Briana sank back to the hard chair. She could scarcely believe it. Was that why she had been whisked off to Bath by her mother? Had the countess wanted to stay away from London because she knew of the mistress? Or had Lady Stotleigh's absence been the reason the earl took the mistress? Their daughter would never know. What she was certain of was the love and closeness between her parents the last months before they died.

"The question I must ask your ladyship is, do you wish to occupy the residence?"

She made her decision quickly despite the taint which had fallen upon her family in her mind's eye. "Yes, I do. Why should I hire a house when I have one? The last thing I wish to do is return to Milburn Place. Mr.

Runton, do I have enough money to keep up the house and to pay servants? Shall I be obliged to seek out a position of employment immediately, or have I a bit of grace money?"

Mr. Runton's countenance brightened. "Lady Briana," he said leaning toward her, "it relieves me to inform you," and here he lifted a yellowed document, "that you are in possession of enough funds to keep this house and a staff with perhaps three thousand per annum over that."

Briana sat up. "Three thou— How on earth? I do?"

"Yes, yes! Quite a tidy parcel for your ladyship to draw upon before such time as your dowry comes into consideration." Mr. Runton beamed as if his had been the benevolent gesture.

"But, my father had to sell Stotleigh Hall to pay his creditors! I fail to understand—"

"This trust, Lady Briana, was set up for you by your grandfather. It is only my conjecture, and please take no offense, but he may have known his son's predilection for, ah, spending the ready rather freely, and, with foresight, made sure your portion was untouchable except by yourself upon reaching eighteen years."

"Dear Grandpapa!" Briana rose to her feet, hardly knowing what to do next. "Mr. Runton," she said, looking earnestly into his round eyes, "how did my father lose all of his wealth?"

"He never told you?" the solicitor asked wonderingly. "No."

Sidney Runton rubbed his smooth hands together and regarded the old wood floor at his feet which smelled of beeswax and gleamed in all the corners of the book-lined cubicle. "Well, you have a right to know," he sighed at last. "It was at Brooks's one night that he laid a hefty wager on one card, my lady—one card was his undoing.

Such an uncharacteristic act on the earl's part followed an argument with his . . . er, the woman."

Briana wanted to hear no more about it. She kept the talk on practical matters until Mr. Runton's coupé halted in Berkeley Square where enormous plane trees dropped colored leaves around an equestrian statue of the king. Beyond was a little pump house with a Chinese roof, ornamental and unexpected in the expanse of green lawn. The house was made of light gray stone three rooms wide, its elegance tucked between larger mansions.

Her comment was, "Affluent indeed to have been given to a mistress, don't you think, Mr. Runton?"

"Ahem, yes."

A knife of anger shot through Briana. How could her father have kept a Cyprian here while his own beautiful wife attended dull musical evenings in Bath with no husband at her side?

"Who was she?" Briana demanded.

The startled solicitor's eyes protruded above the oval frames. "Lady Briana, I feel you are in a more peaceful position if you remain in the dark on that point." Briana had the impression he would prove adamant should she press him.

Could she force herself to pass beneath the Grecian columns gracing the fanlit doorway? What Sinful Woman had vacated unwillingly through the pale blue door which now opened at Mr. Runton's tap of the knocker?

A staff was already in place, hired as promised. Paget, the soft-spoken butler, sent the wiry porter to summon every member. Briana met them all down to the scullery boy, and found no fault with the demeanor of any of her new servants. Briana's first mission for the footman was to fetch her trunks and her relations from the Peacock Inn.

Briana gazed at the flying staircase lifting to a graceful gallery where silk wall coverings shimmered in muted saffron. It was beautiful, but she kept thinking of her mother making lace at night when sleep eluded her.

There was a shell pink drawing room with French furnishings, and an intimate dining room draped in teal velvet. The chamber Briana chose for herself was papered in white, green, and raspberry flowered silk. The gold and white room just below had obviously belonged to That Woman. Chalandra could have it while she was in town.

"I could hardly credit this address to be the one where *you* would have a house, Briana!" declared Mrs. Milburn as she stepped uncertainly into the drawing room where Paget ushered her. "I thought the coachman was hoaxing us stopping here with such mansions on every side."

"Why hoaxing you?" inquired Briana.

"Your father and mother never told me about any of *this,*" complained Mrs. Milburn, waving her hands at the grandeur.

"It was a recent purchase, I believe," said Briana in a preoccupied manner, "tied up by legalities. The papers were drawn up just before Papa died."

Chalandra's bonnet-framed eyes sparkled as she burst into the room and gazed up at the rococo plasterwork ceiling. "This should certainly *do!* Look, Bri! Why they're *cupids!* We're in London, in London! In *style!*" She hugged herself and twirled in bliss.

"I suppose you love me all the more now," Briana said, darting a glance at Mrs. Milburn.

That woman drew up bosom and chins. "We have always felt affection for you—you know that, Briana. So what if I've had to reprimand you at times? I have meant what was good for your character." Oonagh Milburn turned away her eyes and pierced them at the articles of furniture so elegantly set in an oval, their gilt legs gleaming.

Chalandra, seating herself on a shell-pink satin settee, said, "Mother, you could at least be a little sorrier, couldn't you?"

Here was reason for Mrs. Milburn to glare at her daughter. "I am sure Briana is as forgetful as I am. I am not going to remind her of her past little jealousies, and neither should you, Chalandra. We're starting a new Season in town, and what's gone before, we must contrive to forget."

"But Mother, you really should ask her to forgive you, you know. Telling her she's envious when I don't think she was at all—it wasn't the thing."

Mrs. Milburn could not take it. She walked out of the room.

Briana stepped after her. "Come, Mrs. Milburn, if you're not ready for that, just know that I forgive you."

A queer look flitted over the older woman's face.

At the sound of the brass knocker, the porter sprang for the door. Anselma came bustling in with the footmen who carried the first of the trunks. Her eyes widened instantly at the spacious beauty of the hall, and she cried, "Merciful heavens!"

Briana leaned on the gallery railing. "No, it's just a staircase," she said, smiling.

As the spinster tiptoed reverentially up the stairs, she breathed, "Is this really yours? Really yours, this house? I believe I shall swoon away any instant. My oh my, one doesn't dare to touch such elegant crystal handrails. Just feature!—servants in place, and everything of the first stare! Are we dreaming, Lady Briana? Look up at that chandelier!"

Briana was glad to retire her duenna's exuberance to the primrose bedchamber. She had to grin at Anselma's

85

refusal to step foot into the room until those giants left it.

To Mrs. Milburn Briana gave a large room next to Anselma's. She felt it suited her with its two shades of orange with touches of blue and purple chinoiserie in the painted fire screen, drapes, and flower vases.

"For me?" Chalandra shrieked in delight over the spacious bedchamber decorated in gold and white and liberally laced with mirrors, even though bedclothes had been removed and the walls denuded of pictures judging by the shadowed squares in the brocade wallpaper. She flung open the dressing room and declared she never had had such space for her gowns before. "Oh Bri, you are sublime!"

At bedtime, Chalandra remained in a state of exultation at having the most elegant room allotted to her. Briana waved off her thanks, saying, "I'll buy bed linens for it tomorrow. You may sleep with me tonight if you like."

Chalandra wriggled into Briana's bed, drawing the sheet over her flat chest, bereft for the night of its wax bosom friends. "Aren't we utterly in the mink?" she cooed. "Have you thought of what being here in this kind of a house will mean for us?"

Briana wryly heard the "us." "Men, no doubt, are what you're dreaming of." With silver snuffers she clipped the candle wick.

In the semidarkness, Chalandra raised on one elbow and flicked her veil of hair over her shoulder. "Of course, Bri! In London there must be hoards of rich, worldly men. Think what an exquisite time we'll have. No more boredom, no more putting up with country rawbones. We begin to live, Cousin!" She sank back onto the pillow in raptures.

Briana rolled her eyes. Startlingly loud were the carriage wheels and chairmen's shouts, and distracting were the lights moving outside the drawn drapes. "How do you think we will meet *rich* men?" she asked.

"By going to parties where rich men go, of course."

"As I remember so few people here, who of quality will invite us?"

"Mother's friends," supplied Chalandra airily.

Briana had to take pruners to that. "Having never been to London, you do not realize that the friends your mother has are hardly from high society. Don't, I beg, let your hopes rise there."

Chalandra lay thoughtful for a moment. "Well, Bri, you can try hard to remember *someone*. Or else we must cultivate some friends on our own."

"How are you or I to do that? Start banging on knockers around the Square?"

"I would think that if we take a lot of walks roundabout or try bumping into aristocrats, say, outside the House of Lords, we should have no trouble getting invitations."

"Chalandra, how scheming and naive you are!"

"It could work," maintained Chalandra. "I could make it work."

"Listen," said Briana, "members of the House of Lords are a far cry from your country yokels, and will only take you for a doxy if you do anything so foolish."

"Then how do you propose to wedge us into Society?"

"I'll find a way to procure you invitations to some respectable parties somehow," said Briana, her hopes on Rex. "But Chalandra, we must behave circumspectly at all times, or those *who are who* will absolutely cut us, that much I do know. Things are very touchy in polite London circles, so please remember it every hour."

The next morning, Briana and Chalandra finished their scones and chocolate while Mrs. Milburn read aloud from the society columns with a view toward instructing her daughter on the names she should know. Briana, with tongue in cheek, made an occasional correction in Mrs. Milburn's perceptions, and added comments about homes her parents had visited. This went on until the butler cleared his throat in the doorway.

"What is it, Paget?" inquired Mrs. Milburn in a grand manner.

Briana's spine stiffened. Did Mrs. Milburn think she would run this house?

The butler's eyes remained fixed on Briana as he presented her a card upon a porcelain salver. "*Visite*," he said.

"Thank you, Paget," Briana nodded. "Show him to the drawing room." Mrs. Milburn snapped her newspaper.

Chalandra demanded, "Who is it? Someone other than the solicitor?"

"Sir Reginald Channing," Briana reluctantly informed her.

Chalandra and her mother exchanged a quick look and rose as one. They rustled to the drawing room in Briana's wake. Chalandra seated herself with much arranging of her purple gown which Mrs. Milburn lamented clashed with the shell pink settee. "Chalandra, you should have worn *anything* but that to receive callers in this room! Briana, delay our visitor so she can change!"

Rex strode in on the words like a refreshing breeze, attired in a plum coat over a pair of waistcoats. Chalandra trilled, "Sir Reginald! You've made it to London—welcome! Will you take tea with us?"

Taken aback at seeing the Milburns, Rex said, "Yes . . . perhaps." Before ten minutes had passed, his almond-shaped eyes rested on Briana in an imploring look, and he said he must be going.

Descending the staircase, Rex expelled, "I must say how glad I am to have you in London, Briana. But deuce take those two—and the duenna."

Laughing, Briana could see Anselma descending as a shadow after them. Rex took Briana's arm and gently steered her out before him onto the front step, pulling the door shut behind them. Smiling, he extracted a sealed billet from his coat pocket.

The cream-colored card was sealed with the Channing crest in silver wax. "What is this?"

"Oh, exquisite Briana," he breathed, moving close to her. He grasped her hand, and the missive fell unheeded. He raised her hand higher and higher. She looked up to see his lips about to touch her fingertips. The door behind them opened wide. Anselma stood there, staring in consternation at the romantic drama before her.

Briana flushed and pulled her hand back.

Anselma eyed Rex severely. "Behave yourself, Sir Reginald, or I must request you leave."

What awkward things were chaperones, thought Briana, sucking in her cheeks at Rex's gracious bow to the intruding spinster. Anselma, with great suspicion, watched him pick up the sealed note from the step and present it again to Briana.

She concentrated on cracking the seal. Inside was an invitation to a supper and ball to be held at Channing House. It was addressed to Lady Briana Rosewynn and Party.

"Does this mean the Milburns?" she asked, a smile forming.

"If it must."

"That is indeed kind of you."

Rex said, "I look only to save you trouble."

"You do. I look forward to coming, and so will they."

"No need to send your response for I have had it

already . . . from your lips," he said, looking at their cherry beauty.

Alarmed at such a possibility having occurred in her brief absence, Anselma cleared her throat and glared daggers at Rex before she took Briana's hand.

In a mischievous tone Rex concluded, "I will see you at my mother's house on Friday, Briana, where rules are not so strict. Good day, Miss Snivelton."

# Chapter 9

## Measures of Kindness

"An invitation?" squeaked Chalandra, reaching out an eager hand after Rex had left.

"Yes, to a supper and a ball," read Mrs. Milburn when she had appropriated the card. Her mouth could not find a satisfactory position as she saw herself and her daughter tagged "and Party."

"I haven't a thing to wear!" realized Chalandra, stricken into a panic. "Nothing *London!*" she qualified as she received Briana's disbelieving stare. Chalandra's manner melted into a submissive coo. "Mother . . . !"

"I suppose we shall have to move heaven and earth to procure ourselves something," her parent said as she speculated how this was to be done in grand style on her clipped finances.

Briana kindly suggested they ransack the shops, and for once all four females were in accord. As they bustled into Briana's town coach, the footman handed Briana a letter. It bore the unmistakable slashing script of Darnier, of all people.

Dear Lady Briana,

I've discovered a linendraper in Conduit Street with what appears to be a wide array of fittings from which you might enjoy choosing for the chamber at Brocco. Mr. Lyon of Lyon's awaits you this afternoon if you are at leisure to visit him.

Respectfully,

Darnier

Briana's heart gave a leap, but it was hardly for the wide array from which she might choose. Darnier here!

As they wheeled out of Berkeley Square into Bruton Street, Chalandra spied a milliner's window arrayed with extravagantly trimmed bonnets, and clamored to be let down. Briana arranged a rendezvous with the Milburns, and directed her coachman to continue looking for a Bruton Street modiste she remembered from three years ago where she had been taken by her mother for fittings of round muslin gowns.

Yvonne's was a bow-windowed modern shop now, and instead of the moderately high prices Briana seemed to recall, the Persian-carpeted, mirrored salon had turned exclusive.

Anselma's eyes protruded when Briana began to finger exquisite silks. "Lady Briana! I fear the gown that just left this shop was fifty pounds! That's what I saw marked on the bill. We must leave at once before they think you are actually *buying!*"

"I *am* actually buying," said Briana, with a stab of pleasure at the prospect.

Madame Yvonne, a small elegant Frenchwoman with blonde hair piled high, remembered Briana on sight, and her lovely face lit. Then she expressed her sympathy. "*La Comtesse,* how sad, she was one of my loveliest clients. Yet I am so pleased to have you, her *jolie fille,* visit me now. How *ravissante* you have grown!"

*"Merci,* Madame Yvonne." Briana explained that she had just arrived in London and wanted some special additions to her wardrobe.

The modiste's eyes brightened, and she became her most professional. She showed Briana a book of swatches she had just put together that morning, for she had received another private shipment of French brocades, silks, and velvets. "I do not show this to everyone, you realize," said Madame Yvonne, guarding it from the view of other customers. "What is new in *Londres* is already on its way out in Paris. That is why I keep the latest fashions and fabrics from *belle France* so tightly guarded: they are only for my *clientèle elite.*"

Briana, duly flattered, ordered seven gowns, one for Rex's ball, each to be uniquely her own design. As Briana sketched under Yvonne's attentive eye, adding innovative touches to the French styles shown her in the back salon, Yvonne exclaimed that Lady Briana should be a modiste herself with such talent, then immediately begged her ladyship's pardon.

After Briana's measurements had been taken, Yvonne tapped the sheaf of sketches. "They shall be just as you wish, Lady Briana, but I warn you this: you will be copied *immédiatement!*"

"Send them to my home; the ball gown by Thursday, please. Here's the direction."

As Madame Yvonne caught sight of the Berkeley Square address engraved in Briana's new calling card, the gleam grew in her eyes, and she replied, "Your ladyship shall 'ave them *tout de suite.*"

"My word!" Anselma expelled outside the canopied door.

"Your word, dear Anselma," took up Briana as her footman stood ready to help them into her parked carriage, "is likely to be that I must never spend more than a shilling on a frock. Did I hit the mark?"

As Anselma could not deny her train of thought, Briana said, "I have a bit of money at the moment and I see no reason why not to spend it on finery. Now, not a word about how many I ordered; here they come."

As Mrs. Milburn and Chalandra searched the shop fronts for Yvonne's, Briana saw the frustration on Chalandra's face. The reason became evident when she cried, "Oh Bri, do you know where we can have some dresses made? I couldn't believe how much they wanted for one ball gown in that shop back there! They told us in a snooty way that they cater to the queen."

"Come with me," sighed Briana. She passed back beneath the blue canopy and reentered the perfumed interior of Yvonne's. Mrs. Milburn and Chalandra showed signs of being out of their element.

Briana was given precedence over two other customers. "What more can I do for you, Lady Briana?"

"Madame, can you make up two more ball gowns to be ready by Thursday?"

"*Naturellement, pour vous*, my lady, anything you wish."

Within a few moments Madame Yvonne had summoned two aides to whom she relegated the Milburns, and they disappeared upstairs into the fitting salons. "*Pardonez-moi*, but those two," said Madame Yvonne behind her hand. "They do not turn in the same circles as you, my lady, *c'est vrai?* It is obvious, quite."

"I have lived with them for the past year," explained Briana.

"*Mes condoléances*," returned Yvonne.

Moving in her equipage down the busy street, Briana said, "Anselma, how would you like some new day dresses? Happy I am to stop at a suitable shop and have you measured."

"Oh no, I couldn't think of it, Lady Briana!"

"Since I am treating Chalandra and her mother each

94

to a ball gown, you needn't have such sensibilities. Here we are," and she pulled the check-string at sight of a reasonable-looking dressmaker's. She was gratified when Anselma sported spots of high color in her cheeks trying to make her selection from olive muslin, a sprigged tan and pink which she wondered, was it too youngish? or a muted mustard jaconet.

Briana's suggestion was to try them all in front of her face at the glass. Wondering how far away was Lyon's, Briana looked out the window, and there it was, diagonally down Conduit Street. She excused herself to the proprietress while Anselma went behind the screen to be measured.

Summoning the footman from her coach, Briana approached the establishment. The swinging sign next to it showed a pair of boots. The green door beneath opened, and Briana looked up into a strong, dark face.

"Darnier!" she said with heartfelt pleasure.

He looked more striking than ever, likely owing to the immaculate collar and cravat above a scarlet waistcoat and dark gray riding coat. "Lady Briana Rosewynn," he bowed, lifting his beaver, "never tell me you're shopping already for those rooms at Brocco."

"Yes, I have been specifically advised to seek out this shop, and to seek it out today, mind you."

The linendraper appeared on his step and welcomed them into his colorful high-ceilinged shop filled to the rafters with trailing lengths of crepe and sarcenet, satin and brocade, and everything in between.

"How do you happen to be in London, Darnier?" asked Briana.

"Parliament opens in two weeks, but His Grace has preparing yet to do. Your ladyship," he said with a sudden frown, "I must say I fear for your safety, and your prudence, with no chaperone in sight. Surely footmen left at doors do not suffice."

95

"I've left Anselma across the street unaware that I'm not in the waiting room."

"Back at your tricks, I see."

Briana laughed, and with an effort at concentration, managed to look through and ultimately choose some materials for the duchess's wing chairs and for Chalandra's bed.

"If you're through for today, step in next door with me a moment," said Darnier very low. "I must pick up some boot blacking; then I'll escort you to your ill-used duenna."

Several well-dressed gentlemen looked up from being fitted for boots and evening slippers when Briana and Darnier walked through the green door. Instantly Briana wondered if she should have entered such an establishment.

"A cup of tea, ma'am?" asked a footman at her elbow, the hot golden liquid steaming from a porcelain and gold cup on a matching tray.

She took it gratefully. It gave her something to do while a pair of dandies discussed her behind their gloves. There was only one other woman in the shop, and she appeared to be a wife.

Darnier was obliged to step a few yards away to pay for the boot blacking he requested, so Briana looked at walking sticks under glass and sipped her tea while he conversed with the proprietor. When Darnier rejoined her, he accepted a cup of tea from the roving footman and stood sipping and explaining how he had once carved a walking stick with the head of a horse for the handle. The bootmaker made notations on paper, unable to refrain from darting looks at Briana in between his work.

"I must return," she whispered uncomfortably to Darnier.

"Certainly, let's leave. This tea could be better."

The bootmaker was still assessing her form when

Briana quit the shop on Darnier's arm.

"Lady Briana, it is utterly too much!" clucked Anselma, emerging from Mary Alice's back room and finding Briana sitting patiently. "Two expensive gowns for mere me in one day! Such extreme generosity, my lady!"

"Nonsense. Consider yourself deserving of every thread put into them. You have me to watch."

Mrs. Milburn descended from the exalted heights of Yvonne's flushed with importance. Chalandra's elation found words. "Briana! You should just see what my gown will be like: gauze of the most exquisite jade green! I just hope against hope you won't think it too costly with the silver embroidery and all."

"It's my gift to you."

"How can you afford these gowns?" inquired Mrs. Milburn as they bumped wheels with another carriage.

"I was left a little something which I have decided to use this Season."

"Thank you from the bottom of my petticoats," said Chalandra.

"Mmm-hmm," murmured Mrs. Milburn, suddenly fascinated by what was occurring out the window.

When Briana's coach swung into Berkeley Square, there was a crush of smart vehicles and sedan chairs on the move. "I wonder where they're going?" asked Chalandra.

Briana said, "This begins the promenade hours in the parks. I rode out sometimes with Mother on fair days. We went to Hyde or Green Park where she would stop and talk with ladies while I sketched from the perch seat of her phaeton."

"Are you thinking of doing so again, Lady Briana?" inquired Anselma with great interest.

"Not immediately, but soon." She wanted to go without Mrs. Milburn.

"Why, that is wonderful," Anselma prated. "I so like all of your sketches, and I have so many hung up in my room at Milburn Place, but none here yet."

The smiling porter who opened the door referred Briana to Paget, whom she caught polishing the china salver with his handkerchief. He whisked a missive onto the tray. "This has just arrived, my lady."

"Paget," Briana teased, "I cannot pass you without receiving an offering of some sort."

Anselma's nose poked around her shoulder, but Briana, recognizing Darnier's hand, took the letter to her chamber to read it in private. There was a leaf inside: a beech leaf.

Dear Lady Briana,

Should you wish to begin adventuring as men do (that is, unrestricted by chaperones), appear beneath this tree on Rotten Row at the southeast edge of the Serpentine Wednesday afternoon at the hour of four.

The missive was not signed. Briana could picture the twist of lips that must have accompanied Darnier's writing of this. Adventuring! What on earth could he have in mind?

# Chapter 10

## Reputations at Risk

"Chalandra, I have a favor to ask of you. Will you come with me to Hyde Park this afternoon? I don't want Anselma tripping on my train all day long."

"That's a favor, Bri? I'm simply languishing to go somewhere," cried her cousin, halting in the middle of a stretch. "Will there be people?"

"Expect a few. The fashionable crowds arrive about five if nothing has changed, but I leave by three-thirty."

"What about Mother?"

"Do your best to get her interested in something or another so she'll not want to come."

"What on earth would interest her that much?"

Briana thought for a moment. "I know! Tell her I've authorized her to have a *petit souper* for Mrs. Wipplingote and her other friends on Friday, and shouldn't she be getting her invitations written? That should do it."

"Brilliant," commended Chalandra. "What will you do to keep Anselma in her corner?"

"I'll send her shopping for something for the ball tomorrow night. Is there anything you need?"

"I could use some silk stockings to match my shoes. . . ."

"Fine. Give Anselma your new shoes and I'll give her mine, and pack her off to buy the stockings."

"Tra-la." Chalandra left, humming.

The afternoon shone warm and pleasant as the horses trotted from Mount Street into Park Lane, but Briana's heart began behaving in a hammerlike fashion. Why on earth? she wondered. She was meeting the duke's secretary for an adventure. Was she going to turn tail?

As they rounded Hyde Park Corner, Chalandra asked whose could the great mansion with the columned entrance be.

"It's the duke of Wellington's now," Briana informed her. "It is Apsley House, just bought from Lord Wellesley by the government, and given to our hero."

Chalandra looked excited. With nose pressed to the glass in awe, she asked, "Do you suppose, if we were to drive back and forth, we would have a chance of seeing him?"

"Who knows?" said Briana leadingly. "I want to look at the ducks on the Serpentine as I did when I was a girl. If I go walking there, do you wish to come with me, or would you rather drive a few times by Apsley House to catch Wellington coming out for his daily ride in the park?" Briana didn't know if he rode daily or monthly, but hoped her ploy would work.

"You would go alone?" Chalandra asked, brows lifting.

"I can hardly be alone with all these people here. It'll just look like I've strayed a few feet from one of the groups. You might see more of interest driving around than trying to enjoy my reminiscing. Who knows, I may find subject matter for some paintings."

"I'll watch for Wellington. How long may I?"

"You may have half an hour." Briana dared not make

it longer lest Chalandra become suspicious.

When Briana pulled the check-string and alighted, her cousin settled herself importantly into the middle of the seat. Chalandra knew the carriage was smart-looking with the blue and white Stotleigh crest on black, and she was to be temporarily aloft behind Briana's dapple grays and respectable if dour coachman, with the liveried footmen adding éclat on their seat behind.

As the wheels spiraled away, Briana's footman cast a skeptical eye at his mistress left standing alone. Briana strolled with a show of confidence toward the blue waters of the Serpentine. A beech tree rose in full autumn glory in the distance. She made her way toward it, twirling her white parasol and chattering at the ducks she passed. There was no one beneath the tree that she could see, although an elderly couple shuffled away beyond it.

Briana pulled out her timepiece. Two minutes past four. She scanned the park for a man of Darnier's height, but saw none of such heroic proportions.

Taking a seat on a bench, it occurred to her that she was doing precisely what she would condemn in Chalandra. She was aware that the reality of meeting a man, even a duke's employee in a public park, sans chaperone, was far more daring than the idea had seemed on paper. She lowered her eyes as a pair of men walked by gliding interested looks over her. When they finally drifted out of sight, Briana nervously played with her parasol, securing it with its ribbons. A leaf came fluttering down before her nose, which was distinctly odd as there was no branch above.

"Adventure it is then, Lady Briana."

She whirled.

Darnier's face held teasing approval.

"I must at least hear what this adventuring *is*," she stipulated.

"Never tell me ennui has set in at Berkeley Square?"

"In a manner of speaking, yes."

"We must rectify that," he said, offering her his arm to walk. "Pardon me for keeping you waiting, but I saw your carriage with a woman in it, and assumed you had mistaken the place. I followed, but it wasn't you. What is Miss Milburn doing, and what does she think you are doing?"

Briana, somewhat abashed, revealed Chalandra's desire to catch a glimpse of Wellington on his doorstep. "I told her to return for me in half an hour."

"That gives us precious little time."

"For what?"

"For the first step in a plan to give you some rollicking fun and education." He smiled. "I am assuming this is still your wish, Lady Briana? To know something more of the world?"

"Yes, yes! But is it something quite . . . proper?"

"Proper?" His eyes crinkled. "Hardly. Is that what you want to be after all, Madam: proper? As I seem to recall, you rebelled against proper in Warwickshire every hour."

"Knowing that, you must also grasp that I am being driven daily another block toward Bedlam, or Lambeth, or wherever those poor lunatics are housed now. It annoys me to have to dodge Anselma's queries about how I am paying for new gowns and bed linens."

"Tell her it's improper for her to ask."

Laughing with him, Briana observed, "It appears that you're leading me toward that stylish Brocco vehicle."

"Correct. There is something you will need before we launch our campaign," said Darnier. "Since the squeeze isn't on for another hour, we can drive away unseen by anyone who matters to your future."

A powdered footman sprang to help her up. Darnier ordered the coachman, "To the house and spring 'em." He settled into the seat opposite her, and they were off,

Briana leaning uneasily against the black velvet squabs. The white horses with their bobbed tails trotted down Rotten Row, made the required circle, and picked up on the straightaway.

"Here comes my carriage!" exclaimed Briana. There was Chalandra, peering with interest at the elegant Brocco equipage. Briana sank into her corner.

"She can't see you," Darnier said, touching his hat to Chalandra. "Ah, she didn't much see me, either." Briana could imagine Chalandra's coolness when she saw it was only Darnier.

"Pardon her behavior. London is having its effects on her."

Darnier pulled the shades down, leaving only two inches of sunlight streaming into the carriage. Briana wondered as he pulled out a bandbox from beneath his seat. "These are for you, my lady," he said.

She looked at him uncomprehendingly until he lifted off the cover. Within was a pair of long black Hessians.

"Boots? For me? Those look like gentlemen's!"

"They look like gentlemen's, but they were made for you." He seemed to enjoy her disbelief. "I feel it would be much more proper for you to sally forth as a member of my own sex."

Briana's mouth dropped. In spite of herself, her eyes began to dance.

"Now, do you still want to go carousing around London with me?"

Briana locked eyes with him. "Oh, yes!"

"Without reservations?"

"Doubts may come, but there is such safety and dullness in staying in my beautiful home that I cannot be worrying about doubts now, can I?"

Darnier's lower eyelids deepened in amusement.

"Where are you scheming to take me, Darnier?"

"To places where you will never go as Lady Briana

Rosewynn. Don't look so appalled. What novelty would that be if we went to the tame sort of functions to which you'll be invited after the *bon ton* claps eyes on you?"

"What novelty indeed?" she echoed. "If you only knew how heavenly those tame soirées and balls would be after the mourning and quietness of this past year." She ran her hand over the smooth black leather of the boots, smelling the newness. "However did you procure these for me? Will they fit?"

"They should be close," he said, setting one next to her blue kid slipper. "Very close." The coach settled to a stop. "Here we are," he said, hustling the boots back into the bandbox.

Darnier alighted, and a footman's silver glove reached in to help Briana. She emerged beneath an enormous parasol and was escorted quickly by two tall footman through the open front door of a great house.

There she was, in a white expanse from which rose marble columns and a double grand staircase. Lacework gold balustrades rose in such intricate beauty that Briana stood transfixed, following their graceful curves to the landing where three white arches framed a balcony in the center. A soft exclamation passed her lips. Grasping the cool bannister, she looked up at the cupola painted in celestial scenes far above where beams of afternoon sunlight gave a breathtaking impression of heaven.

With only a quarter hour remaining, Darnier, waiting politely for her to conclude her worshipful gaze, urged her up the stairs. He flung open a room where a suit of clothes hung upon a mahogany valet.

"Do you think this will fit your ladyship?" He lifted a black tailcoat of narrow cut with padded shoulders and chest, very much in the mode for gentlemen.

Briana looked at it in comical dismay. "Assist me, please," she said with a grin, holding back her arms for the sleeves. With the coat in place, she went to the looking glass.

Darnier watched her, head to one side while he fingered his dark jaw. "Impressive."

Briana surveyed the back. It met with her approval. Her bosom, however, posed a problem, and she knew that if she were to dress as a man, a tight bandeau was definitely in order.

Darnier had the same thought. "My lady will need to diminish her charms somehow. Is it possible?"

"It is essential," she threw back, casting him a look between her double fence of black lashes. Surely color was rising in her cheeks.

"Fine, I'll have these sent to your back door so your Milburns and Miss Snivelton won't see them." He held the pantaloons alongside her for size, and placed other articles into a traveling case. He took the coat from Briana's shoulders and added it to the stack.

Briana watched him, puzzled. "How did you fit these?"

"Do you recall the intense scrutiny to which you were subjected in Mertonleigh's, the bootmaker's?"

"Yes. I felt I didn't belong there."

"A word to Mertonleigh's son was sufficient. He sized you by looks, recording your measurements on the spot."

"That odious man making copious notes and staring?"

"A man with an eye, wouldn't you say? He can size more than boots," chuckled Darnier. "His brother works for Stultz so he relayed the information over there and had these cut for you. I told him it was for a costume ball, and no one is to know."

Briana, hand to her forehead, was reeling at the idea she had been that intimately examined.

"The boots may need extra stockings, for you're not accustomed to such firm leather, I daresay. You'll find some in the case. Try on the evening slippers; their fit is more critical."

As she sat to remove her blue slippers, Darnier handed her the black shiny pumps with man-style bows. "They only need a bit of tissue in the toes, just the veriest bit."

"What luck. Let me know if anything else needs altering. Can't put Stultz to shame. I had to cross his palm with silver to get him to make these togs without a fitting."

"I can scarcely believe you have done all this. If this is an example of your efficiency, His Grace has got himself a *secrétaire superieur*. Send the bills to me without delay."

Darnier thanked her for such kind if misguided sentiments, after which an argument ensued; Briana asserting that she would definitely pay for her own wardrobe, and Darnier replying that it was not proper for a single lady as Madam was to pay for a gentleman's clothes. She was about to say the same in reverse, but he took note of the clock in horror, and whisked her down the staircase.

There a footman took the traveling case while Trump, the large butler from Brocco, eyed Grosvenor Square through the miniscule window before he swung open the portal. Umbrella and footmen waited. Again they hid Briana from passersby.

When the coach door closed, she fixed her eye on Darnier and asked, "That was obviously the duke of Brocco's house."

"Yes, my lady."

"How well His Grace's menials are trained in keeping a lady anonymous from the world," she said meaningfully.

"His Grace has an efficient staff; did I not just hear words to that effect? We protect your reputation at all costs."

"I am grateful." She extracted her timepiece on its chain from the bodice of her gown. She could see carriage wheels and hooves through the unshaded inch of

106

window. They were all rolling toward Hyde Park. Briana dropped her watch back into her bodice.

"What does the clock say?" Darnier asked.

Briana looked up to see his eyes flicker over the swells above her corsage. Unsteadily she murmured, "Five o'clock," wondering if he paid her words any heed.

He passed a hand over his forehead and muttered, "Being with your ladyship may prove more difficult than I anticipated."

Briana caught her breath. "What may prove difficult, Darnier?"

The coach halted. As the door swung wide, Darnier touched her on the forearm and said, "The sooner you are in gentleman's clothes, the better." He descended to the turf and assisted her down, summoning a smile which bathed her in easy charm. His touch stirred her with its warm pressure, and she was flooded with awareness of her femininity. And how very much of a man he was.

"Miss Milburn is parked beyond the phaeton in front of us. If you walk around that pair of elms, you'll look quite innocent. But stay: are you truly ready to begin your education, Lady Briana?"

"Yes."

"Tonight?"

She cast him a bright look, nodded, and circumvented the trees to remove her flushing face from his sight. If only her heart would stop galloping.

It did as soon as she saw Chalandra leaning out of the carriage window conversing with two attentive men on horseback, one in a red Army officer's uniform. Briana hastened her steps, gave them a cool look, and said to her footman, "Have Jacks drive on."

"Now, why did you do that?" Chalandra demanded plaintively after she was forced to cry quick adieux.

"Who were those men?" countered Briana.

"One was a viscount, Briana—Lord Glenby! His

friend is in the army—a Major Quentin! Why did you have to cut them and drive on?"

"There is no cause to worry, Chalandra. If Lord Glenby or Major Quentin are interested in you, my behavior will certainly not stop them from pursuing you. But we have not met them."

Chalandra appeared to take a liking to the thought of being pursued. "Well, where did you disappear to? I didn't feel like traipsing all over the park so those helpful gentlemen took a canter down that riding lane for me. But they didn't have any luck."

"How kind of them. I was across the way, talking to someone I met in the country."

Chalandra declined to pursue such a boring subject when there was so much to see as they trotted along Rotten Row. She stared at lavishly dressed women stopping their carriages and hailing their friends, but what interested Chalandra to the greatest degree was the line of dandies lifting quizzing glasses or otherwise ogling the passing carriages and tossing comments to one another.

Chalandra observed, "They're discussing our merits."

"And demerits," said Briana. "That's what dandies live to do."

"Then let's discuss theirs," said Chalandra. "Look at that skinny-waisted man with the patch by his mouth. Is he wearing rouge?"

"Likely so. Have you ever seen so many glasses screwed into the eyes? It quite ruins their looks from our perspective, if they only knew."

"Ooh, this is such fun!" Chalandra effused as they passed a curricle which contained two well-dressed bucks. The driver whipped up his horses, and next the men lifted their hats to the occupants of the Rosewynn chariot.

"What is etiquette, Briana?—quick! They're waiting

for acknowledgment of some sort."

"Just keep a little smile on your lips, but for heaven's sake don't wave. You don't know who they are."

Chalandra's secretive smile came naturally. Briana could see in one glance that the bucks were intrigued.

"Never tell me you're attracted to that man in spectacles," teased Briana. "Chalandra, converse with me! Don't keep staring at them like some vulgar rustic."

"Why not?"

"It's not refined."

"Then how will I ever meet them?"

"How many do you need to meet in one day?"

Chalandra let out a huff of disappointment.

Briana looked out her own window, and her eye chanced on a scrap of lace being trampled in the lane. "Oh, all right," she sighed.

While Chalandra watched in total bewilderment, Briana jerked the check-string and hurriedly opened her window. Her coach rolled to a stop, causing a pile-up of carriages behind.

"What are you doing?"

"Are they up with us yet?" asked Briana.

"Who?"

"Your blond buck and the spectacles!"

"Yes—yes, they've stopped, and here's your footman opening the door."

"All right, *now* smile at them."

Chalandra did so with a brilliant flash.

The fair-haired driver threw his reins at his friend and leapt down, striding round his curricle past a barouche loaded with a stout matron and five schoolgirls whose eyes all followed his progress to the Rosewynn coach.

Briana gestured her footman aside.

Chalandra said desperately, between her smiling teeth, "What do I do now?"

"I'll talk. You stop smiling. Just throw one in once in a

109

while. Goodness, I thought you knew all about ensnaring men . . . Good afternoon, sir!"

On close inspection, the man was older than he looked from afar; perhaps four and thirty. He swept off his beaver and made a bow, showing them an abundance of hay-colored locks wisped in silver. "A good afternoon to you, O Ladies."

Briana said, "Pardon, sir, but I let my slip of a handkerchief blow out of my window back there. I was going to ask my footman to go get it, if he can find it."

"She was waving at someone," supplied Chalandra.

"You shall have it back." The large man was gone on his words, ducking before horses pulling at their bits, unheedful of coachmen and passengers straining to see the cause of this new delay.

"Well! Where did you learn such tactics?" asked Chalandra, impressed.

"You are fresh indeed. Enjoy what benefit you can. I'll thank him, but," she eyed Chalandra sternly, "I'm not at all sure he's a breed to cultivate, so don't be come-on-ish."

"His friend holding the horses is being forced on."

"Oh no. Now yellow-hair is left behind. We shall be obliged to take him up!"

"Take him up?"

"You're panicking, are you?" asked Briana. "Maybe we both should be."

The buck dodged a team which was giving them the go-by out of impatience, and at last reappeared at their door presenting a grime-laden scrap of lace. "I'm sorry, ladies, but this looks more like a glove than a handkerchief."

Briana took the article between her fingertips, the dust powdering out. "You're right, this isn't mine. Thank you anyway, Mr.—?" Her dark brows lifted.

"Lord Fitzroyal, at your service, Lady—" He ma-

110

neuvered his sights to the crest on her carriage door, but he did not recognize it. "I presume you're too young to be the mistress of this quality chariot."

A flatterer, thought Briana. "I am not too young. I am Lady Briana Rosewynn, and this is my cousin, Miss Chalandra Milburn." So the deed was done. With a look she tossed the ball into Chalandra's lap.

"We are very grateful, Lord Fitzroyal, for your stopping to assist us," purred that one, lowering her brown lashes coyly.

Briana dropped the glove out the window, saying, "I notice your curricle has been forced to press on. The least we can do is take you up until we overtake your friend." She indicated the opposite seat.

Lord Fitzroyal jumped in without further ado, and the tall footman clicked shut the door with a disapproving look at Briana. The wheels rolled.

"Thank you kindly, your ladyship," their passenger said with a smile, adjusting his large frame into the seat. He made himself a little too comfortable for Briana's notions, and she found she disliked the way his yellow nankeens strained across his widespread thighs. Furthermore, he reminded her of a sheik choosing an evening's entertainment from a new harem. Deciding to appear reserved, Briana did not deign to meet his provocative eyes but gazed regally out the window.

"And thank you, too, Miss Milbank," he added.

"Milburn," corrected Chalandra, fanning herself and casting heavy-lidded looks at him.

"Ah, yes, Miss Milburn—a thousand pardons. Are you ladies new about town?"

"Yes, although my cousin, Lady Briana, has lived here every year, practically."

"I certainly hope we meet again soon," said Lord Fitzroyal, extracting two of his calling cards from a box within his waistcoat and handing them out.

111

"Yes," returned Chalandra, appropriating the card and fanning coquettishly.

Briana's heart sank. Fitzroyal winked at her, saying, "I'll be most happy to call on you and form a happy acquaintance. Let me make it soon." Briana groaned inwardly. Chalandra bathed him in her smile.

They were up to the curricle with its surrogate driver craning back his head, his thick spectacles glinting in the sunlight. Briana gratefully flicked her check-string. "Here is your curricle, Lord Fitzroyal. Thank you for your assistance."

"Thank *you*, ladies," returned he, not taking his eyes off the beauties before him as he fumbled for the latch. He lost his balance when the footman suddenly opened the door. That caused him to sway clumsily, drop his hat in the dust, and turn red. Briana's footman retrieved the beaver, dusted it off, and handed it to his better.

Lord Fitzroyal, under Briana's cool appraisal, muttered, "Your servant, Lady Rosewynn," and bowing, added, "Miss Milbank." He loped off to resume his seat in his curricle where his older friend looked agog at this turn of events.

Safely out of view, Briana let out a huff of displeasure. "Now are you satisfied?"

"Very! He was a *lord*. Rather an attractive piece, too," mused Chalandra. "That's two in one half-hour."

"Chalandra, the way you talk! He has the unmistakable aura of a womanizer. We must keep him at arm's length or further. Did you glimpse the duke of Wellington?"

"No," sighed Chalandra, "but perhaps I will next time if I say my prayers hard enough."

"Forget that plan. After this little incident, I will not give you leave to keep rounding Hyde Park Corner in my town chariot, with my crest upon the door, or it will be said that Lady Briana Rosewynn is setting a trap for the

112

nation's hero."

This stricture did nothing to upset Chalandra's spirits. She kept discussing her pair of lords. As they arrived home, she sighed rapturously, "One more day until Sir Reginald's ball!"

Mrs. Milburn was descending the stairs with her stack of invitations. She looked pleased with herself as she directed the footman to take them round at once, and therefore did not even notice that the girls entered the hall without duennas. When Chalandra gave her embroidered account of her ride in the park, her mother was visibly gratified, for a Lord Fitzroyal and a Lord Glenby both sounded infinitely desirable for her daughter to know.

To Briana, supper seemed interminable even though Paget served onion soup with tiny pigeon pies, carrots steamed with asparagus, baked cheese-and-ale, and an apple pudding with cream and strawberries, all which she found succulent. Her thoughts constantly prodded the long hand of the ormolu clock.

Anselma sat in stark disapproval, for she had heard inadvertently about the park ride. Briana avoided her gaze, donning a nonchalance which her duenna could not penetrate.

"Coffee, please," Briana requested of her butler, "to go with the truffles."

Anselma ventured a criticism. "Lady Briana, you will not be able to sleep if you drink coffee now. Have you forgotten what it used to do to your papa? He confided to me once that it kept him awake the better part of a night when he should have been resting for an important speech in the House of Lords."

"You're right, Anselma, but I have no important speeches to make tomorrow." She wanted to be awake for this night's escapade. She excused herself with cup in hand, saying, "I have a new novel by Mrs. Radcliffe, so

113

you won't see me till morning. Good night, all."

In her bedchamber Briana tugged the bell pull, glad that she had found linens for Chalandra's bed, and that her cousin was blissfully moved into her spacious chamber. Shortly the friendly maid Briana had claimed for herself scratched and entered.

"Mary, can you assure me of your loyalty, and keep a great confidence?"

The maid looked startled. "Lady Briana, I'm mighty glad to serve you any way I can, and of course I'll be loyal to you, and keep my lips fastened."

"Good. I'll raise your wages if you keep me from being found out tonight. What I want you to do is ask Paget if my dark brown traveling case has arrived at the back door. Go now, and don't let anyone else open it."

Mary returned carrying Darnier's valise.

"Thank you," breathed Briana, a thrill of anticipation seizing her. "Now help me dress."

# Chapter 11

## Her Ladyship's Cravat

Mary's eyes widened but she asked no questions when Briana stripped away her chemise and tied a white scarf tightly across her breasts. "Open the case," said Briana. "I'm hoping there are men's smallclothes in there."

Mary did gape at that, but she obediently handed her mistress the skin-hugging indescribables, averting her eyes while her ladyship removed her drawers and tugged the gentleman's garment over her supple limbs.

"The linen, Mary—the shirt," prompted Briana, "and two pairs of stockings, and garters—just give me everything I need in the right order. Although I don't suppose you've dressed many men before."

Amongst giggles they were handed over. Shortly Briana asked, "Are there any braces to hold up these pantaloons?"

There were. When Briana had buttoned the waistcoat of silver gray taffeta, she looked at herself in sudden consternation in the glass. "Heavens above! What am I to do with my hair?"

"There's a wig in the case, my lady."

"There is?"

It was produced; a most natural-looking windswept style in black. "Amazing," murmured Briana, "he is just amazing."

"Beggin' your pardon, my lady?"

"Nothing. Will you help me pin up my hair?" With the wig in place, she had to laugh. She had never been so glad of her height, for she made a dashing figure of a man with the well-padded coat.

Mary grinned widely behind her. "You look mighty handsome, my lady. And did you know there is a wisp left in the case that could very well be a moustache?"

Briana rolled her eyes around. "Fetch it."

To wear a moustache was so new an oddity that only a few such eccentrics as Lord Byron, and now Darnier, had adopted it; the former to add mystery to the exotic native garb he had sometimes affected. Darnier had a sense of humor, to be sure.

Briana glued the feathery wings of dark hair into place above the curve of her upper lip, thinking of Darnier's which so became him. "This helps immensely. Behold the London buck." She cocked her chin and looked arrogantly down at her maid.

"You *are* a gentleman, as I live!" cried Mary, dropping a curtsy.

"Shhh—you must not give me away!"

"Oh la, no!"

"Now see my way clear to the back door—there's a good girl," drawled Briana, picking up the tall, curly-brimmed beaver and setting it jauntily on her forward-swept locks.

"Yes, sir; right away, sir," giggled Mary.

Briana spent the intervening minutes practicing different degrees of bows. She found she had a smirk which looked wonderful with the moustache, so she memorized the proper way of it, twisting the right side of her mouth. She found that by squinting her black lashes together just so, she could look wicked and unapproachable. She tried the effect of a wink. Ah, this would be famous fun.

The cravat! She looped it tentatively round her collar, then finally decided to leave it hanging. She would ask Darnier's advice on how to tie such a starched piece of linen without crushing it irretrievably.

"You can come out now, my lady," whispered Mary from the door. "I'll go ahead to make lock-sure no one comes."

When Briana followed surreptitiously down the carpeted staircase and had just gained the back hall, Anselma strode from the housekeeper's candlelit office, saying, "I'm going up to check if Lady Briana is still reading. She shouldn't strain her eyes, and she might like a cup of warm milk after all that coffee. Merciful Margaret! *Who is that man?*"

At Anselma's screech, Briana's coattails flapped, and she dived through the shadowed back door, jamming her beaver brim over her eyes. Anselma's hysteria could be heard in the doorway next to the high lilacs Briana was cowering behind. She heard Mary's calm voice saying, "Do come in, Miss Snivelton. He came to the wrong house. He wanted a Mr. Brown. I have sent him on his way. No, he wasn't a wild man on the loose, Miss Snivelton— yes, he's gone now. I was just coming to tell you that Lady Briana fell sound asleep, and I shut her bedcurtains. She was exhausted." The door clicked.

Good for Mary, but what a near escape, thought Briana, her heart thumping. She straightened up, adjusted her hat, and left her miniscule garden.

"Right on time," said a deep voice.

Briana jumped, then let out a sigh of relief. Darnier

emerged from the shadow of a tree.

"Now what?" she whispered, looking back at her lighted house windows.

"I show you to the town, or the other way round, if you prefer." He indicated she follow him to the brougham waiting in Berkeley Street. The night air was crisp and carried the sound of horses clopping and harnesses jingling, and Briana breathed in the sweet smell of freedom. Hurrying to match her stride to his, she met the whites of his eyes, laughed breathlessly, and said, "I've fooled Anselma so far."

"Good." Reaching the glow of a street lamp, Darnier scrutinized her from hat to boots. She grew uncomfortably aware of her snug-fitting black pantaloons, and vaulted past him into the brougham in decidedly unfeminine haste.

"You do look splendid!" he marveled, his look full of admiration.

The footman checked at that, gaping queerly from Darnier to the young gentleman.

Darnier pulled the door shut with force. "Blast his ears!"

Briana choked on a laugh.

"What do you plan to do with that loose cravat?"

"Will you show me how to tie it?"

"Certainly." With a series of tugs and loops, he accomplished a chin-lifting arrangement. She enjoyed his movements, and watched him through her lashes. As the brougham jostled through the streets, light came and went, and Briana noted how the planes of his face were dramatically shadowed then warmed by lantern light. She took a careful, deep breath. There was something unspeakably sweet in the way his fingers ran along her neck as he smoothed the inside of her collar. He lifted the crisp points of it to graze her jaw, and gave her chin a

118

tweak. He sat back in his corner to survey her. "I do say," he said in satisfaction, "it's far easier to make a *trône d'amour* for someone else."

A throne of love—is that what he called this cravat style? Briana found herself tongue-tied on that theme, so she said flippantly, "You should have been a valet."

"Thank you, no! To be obliged to spend my days in a closet pressing cravats would turn my head into a snuff box. By the way, have you thought of a name?"

Briana deliberated. "How about Radcliffe? Mr. . . . *Brian* Radcliffe."

"Only a reader of novels would choose such a name."

"I admit to my shameful proclivities." After the brougham waded through a crowd of theatre-goers, she felt a twinge of panic. "How is my voice supposed to sound?"

"Can you lower it?"

"How's this?" she rumbled, imitating Wookey.

"You couldn't sustain that for long," chuckled Darnier. "Try for a tone lower than normal."

"All right," she tested, and Darnier nodded.

She realized that the streets they were passing through sported crowds of women posing beneath every light. Some looked to be accosting male passersby, and who knew what was occurring in those shadowy recesses. Briana shot Darnier a wide, questioning look.

His eyes twinkled, and in a deep, teasing voice he began to sing:

> London Town's a dashing place
> For everything that's going,
> There's fun and gig in ev'ry face,
> So natty and so knowing . . .
> Where novelty is all the rage,
> From high to low degree,

119

> Such pretty *lounges* to engage,
>     Only come and see!
> What charming sights,
>     On gala nights—

The coach rumbled over uneven cobbles and as Briana laughed at the effect on his voice, she wondered how on earth women could parade the streets in such abandon. And how could the poor things bear such sleazy-looking customers?

Their carriage halted. Briana looked askance from Darnier to a gaggle of females running to surround the brougham, one bosom pressed against the glass inches from Darnier's profile.

With a look of dry amusement, Darnier winked and said, "Try not to get separated from me." As the door opened and he backed out, he admonished, "And, Radcliffe, don't get foxed."

"Foxed?" gasped Briana, womanlike, as she followed him down the step and into the press of odorous women. Instantly she realized what a prime victim she must appear as she eyed them in amazement. She dodged and strode away from clutching hands, squaring her shoulders against the cries of, "Good sir! Want sweet company tonight?" and "I'm the best, take *me*, milord!"

"Thank you but *no*," said Briana, pulling away with finality from a painted redhead. Blushing under Darnier's mirth, Briana tightened her beaver on her wig and followed him into the foyer of Stevens's Hotel.

"I hope those women left you unscathed? Tell me, is this the kind of eye-opening sortie you had in mind, hmm?"

Briana retorted, "It beats embroidery."

Darnier's handsome laugh caused military men to look up from their plates. Briana schooled her features into the most bored look of worldliness she could muster. It was difficult to maintain, for one disastrous look at Darnier, and she had to cover her mouth with her glove.

No sooner had he ordered the only dishes the establishment served—boiled fish, fried soles, and joints—than Briana caused him silent whoops by tossing her beaver onto a vacant chair only to see it bump to the floor and go rolling. Her embarrassment turned to chagrin as a party of men on the spree jostled into chairs and the largest of them picked her beaver off his shoe and looked around for its owner.

Briana turned her shoulder, her eyes fixed in desperate appeal on Darnier. He rose and accepted the hat with thanks.

Resuming his chair, he asked, "Do you know that gentleman?"

"Yes!" she whispered. "I met Lord Fitzroyal in Hyde Park. He must not recognize me, Darnier. But—I should definitely learn more about him."

"Ah, intriguing. I shall endeavor to help you. But never fear, there is no way in the world he would recognize your ladyship now."

As she and Darnier were served their steaming plates, Briana heard the unmistakable voice of Fitzroyal above the laughter. "I've got me another ladybird, gentlemen! This one I'm plucking from the nest . . . maybe from the egg!"

Briana alerted, her hand stilling Darnier to listen.

Fitzroyal tacked on, "All for rescuing a scrap o' lace."

At that clarifying remark, Briana banged her fist on the table, sending the goblets chiming together. "He will *not* pluck her from the egg!" she gasped.

Darnier's expression danced lively. "He won't do *what?*"

"Take Chalandra as his, his . . . whatever!"

121

Darnier cocked his head at her in considerable interest.

She cast a malevolent eye over her shoulder. "Just listen to him; he is in such a great good humor! I knew I made a mistake the moment that man entered my carriage."

Lord Fitzroyal rose with a scraping of his chair and came their way. Briana saw him swagger, and an impulse rose to trip him with her boot. She stifled it at the last instant, knowing she would draw unwanted attention, not to mention a parcel of trouble for Darnier.

Lord Fitzroyal must have felt the force of her glare, however, for as he passed he turned and looked her curiously in the eyes.

Briana stuck her nose in her wine glass and tossed off the remainder in cool style, much as her father had done. Her heart beat erratically as Fitzroyal placed his beefy hand on their tablecloth.

"Sir, you look familiar," he said to her.

Darnier rose, and Briana did likewise, bowing her head with the slightest deference. Thinking quickly, she said in her Radcliffe tone, "I regret I have not had the pleasure, sir."

"Lord Fitzroyal of Northampton." Scratching his broad cheek, he said, "Must be family—you must be! Whom am I addressing?"

"Radcliffe, M' lord. Of Warwickshire."

"And I am Darnier, the duke of Brocco's secretary."

"M' pleasure," waved Lord Fitzroyal, returning his scrutiny to Mr. Radcliffe. "Do you know a Lady Briana Rosewynn, by chance?"

That lady's heart jumped painfully. "My cousin," affirmed she in a cold manner.

"Ahh!" Fitzroyal smiled in satisfaction. "A diamond, is that one."

Darnier inquired, "Do you know the lady, my lord?"

"Rode with her today in Rotten Row. Give her my best, Radcliffe, if you see her before I do. In fact, I'd appreciate direction so I can send her a bouquet."

"She's not interested in anyone like you," snapped Briana before she could stop herself.

Fitzroyal turned back in deadly stillness, eyeing her over his collar points. Darnier shifted.

Briana, keeping a deliberate hauteur, drawled, "Likes her men a lot older, sir."

Fitzroyal slid his eyes at last away from the elegant buck with the neat moustache whose words had quickened his anger. "I am getting older every minute," he said distinctly.

Briana, her heart erratically bouncing, gave him another bow of her head. Then she signaled the pausing waiter to bring more wine.

Her act was fascinating Darnier to the fullest. As Lord Fitzroyal moved away calling a greeting to an acquaintance, Darnier shook his head and mirthfully mopped his brow.

Between her teeth, Briana said, "Now do you see what I did by taking him up in my carriage?"

"He has doubtless set his quizzing glass on *you.*"

"It's Chalandra who's interested in him!"

"Why shouldn't she be?"

Briana's mouth dropped. "Why shouldn't she be? Because he is nothing but a womanizer! You heard him boasting."

"Such a man could never take advantage of you, could he?"

"Never. Thanks to you, I've seen with my eyes and heard with my ears what I suspected about that man. I was sorely tempted to put my boot in his path, and I may end up doing so yet on his return unless we leave this place."

Lord Fitzroyal was, in fact, returning, so Darnier did not put her forbearance to the test but gathered his cape and beaver and said, "Radcliffe, shall we be off?"

Briana had imbibed wine unthinkingly as something to do in her distress, so when she stood and wavered, Darnier caught her about the shoulders, winked at Lord Fitzroyal, and confided, "Too much of Hungry Sally's brew earlier."

Out on the flagstones, Briana repeated, "Hungry Sally's?"

"I told you not to get foxed," chuckled Darnier.

## Chapter 12

## Double Debut

Sir Reginald Channing emerged from between the columns of Park Crescent to offer his hand to the three ladies whose carriage had at last gained his door. "How long have you endured this crawling pace?" he exclaimed, assisting the heavy Mrs. Milburn down.

"Much longer than I have ever waited for anything before, Sir Reginald," returned she. "You must have all of elite London coming to your party."

"A few friends," he said, smiling as he handed the breathless Chalandra and then Briana onto the walk at the edge of the crescent where gaslight radiated from ornate lamps. All three women were a credit to the genius of Madame Yvonne. Chalandra's silvery *crêpe lisse* tucker and bouffant sleeves over jade green gros de Naples did homage to her small proportions whereas her mother's stoutness was diminished in deep purple velvet trimmed at corsage and hem in blond lace.

But it was Briana who made Rex's eyes darken. From her dusky hair in *grandes tire-bouchons* to her stark white sarcenet and lace gown with black velvet sleeve draping, she looked regal and nubile and fresh.

"London, raise your quizzers! Lady Briana has arrived," he said with a grin for his mother before Lady Channing grasped Briana's hand and added her welcome. Briana found her ladyship white-haired with fine skin and a warm handshake, fully in control as she greeted her dozens of guests snaking up the staircase. The difference, slight though it was, between Briana's reception and that of Mrs. Milburn and Chalandra was noted by Briana who remembered her mother's instructions in the subtleties of preferment to people of rank.

Chalandra certainly hadn't noticed that she wasn't greeted with anything less than her usual rapt audience. At the columned entrance to the ballroom, she paused for effect and said with a breathy smile, "Briana, can you see over everyone's heads? Is Lord Fitzroyal here?"

Another jab at Briana's height, but she obligingly cast her eyes over every large man. "He's not here, and I doubt he will be. I'm convinced he has no ton."

Chalandra gave a pretty pout and slid rather too quickly into dialogue with two young men in waist-nipping corsets who had their eyes fixed on herself and Briana. Mrs. Milburn intruded on her daughter's circle to add tardy respectability to the group and to undertake the pleasing prospect of self-introductions.

Briana felt the full force of the honor given her when Rex returned to her side after having welcomed one of the royal dukes. She could see that every eye in the room recognized the quality of the tall, handsome, and wealth-backed son of the late Sir Kester Channing.

Chalandra materialized in front of Rex. "What a profusion of jewels in this ballroom!" she exclaimed. "How could you forget, Rex, to tell us it was going to be a night of display? We would have worn some stones ourselves."

While Briana, with visions of the glass beads in Chalandra's casket, fought to keep from laughing, Rex said, "You have no need for them, Miss Milburn; your wit sparkles enough."

As soon as he could politely do so, he drew Briana aside. "Will you open the ball with me?"

Briana could scarcely believe it. Out of all these beautiful women? As she danced across the gleaming parquet floor with her gloved hands in Rex's and a frightful kaleidoscope of eyes following her, she felt she was spinning into another sphere, and elation brought a dainty flush to her cheekbones.

"I take it you're enjoying London?" smiled Rex, sending her lace scallops lifting in the twirling cotillion. "You're positively radiant. What have you seen?"

Briana did not tell him she had seen the inside of Stevens's Hotel at the hour of midnight, nor did she mention she had entered the portals of Brocco House under cover of a parasol like a Cyprian. Between the movements of the dance, she confined her report to the general sights and the parks and Yvonne's.

When the candles in the chandeliers had shortened by an hour, Briana, in need of drink from dance after dance with talkative, admiring society men, approached Chalandra whose tinkling laugh could be heard over the buzz of voices at the punch table. "Cousin, have you a supper partner?"

"Why, what a question!" drawled Chalandra. "Here he is now." Briana looked round into the face of Lord Fitzroyal.

"Your servant, Lady Briana," said he, presenting stiffly coiffed blond curls. "I looked to dance with you, but have so far been particularly unfortunate."

She had seen him on two occasions making his

purposeful way toward her, and had practically turned into the arms of the nearest gentleman.

"Good evening, Lord Fitzroyal," she said. How could she remove him from her cousin without taking him on herself? She had tried to impress upon Chalandra that the man was undesirable, but how could she prove it without revealing exactly what she had heard him say in Stevens's Hotel while she was out on a lark dressed as a man? Chalandra had dismissed Briana's warnings as totally unfounded.

Briana grit her teeth to see Chalandra place her gloved hand possessively in the crook of Fitzroyal's arm and say, "Lead me to the feast, your lordship."

He would lead her to a feast, all right, thought Briana. She knew it was Lord Fitzroyal's interest in more than one little morsel which led him to say, "Lady Briana, will you do me the honor of taking my free arm? I have met your cousin as well as you so I feel at liberty to request your gracious company at table."

Briana regally replied, "Thank you, but no." She was relieved he had not mentioned her "cousin" by the name of Radcliffe. Chalandra must credit the reference to herself.

A firm touch on her elbow brought Rex saying, "May I take you in to supper now?" Two other gentlemen fell back.

"Thank you, I—" Past Rex's shoulder her eyes fell on a stunning golden-haired woman. Her arm was linked in a man's who turned to smile down at her: Darnier!

Briana's smile wavered. Hastily she flicked her eyes back to Rex. Quelling the strange stab in her heart, she said, "I would be honored to be your supper partner, sir."

"Please! Call me Rex," he reminded her. "I adore having the privilege of calling you Briana."

# MORE PASSION AND ADVENTURE AWAIT... YOUR TRIP TO A BIG ADVENTUROUS WORLD BEGINS WHEN YOU ACCEPT YOUR FIRST 4 NOVELS ABSOLUTELY *FREE* (AN $18.00 VALUE)

Accept your Free gift and start to experience more of the passion and adventure you like in a historical romance novel. Each Zebra novel is filled with proud men, spirited women and tempestuous love that you'll remember long after you turn the last page.

Zebra Historical Romances are the finest novels of their kind. They are written by authors who really know how to weave tales of romance and adventure in the historical settings you love. You'll feel like you've actually gone back in time with the thrilling stories that each Zebra novel offers.

## GET YOUR FREE GIFT WITH THE START OF YOUR HOME SUBSCRIPTION

Our readers tell us that these books sell out very fast in book stores and often they miss the newest titles. So Zebra has made arrangements for you to receive the four newest novels published each month.

You'll be guaranteed that you'll never miss a title, and home delivery is so convenient. And to show you just how easy it is to get Zebra Historical Romances, we'll send you your first 4 books absolutely FREE! Our gift to you just for trying our home subscription service.

## BIG SAVINGS AND FREE HOME DELIVERY

Each month, you'll receive the four newest titles as soon as they are published. You'll probably receive them even before the bookstores do. What's more, you may preview these exciting novels free for 10 days. If you like them as much as we think you will, just pay the low preferred subscriber's price of just $3.75 each. *You'll save $3.00 each month off the publisher's price.* AND, your savings are even greater because there are never any shipping, handling or other hidden charges—FREE Home Delivery. Of course you can return any shipment within 10 days for full credit, no questions asked. There is no minimum number of books you must buy.

Unfurling her fan to cool her cheeks, she allowed herself another glance, but could not bear the contrast of such fragile femininity next to the dark ruggedness of Darnier in ball dress.

As she moved through the crowd with Rex, she became the object of speculation by the haute ton. Sir Reginald Channing, their popular host, had singled out an exquisite newcomer, the daughter of an earl.

Very casually, Briana asked as they moved along the balcony to the banqueting rooms, "Was that Mr. Darnier?" She felt horrid at the sound of her own words while her heart was in such an uncharitable state towards the china doll creature at his side.

"Darnier—yes. I suggested Mother invite him. The duke couldn't come tonight, but I thought his hard-working secretary deserved a night in the society of beautiful women."

"Why, naturally he deserves it. How kind of you," said Briana. The remainder of the hour was marred by the maddening glimpses she had of the back of Darnier's dark head next to that spun gold one interspersed with silk leaves. Why should the sight prick her so? She knew she should glory in her seat at the head table between Rex and His Royal Highness, the Duke of York, for Mrs. Milburn's envious countenance told her so.

But *leaves*. Did Darnier also write assignation notes to that lady, with leaves as his clues? Did the clever thing wear them now as a reminder in her hair? The thought made Briana flash a severe look at the Duke of York's request to pass the salt cellar.

"My request isn't apt to break our friendship, is it?" he asked, eyes askance. Thereafter Briana tried to ignore Darnier's part of the room and be laughingly sweet to her dinner companions.

Her worry over the progress Lord Fitzroyal was making

compounded when she saw him lift a dried apricot on a fork and convey it into Chalandra's open mouth. Horrors, didn't Chalandra realize what fast behavior that was? Briana, powerless to stop her, could only watch with quaking heart as Chalandra took center stage at her end of the far table, drawing male guffaws and baited questions from the boldest. Old men and dowagers turned to look once at whom it was who so conducted herself. Briana knew Chalandra interpreted every look as admiration or envy.

Upon returning to the ballroom, Rex and Briana came face to face with Darnier and his supper partner. Darnier bowed low, saying, "Lady Briana, it is an honor to meet you again."

Briana smiled in a misty way, unable to honestly meet his eyes. "Mr. Darnier."

He said, "May I present Miss Cordelia Landers to Lady Briana Rosewynn."

The lovely Miss Landers curtsied. Briana summoned all her forces into a gracious smile down at the flawless face. "My pleasure," she lied.

Then followed the well-modulated phrases of the woman who had been asking Darnier if he might not introduce her to the beautiful lady in the white lace gown with such arresting sleeves. Briana's heart sank as she watched those violet eyes look up at Darnier for verification.

To Briana's relief, Rex maneuvered her away the next minute. He presented her to Countess Lieven and Lady Jersey, the legendary queens of the ton.

"I remember you, Lady Jersey," said Briana, "for you visited my mother."

"I was wondering if you would. I recall a time we had dinner with your parents, Lord Jersey and I, and you sang for us. Do you still sing, Briana?"

"No, since my parents died last year, I've been in mourning. I've only sung at Shipston church."

Rex inserted in timely fashion, "But she would like to waltz with me, if you will sanction her, dear ladies." His slow smile at each in turn would have melted the objections of the most rigid mother superior.

In the arms of Rex, Briana could not help asking, "Who is Miss Landers? A friend of yours?"

"I believe her father is in banking. She's the second sister to come out; the first married a shipping merchant. I hear say titles aren't important to that family, for their coffers are bulging. Miss Cordelia, naturally, has many men clamoring for notice."

"You among them, no doubt?"

"Oh no! She's hardly my style. I prefer raven-haired goddesses to pale diminutive chits." He twirled Briana, looking at her in a way that caused other feminine hearts to lose hope.

Would Lady Stotleigh have been proud of her daughter at this moment? Briana felt she would have been. She would have declared that it was what Briana could expect: to be courted by the handsomest and the most eligible men of the peerage.

Briana's spirits rose with the lilting music and Rex's attentive words, but when the dance ended and he bowed himself away to dance with Countess Lieven, a frustrating thought returned to Briana: Mr. Darnier liked pale, diminutive misses, and that Cordelia miss in particular.

The knowledge haunted her all the evening until she turned from her final curtsy to Lord Alvanley to find Darnier standing there, two winking goblets in his hands. "Could you use some wine? I've only filled it halfway, you'll notice."

Briana dimpled. "Yes, I see." They laughed. She felt a sudden relief.

Darnier lifted an eyebrow in invitation, leading the way to a nearby statue alcove. Leaning on Handel's pedestal, he sipped and said, "Are you still concerned about that predatory Fitzroyal?"

"Yes," sighed Briana. "Chalandra has danced with the man twice since supper, and now they're playing cards."

"I noticed," said Darnier wryly. "Do you feel it is your responsibility to protect her?"

"If there is any way to do it, I must!"

"Then, what do you think of this plan?"

# Chapter 13

## Challenge at Vauxhall

Briana adjusted her snow white turban and smoothed down the chin beard Darnier had affixed to her jaw. Her padded shoulders shook with her giggles beneath the white tunic as she surveyed herself in the dark window of the coach. "I feel the need for a camel," she said.

At the look of her white grin beneath the moustache and beard, Darnier slapped his thigh. "See if you don't catch a string of women tonight, you lucky Turk!"

"Stop laughing! I'm doing this not for your enjoyment, but for my little cousin's sake. Aren't we ever going to move?"

Darnier pushed the door lever. "Let's abandon this hearse; otherwise we'll sit here 'til dawn." The neighs of horses, the shouts and the jingle of harness backed by music wafting from an orchestra filled the air as Briana tucked up her flowing robes and descended. Darnier, splendid before her, wore fitted hose in the sixteenth-century style, complete with black and white codpiece. When Briana first clapped eyes on him in the dimness of the garden, she had given it a shocked scrutiny. He had laughed hugely. He looked rakish and virile in the dark, with one leg white and the other black vertical stripes. Adding authenticity to his Renaissance theme was a red velvet and silver doublet with slashes in the sleeves and a fine lawn shirt seen as a frill at his neck and wrists.

"Sir Walter," Briana called pointedly, reaching back to the carriage seat, "Your cap, sir."

Darnier presented his head with a bow. Briana sank the velvet cap onto his crispy locks, and felt daring at the contact.

"Your kindness overwhelmeth me," he said, looking fondly into her one eye not hidden by the black eye patch.

Briana felt a sudden need for forced playfulness, so she adjusted his cap until the red plume arced roguishly over his ear. "*Vous êtes trop ravissant, monsieur,*" she pronounced. Yes, utterly too ravishing for her peace of mind.

"On the other hand, I liked you best in that filmy gown you were wearing at Rex's ball: the one with the designs on the sleeves, and that transparent lace."

"It was not transparent!" refuted Briana, remembering the bodice.

Darnier grinned. Looking over her masculine robes, he shook his head regretfully. "What you won't put yourself through for that cousin of yours."

While impatient passengers in shrill voices admonished their drivers to action or abandoned their carriages, Briana wondered how they would ever find Lord Fitzroyal in such a crush.

Darnier, unable to see an opening in the line of vehicles, ducked beneath the belly of a carriage horse, and Briana was forced to scramble after him, but not before she gave its coachman the admonishment not to touch his whip. They were hailed by an individual in the

134

pressing line of humanity outside Haydn's gate. The man was instantly recognizable as Major Quentin with whom Chalandra had spoken in Rotten Row. He wore a Wellington hat with his red-coated military uniform as costume, and his lively brown eyes lit on Darnier. "You and your wicked-looking Persian, step right in here. Never so relieved to see a familiar face."

When Darnier introduced Briana as Mr. Radcliffe from the country, the major said, "So you've never been to one of these *ridotto al frescoes* then, eh, Radcliffe?"

"Never had the chance," Briana said in her low timber.

Major Quentin leaned an arm companionably on her shoulder. "You'll tolerate it mighty well, I daresay. Look there!" Quentin's attention fastened on two young ladies whose attractions were their bodices, cut so low that their bursting orbs could be examined by every passing ogler. "Take a look, Radcliffe, that's only the first course. There are bound to be more in the walks. I'm meeting someone myself, but I'll show you, my boy."

Briana's one eye met Darnier's crinkled ones in an uncompromising glare. She feared her cheeks were aglow.

"Quentin," said Darnier, "this rake Radcliffe, wicked devil that he is, has no time for ladies tonight. He and I came for the sole purpose of locating Lord Fitzroyal. We'd appreciate your pointing us in his direction should he come across your sights."

"What need would you have of Fitzroyal?" asked the major. "I watched him at Watier's tearing an estate from a doddering old peer with a slap of a card. He's bad news."

"I can well imagine," Darnier remarked. "But we have other reasons to spy on the man."

As they paid their half a guinea to enter Vauxhall Gardens, Major Quentin promised to meet them at the Chinese Pavilion in an hour and report on his search.

"Don't expect to see him again," Darnier told Briana. "He's winging after the ladybirds."

Briana was shocked at the raucous atmosphere which prevailed among the outlandishly costumed throng, and could see little hope of finding the man they sought when hundreds of people milled about, many of them masked.

When they approached the music issuing from a pavilion of ornate boxes, Darnier said, "Voilà," and indicated a large figure in a long brown wig and tricorn. Lord Fitzroyal it was, roaring at some witticism made by an opulent shepherdess in pale blue and panniers, her hair a high powdered wig.

As they hurried toward Fitzroyal, the shepherdess playfully rapped her staff at the brim of his hat, knocking it off. He jerked his wig back into place and scowled at her.

Darnier, smooth as silk, strode forward, retrieved Fitzroyal's hat from the ground behind him, and presented it to the surprised woman.

"La, a man of honor, as I live! *Merci, merci mon cavalier!*" The laugh of the shepherdess turned on Fitzroyal. "I wonder what this kind stranger would've done for me had I slit your trousers and *they* had fallen to the ground?" The crowd's laughter rose around her.

Lord Fitzroyal snatched his tricorn from her. Menacingly he said, "Emmaline, I have need of a few words with you . . . !" He pushed her before him.

Emmaline threw a regretful glance at Darnier over her shoulder. Then she caught sight of Briana moving to his side, outstanding in her white turban and eye patch. "Fitzie, do stay a moment! I have not been presented to those two grand gentlemen."

Lord Fitzroyal, exasperated, turned his eyes on Briana. He blinked in surprise, crossed his arms, and drawled in a voice of discovery, "It must be the cousin of Lady Briana Rosewynn again."

Briana quaked but said, "Correct. Radcliffe, my lord."

"I'm Emmaline Clifton," inserted the woman with a bright pink smile.

"Did you convey my greetings to Lady Briana?" Fitzroyal demanded.

Briana fingered her beard. "Did I remember to do that, Darnier?"

Lord Fitzroyal's face grew red.

Darnier said, "I am certain you did." He gave her a look, wondering at her deliberate needling of the fellow.

But Briana seethed at the way Lord Fitzroyal was making inroads into her household through Chalandra. Now he trumpeted her own name in this public place.

Emmaline Clifton curtsied, affording Darnier and Briana an unobstructed view of her mountainous properties. "La, Mr. Radcliffe, you are your first time here at Vauxhall?" At hearing it *was* the first visit, she said, "Come, Fitzie, I must have a dance with him, he is so new and bewildered. And then with the cavalier. It is only polite, no?" Emmaline seized Briana's hand before she could protest and pulled her toward the couples flocking to the floor below the orchestra.

Briana, uncomfortably in tow, heard Darnier say, "Your Miss Clifton is indeed kind, Lord Fitzroyal. Radcliffe never would have asked a woman to dance of his own volition."

As Emmaline poised, elbows raised, waiting for her turbaned partner to take her into the waltz, Briana sinkingly realized she must take the lead. She put her hand on Emmaline's corseted waist and tried to think how the man must move, opposite to the woman.

Emmaline giggled. "Are you afraid of me, Mr. Radcliffe, or don't you dance much?"

"I don't dance at all, Miss Clifton."

"Well, do give it your best effort for half a minute. Just move me past this knot of commoners; swing me out of

137

Fitzie's sight," she directed, "so we can talk without his frown aiming at us."

Briana concentrated on dancing the woman toward a hedge-lined walk.

"You are right: you cannot dance, Mr. Radcliffe. All the better, I am parched. Will you get me a champagne?"

"At your service," Briana murmured, stepping into the path of a servant and lifting two glasses from his tray. Although this was unplanned, a talk with Fitzroyal's mistress could shed light on how tight a liaison it was, and Darnier could try to discover whether Fitzroyal had serious intent in Chalandra's direction and try to ward him off with their story of an attachment in Warwickshire.

"You must call me Emmaline, and come calling one day," that woman said suddenly with a bat of her darkened lashes. "Soon," she added, licking her lips.

Briana achieved a sardonic look down her nose. "Indeed? Does not yonder lord take care of you?"

"He has a roving eye, does Fitzroyal." She nervously fingered her face patch. "I am likely to part ways with him. I'd be glad to leave him in favor of you, Mr. Radcliffe."

Briana gulped at the champagne, and heard herself say, "And what is your address, Miss Emmaline?"

The woman dipped into her bodice and produced a warm pink card. "I will receive you at your convenience any day but Saturday and Thursday. I implore you not to drop a *hint* of this to Fitzroyal."

"Doesn't he let you receive callers of an afternoon?" Briana drawled on, not quite sure into what deep waters all this would lead, but growing positive that the more she talked to the woman, the more she would have to tell Darnier.

"No! He considers me his exclusive piece which is a bore, seeing as he's neither generous nor as respectable as was Lord Stot—" The woman cut off her own words with a quick sip.

Briana's heart galloped. *"Lord Stotleigh?"* she demanded.

Emmaline swallowed. "He's dead now."

Beginning to tremble, Briana stared at the woman. She just could not picture her father taking this outspoken beauty into his arms, and more!

"I have been very sad," Emmaline said, "and very ill since Lord Stotleigh left. And I've been forced to leave the home he gave me besides." Her voice dropped as she clamped her warm hand around Briana's wrist. "I admit to you alone that Lord Fitzroyal does not take my late earl's place in any way. But you—you are his late lordship's relation, are you not? Fitzie told me he had met a Radcliffe who was. We could take up, my dear Persian, at once."

"I am *not* in need of a woman!" snapped Briana at her most forbidding. Icy anger had been shooting through her, and now glinted in her eyes.

"But you do not know that yet, dear Radcliffe! You are too young and inexperienced to know!"

Briana spotted Darnier's red plume moving through the crowd, and behind him, Fitzroyal's gold one.

Emmaline, oblivious, grasped Briana's robes and said, "I will teach you how to dance," and she moved suggestively from side to side, "and to do many other positively delightful things—!" The woman pulled on Briana's neck and planted a kiss on her startled lips.

The next thing Briana saw was the disbelieving look beneath Darnier's skyrocketing brows, and then Lord Fitzroyal's thrusting frame as he strode furiously toward them. Emmaline looked over her bare shoulder and gasped, "Tell him you kissed me! Tell him, please! You're a man—he'll beat me!"

*"Beat* you?"

"Emmaline!" Fitzroyal roared.

"Yes, Fitzie?"

"Was that a kiss I saw between you and this fancy whelp?" He slapped his gloves, hard and cruel, across her eyes. Emmaline shrieked in pain.

Briana and Darnier both reacted: Darnier catching the tearful woman, while Briana, her dam of fury bursting, snatched the shepherdess's staff falling from Emmaline's limp grasp. With a hefty blow, Briana cracked it in two on the back of Fitzroyal's neck.

Cries of excitement went up from the gaping crowd as Lord Fitzroyal staggered. He renewed his forces and lunged at Briana, his eyes alight with murder. In a flash of red and black, Darnier leapt between them.

In the scuffle that followed, Fitzroyal could be seen thrashing about trying to catch Darnier's quick body, and redoubling his fists in increasing rage. To Briana's elation, Darnier sent a hard, swift jab to the stout jaw between the brown curls. As Fitzroyal fell backward, spectators tightened the crowd to gaze and Darnier said distinctly to Briana over the press, "The time has come to depart, my friend."

Leaving Emmaline nigh fainting onto a masked matron, Briana made haste to elbow her way through the onlookers. She heard word spreading like the Fire of London that two doxy-chasers had put out the lights of a bruising peer.

In a maze of shrubbery, Darnier said, "Quickly, off with that beacon of a turban!"

Briana bent her head and unwound it as they raced along. "Here," she said, thrusting Miss Clifton's card at him, "what do you make of that?"

Darnier halted and turned it toward the distant light. He gave a shout of laughter. "Behold the lightning conquest! Yo-ho! Especially for a raw up from the country."

"Hush, Darnier, it was awful! I *refuse* to go near that woman again."

"Then why did you accept her card? For me? Oh no!" He looked slyly from the corner of his eye.

"Absolutely not. Men should never take mistresses! They—"

"Yes?"

How could she possibly put it? "They positively ruin one's life," she said with feeling. "Women are the first to suffer, but men regret their entanglements sooner or later. Most importantly, it's against the Bible." She knew she was preaching, and she didn't care. She could only think of her lovely mother wronged.

Darnier's expression was attentive and he looked about to speak. But to ruin all, a little scream came from an intersecting path and a golden-haired lady ran at them, arms outstretched. "Help us, please, if you're kind gentlemen!" she cried. A quick look into Darnier's face, and she threw herself into his arms with a cry of joy.

Addressing his armful, Darnier exclaimed, "Miss Landers!"

Another damsel appeared from the shrubbery, struggling to pull herself from the clutches of two disheveled bucks. With great lung power she cried, "And if you're not kind, show your unkindness to these two!"

"Excuse me a moment," said Darnier, thrusting Miss Landers at Briana while he strode to the scene of altercation.

Briana fended off Cordelia's effusive expressions of gratitude by saying coldly, "You're welcome, miss. Please to calm yourself." Her heart sank. Why must this china doll appear upon the scene in such fetching distress?

The lecherous young bucks rushed at Darnier of one accord. The damsel with dark ringlets scuttled to freedom, cheering Darnier on as he ducked and threw one of them with a loud thud upon the path. Briana had an urge to even the odds against the two frisky youths so full of their whisky, but saw in an instant that Darnier needed no help. He dodged and punched until both lay panting in the shadows of the hedge.

"Oh, Darnier!" breathed Cordelia, lifting her white draperies and rushing to him. "You saved us! I'm infinitely relieved that you, of all men, were here. How can I ever show my gratitude to you?"

Briana had just been wondering the same in regard to Fitzroyal. Now she noted the look of pain that shot across Darnier's features as he massaged his shoulder through his doublet. "You can show your gratitude, Cordelia, by staying away from such unlit walks where ladies should never wander."

Between clenched jaws, Briana added, "*Exactement.* Ladies should not set foot in lanes of such dalliance." To Darnier she said, "And you should not have to toss dandies through the air, no matter how light they look."

In spite of himself, Darnier laughed, but Briana turned on her boot heel.

As she stood apart with folded arms, she heard Miss Landers asking when she would be seeing Darnier in her father's parlor again. Briana turned and saw the look with which Cordelia coaxed him. Granted, she was a vision of frailty in a Grecian robe crisscrossed about the bodice in laurel leaves with a wreath of the same gracing her tumbling curls, but did Darnier have to succumb with such an attractive grin? Briana swallowed against a lump in her throat.

Darnier said, "That we will discuss when I've seen you safely to your mother." With a motion to Briana to follow, he offered his arms to the ladies.

Furious, Briana made a bow of dismissal, maintaining the most disinterested, Byronic look she had practiced before her glass. Those ladies must be made to lament

142

that they had failed to interest at least one man who trod British soil.

"Well, I'll be back soon," said Darnier to Briana.

She nodded curtly, not looking at him. When they had gone, she squeezed her turban muslin into a large ball and could have thrown it at him.

"Ho there! Radcliffe!" came an angry bellow. It was Lord Fitzroyal. Bereft of wig, his pale hair rose in spikes, and he strode straight for her, his muscular thighs rippling in his torn hose. "I want you, Radcliffe!" he said without demur, pointing at her face. Darnier was out of sight.

"What for?" she asked, squaring her shoulders despite her fear.

Glaring, Fitzroyal threw his gloves at her feet. "Rascal! I'll teach you to meddle with my property! Name your second!"

Briana looked up from the gloves on the ground. "Second?" she repeated. "A *duel?*"

"Amazing how brilliant you are. I challenge you, you ladybird thief!"

Briana's fists tightened. "How dare you!" she said between her teeth. "You behave unjustly, your lordship." She kicked the gloves back onto his boots.

Swearing, he picked them up with a snap, and Briana gave a desperate look around. Where was Darnier when she needed him?

Fitzroyal advanced. She smelled the brandy on his breath as he enunciated, "I know what I saw. You not only danced with my mistress but you *kissed* my mistress! Practically under my nose, and before all of London!" Fire leaped in the closely set eyes.

"You misunderstand!" She hoped that, like a strange dog, he didn't hear her heart pounding or sense her fear.

"I understand," sneered Fitzroyal, "that she gave you her card. How can one misunderstand that, you villain?"

143

Briana wondered in her desperation if she should tell him she was a woman. No, never, for that would effectively ruin her. Since she'd taken on the role of her fictitious cousin, she must act the honorable gentleman or hear her family name smeared in all the clubs and drawing rooms of London.

"I am no villain, your lordship. It would have been the utmost rudeness to refuse a woman's card, but I have no plans to see more of your Miss Clifton."

"And pray, what decided you that? Is she not good enough for your fancy pants?"

Briana didn't know what to do or say. She managed, "Of course she is attractive, but I will not meet her again, I assure you!"

"Then meet *me*, you coward!" shouted Fitzroyal, coming after her as she stalked away.

Briana was aghast and frightened when he grasped her arm and she was spun around to face him. A cold fury rising, she jerked away, expelling slowly, "I am no coward!"

"Then name your second," Fitzroyal mocked.

Briana, unable to think, heard herself say, "I must consult with my friends."

Around the plantation of shadowy trees came Darnier. He was visibly taken aback at the sight of Briana, horns locked with Fitzroyal. "What can we do for you, your lordship?" he called in a congenial tone.

Fitzroyal swiveled around. "*You* can do nothing! Radcliffe, however, must give me satisfaction. We shall meet tomorrow morning in the Field of the Forty Footsteps."

Darnier's look of disbelief wavered over Briana. To Fitzroyal he said as though joking. "Surely you have not coerced our young Mr. Radcliffe to a duel, your lordship!"

"Of course I have. And the dastardly coward has at

last accepted."

Briana shot Darnier a wild-eyed look.

Earnestly Darnier said, "I recommend that you reconsider, your lordship. Radcliffe did not mean anything toward Miss Clifton. Surely you could see it was all her idea."

"You keep out of this!" snarled Fitzroyal. "This rake will pay for his interference!"

Briana, bristling, said, "You treated your mistress cruelly."

Fitzroyal grabbed Briana's robe front. "She's my property," he punctuated. "I can do with her as I bloody well please. Now name your deuced second or we'll do without seconds!"

Darnier yanked Fitzroyal off. "I will meet you myself," he said. "How's your jaw?"

Fitzroyal looked sorely tempted to return the injury, but he looked wary and merely pushed Darnier off. "It would please me to do away with you, but I don't stoop to accepting challenges from nobodies. So quit your distractions. I aim to sink my blade through this handsome puppy in the morning."

"Then I would be honored to be Radcliffe's second," Darnier said in clipped tones.

Briana's brain reeled. How had her masquerade turned into such dreamlike, frightening consequences?

"Suit yourself," Fitzroyal said to Darnier. "Daybreak, then."

"Not so," Darnier said curtly. "Radcliffe is promised to his relations in the country, and leaves in the morning. You'll have to make it after Thursday se'nnight; isn't that right, Radcliffe?"

Briana nodded, totally bewildered. He was buying time, but for what?

"Thursday se'nnight, then. Daybreak," barked Fitzroyal.

"Who is your second?" Darnier inquired.

"Clewes will stand for me."

Darnier asked Clewes's direction. "Now for the weapons," he said.

There was a distinct thud in Briana's breast.

"Swords," said Fitzroyal with finality and a ring of superiority.

"This is not the continent," said Darnier dryly. "The choice is Radcliffe's."

Briana stared.

Darnier said, "Excuse us, your lordship," and he pulled her into the maze. "I don't suppose you've ever learned to fence."

"Of course not!" she whispered back.

"Can you handle a flintlock musket, then? What a question—how about a rapier?"

"Darnier, I can handle *nothing!*" she said fervently.

"Then it'll have to be pistols."

"But I've never held one in my li—"

Darnier stepped out and she heard him say, "Pistols it is."

Briana, her knees weak, emerged to face Fitzroyal. She squinted formidably.

"Pistols," mocked Fitzroyal, looking Briana up and down as he rubbed his palms together. "I'll enjoy blasting a hole through those robes. Better yet, through that eye patch."

"Go easy, your lordship," warned Darnier. "Radcliffe is cousin to Lady Briana Rosewynn, remember? If you kill or maim her beloved kin, she'll have you sent before the House and very likely exiled. Do think."

Lord Fitzroyal gave them each a venomous look, turned on his heel, and strode toward the Chinese Pavilion in what appeared to be high dudgeon.

# Chapter 14

## One Voucher for Almack's

"Lord Fitzroyal is here to see you, my lady," said Mary in an urgent voice as she parted Briana's bed curtains.

Briana jumped to a sitting position and stared at the maid through sleep-hazed eyes. "That man is here?"

"Here is his gaudy card. He said he'll wait until Lady Briana Rosewynn is ready to receive him."

"I will not receive him!" said Briana with feeling, pulling up the lacy coverlet and flouncing back onto her pillow. He is going to blow a hole through me in a se'nnight, she added to herself.

"He will wait, my lady—he has that look about him. And Miss Chalandra was on her way to the drawing room as I came up, so he'll be talking with her for ages if you don't go soon," finished Mary.

"Heavens! I must put an immediate halt to that tête-à-tête. Run and tell Mrs. Milburn that her chaperonage is needed in the drawing room on the instant. Or Anselma, or Frances—anyone."

Sliding out of bed, Briana thought that here was her chance to try to persuade the man from shooting her "cousin Radcliffe."

Twenty minutes later, when Briana strolled confidently into the drawing room, she made a strikingly feminine sight for Lord Fitzroyal and her relations. A grand leghorn hat perched on her dark mane, its pink and aqua ribbons curling to her waist. An aqua jaconet round dress covered in teal French work round the hem and puffed shoulders showed off her sumptuous figure. A white lutestring spencer was thrown over her arm and she held the ferule end of a bright pink parasol. "Lord Fitzroyal?" she uttered politely, careful to sound as different as possible from Mr. Radcliffe.

"Yes, Briana," interjected Mrs. Milburn importantly, "he has come to see us."

Lord Fitzroyal rose from his seat at the window where he had been sipping breakfast tea with the two Milburn women. "Lady Briana!" he vibrated in a voice of pleasure. She noticed his jaw had been touched with theatrical face paste. "I beg your forgiveness for calling so early," he continued, "but I did promise you I would do so after your kindness in giving me a lift in the park. I could not in good conscience pass through Berkeley Square without looking in to thank you."

"You are welcome. I regret, however, that I am on the point of departure and cannot stay to visit this morning."

Mrs. Milburn's chins dropped.

"Then, ladies, will you excuse me if I speak for a brief moment with Lady Briana? In the hall, perhaps?" he addressed first his attentive two, then came to Briana's side, smiling down at her in a manner calculated to charm.

Mrs. Milburn called, "Well, I do believe I'll countenance the hall as sufficiently proper in this case, since Paget is there."

Briana, with spine straight, swished out of the room, Lord Fitzroyal in her wake. He said sympathetically,

"Tries to mother you, does she?"

Briana turned to him. "A word, you said, your lordship?"

"Yes, I—" He halted as if overcome by her dark blue eyes beneath the hat brim, then took her slim arm in his two hands. "Yes, Lady Briana, I cannot exist another day—that is, without telling you that I have been living but for another glimpse of you. Never have I seen a more statuesque beauty than yourself." His eyes traveled. "I wish to see more of you, for my thoughts are of nothing but—"

"Have done!" ordered Briana, pulling her wrist out of his thick hot fingers. Mustering a playful tone, she said, "It does not please me to listen to such a flow of idiocy." As she saw Fitzroyal's countenance all at sea, she heard a latch click, and knew Chalandra and her mother listened at the crack in the door.

"It is the gospel truth! You are not a vain woman, or you would acknowledge my words as due tributes at your shrine. Say that I may take you riding in the park this afternoon."

"No, Lord Fitzroyal, it is not possible. I have other commitments. Anselma?" she called.

Anselma and Mary appeared from the back hall where she had instructed them to wait. "You may walk me to my carriage, your lordship," Briana said as Paget flung wide the portal to the sunshine and birdsong.

"You were so kind to me the day we met," Lord Fitzroyal murmured. "Why will you not ride with me?"

Briana waited until she was out of earshot of her attendants waiting at the door of her town chariot. She looked squarely into his eyes. "I hear you are engaged to duel with my cousin," she said levelly.

The statement took him by surprise. Surely he had not expected word to reach a lady's bower by morning. "Well, well! How do you know?"

Briana gave him a frozen look and stepped into her glossy vehicle. Her female troops closed in behind her. Would that slosh of cold water on his suit make him cry off the duel? She dearly hoped it would, but her doubts rose as her chariot rolled into Bruton Street.

Briana alighted at Lyon's Linendrapers, and spent three-quarters of an hour feverishly choosing the remaining fabrics for the duchess's rooms at Brocco Park. She was relieved to find a watered silk in Mr. Lyon's newest shipment from Brussels, for it had very similar shadings of pale mint, French blue, ivory, and pink to the design she had done in watercolors for the fireplace border. She bought the silk for the outer bed hangings, planning to line it with Valenciennes lace.

She felt much better for this exercise in the creative. She felt certain she could transform the Brocco rooms into a fairyland like none she had yet seen. If only she could do it before this frightening duel business commenced.

As she ignored Anselma's prattle about damask velvet for the antechamber chairs, Briana's mind left the realm of patterns and fabrics to ponder her predicament. Darnier had confirmed, as they hastily left Vauxhall Gardens by hired boat, that unless she learned to shoot a pistol before the duel, her cousin Radcliffe would be a disgrace to the Rosewynn name.

"What?" Briana had uttered. "I must really shoot that pompous lord?"

"Frankly, I would delope if I were you."

"Of course," shuddered Briana, unable to imagine actually shooting a lump of lead into a living being. "But what if he shoots me, Darnier?" she asked in a small voice.

"I will meet with Clewes in the morning and work to effect a reconciliation. You should write a formal apology without delay."

"Apology! But you and I both know I did nothing wrong. His woman absolutely threw herself on me."

As the river men rowed the boat past the houses of Parliament and into the darkness beneath a deep arch of Westminster Bridge, Darnier said, "Write the apology. But you would still do well to practice shooting." The last word echoed off the water and off the stone.

"Yes," whispered Briana, shivering. "If he does not accept my apology and insists I appear, I must know how to do it, mustn't I? But what if I told him who Radcliffe really is?" she said in a moment of weakness.

"You'd be another Caroline Lamb."

"Heaven forbid." Briana imagined her name bandied about behind fans, her unladylike deeds seen in print and caricature. It was half after two when Briana stood waiting for the knot of her servants to leave the back door where they were smoking tobacco and telling stories. Darnier had left for Brocco House at her insistence: she begged him to go home and rest his painful shoulder. When she had asked him how he received his injury, he had said he would explain it to her some other day, that it was her situation that bore thinking of now.

Briana grew stiff hiding in the shrubbery, and furious with memories of Cordelia Landers asking when Darnier would next be in her father's parlor.

Briana snapped out of this review of Vauxhall night when Anselma pressed her with a direct question which Briana must needs hear repeated. She curtly ended her duenna's dreams of contributing to the decorating process by stating, "I will choose the chair coverings myself after I've found lamps, Anselma."

Anselma chirped in distress.

"I'm sorry," sighed Briana. "I'm preoccupied; forgive me."

As clouds scuttled over London and it threatened to rain, Briana stopped at Madame Yvonne's to check on the

151

progress of her wardrobe. When she emerged from under the blue canopy, Darnier stood leaning his shoulders against her parked chariot, holding his hat in the breeze and chatting congenially with Jacks, her coachman.

"Darnier! What are you doing here in front of my modiste's?"

"Where better to see beautiful women?" he tossed back, his eyes deepening in appreciation of her lifting skirts. He looked fit, but Briana sensed a difference in his movements.

"You were injured last night, weren't you?" she whispered, looking into his eyes for truth.

"A little," he admitted. "But I've seen Fitzroyal's second, Dr. Clewes. He checked my shoulder and then he went to plead with Fitzroyal."

"And?"

"Clewes said the apology you wrote is not viewed as genuine. I will see Fitzroyal myself this afternoon. But, Briana," and here Darnier looked down at her in great concern, "I think I had better teach you to shoot . . . immediately."

Her hand went to her throat.

"I couldn't send a note of assignation to Berkeley Square, for what if it fell into the wrong hands?"

"Yes, what if? So that is why you're here."

"Paget said you'd come here."

As Anselma and Mary bustled up laden with bandboxes, Darnier said, "Here is the book you wanted on stringcourse designs, Lady Briana. How are you progressing with the decorating?" he asked, nodding to Anselma.

"I am on the homeward stretch. I believe His Grace is in a hurry to have it completed."

"He hasn't secured a duchess yet, if that is what your ladyship means. But he hopes to soon rectify that." He withdrew two sealed missives from his waistcoat pocket. "Here you will witness the commencement of his *campagne d'amour.*"

Briana stared at Darnier for a curious moment, then took the gold-edged card and cracked the Brocco seal. "A ball at Brocco House!" she exclaimed under her breath. "The duke is really giving one? The duke who doesn't want women looking at him?"

"He plans to have a look at Society," affirmed Darnier, his eyes twinkling.

Mrs. Milburn's reception of the duke of Brocco's invitation was not what Briana expected. With gilt-edged card in hand and Chalandra nearly dancing in her wake, she came to Briana's library and demanded, "You aren't really going to accept, are you? After he refused *all* our invitations to dine at Milburn Place?"

"I'm afraid that I, at least, am obliged to attend," Briana said, hiding a smile and sketching ribboned bolsters for the duchess's bed. "I work for His Grace."

Mrs. Milburn effected a shudder at Briana's occupation, for after one rout party with her social-climbing acquaintance, she pretended to despise anything which "smelled of the shop."

Chalandra asserted, "Mother, *I* certainly am going! Briana, just consider! Do you suppose we will be treated to a glimpse of His Grace's face?"

"If he has unmasking at midnight, we will. That reminds me, we must buy our masks."

"Ohhh . . . !" pouted Chalandra. "Why must it be a masked ball?"

"Yes, what a piece of annoyance," Briana agreed. "You shall have to cover half your lure-bait."

"Briana!" expelled Mrs. Milburn.

Paget entered the library with a bouquet of violets and a card with its corner turned up. He presented both to Briana.

Mrs. Milburn, ignoring the flowers, queried, "What does one wear to this Brocco House affair?"

Briana took her flowers and followed Paget onto the gallery without replying. Her relations would pester her for more ball gowns and Briana knew she would pay for them once again, but she would let them ponder their situation and learn in the meantime to treat their benefactress more cordially.

"*Bonjour*, Rex!" Briana called happily, descending the staircase. "Oh, Anselma, here *you* are. Rex, will you take a dish of tea with us?"

"That I will. Good afternoon, Miss Snivelton."

Anselma fluttered back her greeting and they repaired to the first floor and settled into a cozy circle in the drawing room.

"I have something here for you, Briana," Rex mentioned when the tea biscuits had been passed around. He rose to lay a card on her lap. "This, most honored lady, admits you to the Inner Sanctum. Will you be my guest tonight?"

"Almack's?" breathed Briana, staring delightedly at the voucher.

"It was a snap to procure for you, which you must take as the highest tribute. After the ball at my house, four of the patronesses all had the same idea: to admit you."

"Dear Lady Jersey!"

"Are you free to come tonight? My mother will accompany us."

Chalandra appeared in the doorway. She had pinkened her lips. "Briana—oh my, I see you have a visitor. Oh, it's Rex! How are you faring? I suppose I must run away."

"Good day, Miss Milburn. Actually, I was just leaving." He set down a half-drunk cup of tea.

As Chalandra walked in and held out her arched hand, Rex took it briefly and questioned without interest, "Did you enjoy my mother's ball?"

She perched herself in a pretty attitude on the edge of the settee next him and motioned for him to resume his chair. "I had an utterly marvelous time! So many of the best people, weren't there? By the bye, are you going to the Brocco ball?"

Rex looked at a loss. Briana said, "The invitations are being sent out today, for I've just had mine when I happened to meet Mr. Darnier in town."

"Ah, then that remains to be seen. If you ladies are going, then I hope I'm on the list. If I'm not, I'll come disguised as a waiter."

Chalandra tinkled with laughter. "We'll require lots of refreshment."

Briana rose to escort Rex out, the voucher for Almack's sliding from her lap. "You dropped something, Briana," said Chalandra, scooping it up. As her hooded eyes ran over the ticket, she suddenly realized its significance.

Rex said, "Lady Jersey sent me to deliver that to Lady Briana. Sally knows I will act her footman whenever she calls." He gave Briana a look of regret at the misfortune of Chalandra's seeing it.

At the front door, Briana said, "I know Chalandra will want to go."

"She cannot," said Rex in finality.

Sure enough, Chalandra came hastening out to the hall calling sweetly, "Rex, do be a dear and try and see if Lady Jersey will acquire another voucher. You see, I was meeting so many people at your ball that I didn't get to her, so she likely does not know there are two of us cousins who go everywhere together."

Rex said crisply, "I shall mention it, surely, but only a few are given out by the patronesses, you understand. Good day, Miss Milburn."

"It's time you called me Chalandra."

When he bowed over Briana's hand and away from Chalandra's view, he mouthed, "Tonight?"

Briana smiled down at him and nodded.


Almack's, as Briana explained to Mrs. Milburn and her sulking daughter, was the club of clubs, the crème de la crème of places to be seen in Society, and unless one was given an approval ticket which signified that the queens of that kingdom had decided to favor one with admission, one simply did not go.

"But Briana! It is only an oversight! I wasn't presented to any of those patronesses—how was I to know?" wailed Chalandra.

You were too busy making a stage for yourself, thought Briana, but she replied, "You heard what Rex said, that he would try; but do not get your hopes up. I feel sure I am being admitted because of my parents. Mother was a friend of Lady Jersey's." She hoped that that would soothe their pique a bit.

Mrs. Milburn spoke up from her corner of the sofa. "Now that we are residents of Berkeley Square and you will see Lady Jersey at this club, you can get Chalandra an *entrée* without any fuss. And I, naturally, must accompany you."

As Briana settled into the Channing's town coach that Wednesday evening, Lady Channing made a compliment on Briana's gown. It was an expensive ice-pink confection with pearl swags framing the low corsage. Briana felt it displayed more of her young bosom than her mother would have thought decent, but Madame Yvonne had insisted that it was more than *de rigueur;* it was essential in catching a gentleman for oneself these days.

When Rex leaned toward her at the door to Almack's, he ran his hand down the cascade of curls ending at her waist and whispered, "You will be the most fragrant partner of every lucky man tonight."

"Thanks to you," she murmured with a smile, for the pink roses he had sent were tucked amongst her tresses.

The lucky men, as it turned out, were to follow none other than the decorated hawk-nosed gentleman who stood directly in their path as Rex ushered Lady Channing and Briana into the chandelier-lit sanctum. Could it be? Yes, Briana decided, it was indeed the duke of Wellington posing there.

She looked at him for a curious instant, thought of Chalandra driving up and down past his house for a glimpse of this man who wanted to be glimpsed, and broke into a smile.

His black brows lifted at that, and he eyed her with interest.

While Briana was introduced to a pair of dowagers, she saw His Grace move closer. Lady Channing got into conversation with two voluble ladies, and Rex turned to answer a young man's hail. Briana shot another look at the duke of Wellington. His lips were curving and his curiously rounded eyes checked her over thoroughly.

Taking a step sideways, he said with a trace of humor, "I see we must present ourselves to one another, fair lady. I am Arthur Wellesley."

"Yes, Your Grace, I had realized that you must be, and was just fitting your face into Mr. Phillips's portrait of you. I am Lady Briana Rosewynn."

"Ah! Lady Briana Rosewynn—grown up already! They are sawing out some music in there; do you care to dance?"

And the nation's hero led her past Emily Cowper and Mrs. Drummond Burrell and the other ornately frocked patronesses without even giving her the chance to acknowledge them. Gentlemen connected their quizzing glasses to their eyes as Briana, in her willowy beauty, passed by on the arm of the most famous man in the room.

"And tell me, Lady Briana: did it fit?" the duke asked her as he touched her waist and they came nearly nose to nose in the waltz.

"Your likeness? Yes. But I find that you have livelier eyes even than he gave you, Your Grace."

The duke laughed immoderately, for his gaze had indeed dipped to her creamy curves. "You have, indeed, caught me. I hoped I had learned the art of subtlety by now."

Briana confided, "It's hardly your fault. I told Madame Yvonne she used too little fabric."

"Not quite little enough," returned the duke, his look full of mischief.

My! thought Briana. The tales of his exploits with La Grassini and Madame Recamier and the others must be true. "Be truthful, Duke; haven't you received more than your share of adulation from the ladies since your heroic victories for England?" she asked.

"Oh yes! Plenty of that! Plenty of that!" he replied breezily.

Briana reflected that she, too, had received more than her share of attention, judging by Sally Jersey's remarks over sips of lemonade. "Why, dearest, all the men see no one else at all, it is so provoking. And Sir Reginald is likely going wild with fear that his new-found gem is dancing with too many others, especially now the duke's noticed you."

Rex was indeed a dashing escort. Briana felt proud moving from one room to the next at his side, for he had a princely way about him and unwittingly drew notice. Women could be seen following his every movement. To how many of them had he shown favor? Briana wondered. She had heard nothing of his life before she met him.

"May I see you tomorrow, Briana?" he asked as Paget

let them in at Berkeley Square.

"That would be nice, Rex, but I must finish shopping for the rooms at Brocco."

"Briana," he said, taking her hands in his, "since you show such devotion to your decorating tasks, I wish to commission you to redecorate my front parlor in St. James's Square. Will you come and have a look at it?"

Briana considered his sly, hopeful face. The prospect pleased her, for Mrs. Milburn and Chalandra had a way of ruining every one of his visits to her house. "I could arrange to do that," she said.

"My lady!" sighed Rex, lifting her gloved fingers to his lips. "Now I have a reason for living."


Briana drew off her swansdown wrap, wondering how seriously Rex spoke—or did such words roll off his tongue to other women?

As she said good night to Paget and mounted the flying staircase, a sharp scream pierced the silence. Briana heard something fall, and then Chalandra's voice shrieking, "No-oo! I never agreed—no!"

Briana dashed up the last steps and down the gallery to Chalandra's room, pushing on the door lever. It was locked. She set her ear to the panel, and was stunned to hear a male voice inside. The words were not clear; they seemed to be muffled against something, and Briana soon realized from Chalandra's protests that that something was Chalandra herself.

How could her cousin be so disastrously witless as to let a man into her room? Judging by the sounds of altercation, Chalandra must be repenting her foolishness.

Racing upstairs to her own chamber, Briana snatched her household keys and returned to push one into the lock. An unprecedented sight met her eyes. A man was bent over Chalandra's tiny form, forcing her against the divan. One of his hands covered her mouth but not her wild eyes while he tried to unfasten her dressing gown through her masses of rumpled hair.

"Ha! Get rid of those!" he laughed, and one of Chalandra's wax bosom friends fell to the floor.

Briana, in disbelief, dropped her bunch of keys on the hard wood at the edge of the carpet. The man jerked his head around.

"*Lord Fitzroyal!*" Briana shouted in horror.

"Chalandra!" expelled Mrs. Milburn, looking over her shoulder. "Lord Fitzroyal! What are you doing in *here?* And with *my poor daughter?*"

Fitzroyal snatched his rumpled coat off the bed, eyeing the women uneasily.

Briana pushed Mrs. Milburn toward her panting daughter, and with an eye on Lord Fitzroyal's every move, said, "You have a lot of explaining to do, Lord Fitzroyal. How did you get my cousin to let you in here?"

Chalandra cried, "He came through the dressing room! There's a door there!"

Scandalized, Briana demanded, "Is that true?"

"I've had a welcome from Miss Milburn to visit her alone, and since I knew the most convenient way to avoid besmirching her name before her relatives, I used it."

"Most convenient way? To avoid besmirching her name? Ohhh, I could throttle you!" With fists clenched, Briana advanced on Fitzroyal, her blue eyes ablaze.

"As I said, Chalandra gave me welcome," he reiterated, backing away.

"Hasn't this been your plan all along since that day in the park when we so imprudently took you up, Lord Fitzroyal—to make one of us your ladybird? *Well? Hasn't it?*"

"I—ah—"

"You mean you wonder how I know that!" spat

160

Briana, her height bringing her eyes to the tip of his nose. "And how in the name of all lecherous peers did you know how to gain access to this room?"

Lord Fitzroyal, grabbing his hat, reached for his riding crop, but Briana whipped it off the bureau. "Answer me!" she roared, the black leather trembling in her grip.

"Lady Briana, there's no need to get defensive," Fitzroyal said, cajolingly, holding out his hand for the crop.

"Yes, there is! Tell me this instant, or all London will know what you have just tried to do!"

He gulped. "After your father died, Emmaline—that is—"

"Yes, I know: your ill-treated Emmaline Clifton resided in this house when she got tangled up with you." The Milburns were drinking in every word.

Fitzroyal declared in a pompous tone, "Miss Clifton opened this house to me, to visit her through the hidden staircase. A common convenience in London which beautiful ladies provide for their protectors, as you would know if you were more worldly wise, my young friends." He headed for the dressing room.

Briana took three long strides and cried, "We're not your friends! And don't ever *dare* to come up that staircase again!"

She would have left it at that, but Fitzroyal turned to pull his forelock in mockery. Briana, riled, whistled the crop through the air and cracked it across his face.

While the women gasped, Fitzroyal bellowed in terrifying volume. Briana, sharp with fear, knew she must needs continue now until he was thoroughly cowed. She administered another singing lash which sliced his flailing hands, and the third she mercilessly let fly at his pantaloon buttons.

That was the *pièce de résistance*. In an outpouring of filthy oaths, he jabbed at a knothole in the wood. A panel

161

behind Chalandra's gowns slid sidewise, leaving a gap in the wall.

"Bring a candle!" cried Briana.

Anselma rushed forward with a smoking candlestick. Lifting it high, Briana watched the mussed locks of Fitzroyal diminish into the darkness at the bottom of a narrow carpeted staircase.

Her voice gave him one last warning. "You can be assured that we will not speak of this to all your acquaintance if you do one thing, Lord Fitzroyal." She took a step down and closed the door behind her. She could hear Anselma's squawks of warning.

"And what is that, Lady Briana?" His voice was sarcasm itself.

"You will not shoot my cousin Radcliffe."

Silence fell for a moment at the bottom of the stairwell. Then he said derisively, "He deserves to be shot."

His groping at the door sent a wave of cold air rushing upward. It blew out Briana's candle flame, and with it, her hope.

# Chapter 15
## Triggering a Response

"Darnier, if I don't shoot him, he'll shoot me!" Briana whispered as soon as she saw Darnier's dark head bent over a large tome in the Brocco House library the next day.

Across the expanse of desk Darnier looked concerned. "I suspect you're right," he replied, gravely fingering his moustache.

"A minor point, but Anselma will soon discover I'm not following her with these sketches. How can we ever talk, Darnier?"

"Miss Snivelton must be sent somewhere." He pulled the bell.

The Brocco butler soon towered in the doorway. "Yes, Mr. Darnier?"

"Trump, send in Janice, if you please."

The maid in question soon strode into the room. "What'll you have, Mr. Darnier?" she asked, tossing back her red ringlets.

"Go find a lady's promenade dress from the late duchess's wing. Don it and be in His Grace's antechamber in a quarter hour. You must be our duke's distant relation. Pick a name."

When the girl nodded and left, Briana gaped at Darnier.

"It's a way to rid ourselves of Miss Snivelton," he said. "Have you an errand for her?"

"We do need masks for the Brocco ball . . ."

At the sound of footsteps, Darnier crossed the thick carpet to open the door. "Ah, here you are, Miss Snivelton. You've not disappointed me. I had hoped you would seek me out."

"Mr. Darnier, I was just—I mean, I'm looking for Lady Briana." Her eyes raked over the book-lined room until they lit on her mistress. "Lady Briana! Oh, you've been showing your sketches to Mr. Darnier. Mr. Darnier, you must have noticed how Lady Briana's ideas are always so to the point. Always coming up with original designs—she doesn't copy from the shops at all. Oh, doesn't she make a striking picture in that hooded burgundy chair with her pale blue ruffles? I do declare, this is the most enormous town dwelling I have ever stepped foot into. Such elegant hugeness. Of course, Brocco Park was like a palace in the country, but this— oh, are we removing?"

Anselma skittered after Briana and Darnier to the north wing. Armfuls of lace and watered silk lay on the tearoom table where Anselma had conveyed them for the duke of Brocco's approval.

Briana determined to see the man this time, but Darnier told her not to entertain such a request today because His Grace was sadly suffering from painful limbs. Briana watched Darnier enter an adjoining room with her samples of materials.

Anselma worried her handkerchief round her fingers. "If he doesn't like them," she whispered, "we'll know he has no taste. Most men don't. But he'd better, Lady

Briana, because you have already spent his money, and I would hate to think—"

A door banged against a stop on the other side of the wall. "Tell her," cried an irate masculine voice, "that all this is a waste of my time!"

Briana crumpled against the sofa back. Anselma gasped.

"Why did I hire her? She knows what she's doing, Darnier. Get this fribble out of here!"

Briana opened her eyes, then shut them in relief.

As Darnier reappeared, the hall door opened. "Miss Jane Attington," boomed Trump, shooting Darnier a look. In walked the maid in an embellished peach ensemble. Darnier welcomed her as Miss Attington, the cousin of His Grace. It took him only a few sentences to get around to proposing Briana show her the shops in Bruton Street. "The duke is not inclined to see anyone today," he explained, "and Miss Attington wrote she was coming expressly to shop."

Briana said aside, "I can only do this if you, Anselma, will go to Madame Yvonne's and order masks for Mrs. Milburn, Chalandra, and myself. Go home and find out what colors they want and have Yvonne match mine to my gown. I'll see you at dinner."

Anselma hesitantly accepted the office, saying, "I expect you'll be in fitting company with Miss Attington." When the duenna had been bundled into a hackney, Darnier thanked the maid for a convincing performance. As his hand brushed Briana in gesturing her back into the library, an oddly sweet sensation went through her. How reckless she was meeting an attractive secretary alone after deceiving her faithful duenna by means of an accomplice maid. She had no business feeling so breathless near a man of Darnier's station, either. But her plight was unusually grave, and she had to concentrate on enlisting his help.

"Take some fresh air at the window," he said, pushing it open, "and tell me what's happened."

Fitzroyal's final words at the bottom of the stairs still haunted her. "I'll very likely die, Darnier," she evoked at last, gripping the window sill.

"Briana! What is it?" Darnier asked urgently, turning her toward him. "Tell me, *m'amselle*." He moved his warm hands down her arms, watching her troubled face. He made her long to totter forward and lay all her worries on his waistcoat. He must have felt her helplessness for he drew her close to him, and when she raised wet frightened eyes to his, she saw those ebony lashes close, and the next thing she knew, he kissed her on the mouth.

Stunned, she gazed at him. Her nerves were tingling, her heart was galloping.

"Briana," he said in the gentlest of voices, "life is not as hopeless as you think."

"Oh, but yes it is!" she managed confusedly. For her own stability of heart she must ignore the fact that he had kissed her. "Darnier, you won't believe this, but he was in Chalandra's room last night!"

"Who was?"

"Lord Fitzroyal."

"And?" he asked ominously.

"I'm afraid I . . . whipped him. With his crop."

"You did."

Encouraged by his seriousness, Briana explained. "After that, he left by a concealed staircase he used to use when he . . . when he visited Emmaline Clifton after my father died. At least, I think it was after my father died." Her voice faltered. Her lashes fell to her pinkening cheeks, but at the same time, angry tears spurted out.

"Ah, my lady, you seem to have done particularly well with the crop. Fitzroyal bore a brilliant welt this morning at Stevens's, which he attributed to a passing coachman's clumsiness."

166

Briana flushed and regarded her shoe ribbons. "I was very, very provoked when I struck him. He might have used that crop on us if I hadn't snatched it first."

"Good thinking!" Darnier produced a key, opened a drawer of the desk, and laid two pearl-handled pistols on its gleaming top.

Briana stared in dismay.

"Dr. Clewes and I tried to persuade Fitzroyal to drop his argument," said Darnier, "but to no avail. He's bent on firing his weapon. Briana, either you must have Radcliffe emigrate to America or kill him off with some disease."

"I can't!" She had already thought over every possibility of the sort. "My father would sit upright in his grave if I did anything so dishonorable."

Respect grew in Darnier's eyes. "Then you leave yourself no option but to learn to shoot. Is that what you've decided?"

"Yes. But I've been praying that you can convince him to agree not to shoot to—to kill."

"Clewes and I will do our best. But it will behoove you to know exactly what you are doing when you're tossed one of these the morning of the assignation."

Briana's mouth went dry as she received one of the cold beautiful weapons. The sight and feel of it scared her even though she knew it wasn't loaded.

"There is something else you can do to possibly forestall his shooting you."

"What is that?" she queried.

He leaned against the desk and gave her an open look. "If you were to write him a pretty apology for slicing at him with that crop, deserved as it was, and perhaps say something to the effect that Miss Milburn, being new in town, had innocently led him on to believe, et cetera, and that you had been so overcome with the impropriety and so on, I believe you could bring him round to seeing you

167

again as a charming and desirable woman. And then," he held up a hand as she sputtered, "you can persuade him from that standpoint into refraining from shooting into you as Mr. Radcliffe. You can say your love for your cousin Radcliffe will put you forever into a nunnery or some such garble. You'll think of something."

So Briana penned Lord Fitzroyal an apology. When it was dispatched, she, with Janice's aid, donned a new suit of male garments Darnier gave her, and bowled into town at his side in his own curricle. In the succeeding two hours, her fingers squeezed the trigger time after time in Manton's Shooting Gallery. Her arm ached with the weight of the pistol as she strained for concentration aiming down the long barrel. Cracks and explosions coupled with guffaws and cries of triumph from male lungs unnerved her feminine head, yet at the same time gave her impetus to conquer her fear of the weapon.

She at last began to hit the wafer. As Darnier congratulated her, Briana let him reload the pistol. She cocked it with determination, leveled her arm, and shot a hole in the upper corner of the new wafer.

"Famous!" Darnier cheered, bathing her in a proud smile. Her inner glow reached her eyes as she smiled back. With a sore shoulder from the kick of the gun, she emerged from her first day of frenzied practice amongst rowdy bucks thinking what a blessed shelter the life of a lady had been.

Her second entry into Manton's was accomplished the next day when Briana sent the Milburns and Anselma to the shoemaker and she took Mary with her to shop for fixtures. She gave money to Mary to buy a lamp—any lamp—and to shop or visit as she chose until their appointed meeting time at Brocco House.

Darnier concentrated on perfecting Briana's stance, her eye, and the steadiness of her arm. Briana accused him of privately indulging in grins at the less-than-masculine figure she cut.

"On the contrary, you're most convincing," he whispered.

Briana felt a second surge of pride when a stranger from the adjacent shooting alley came to say, "You've improved mightily, young man, since you walked in here yesterday."

"Thank you, sir," she returned.

They were joined by the man's son who proposed to Briana that the four of them take a glass of wine together. "And then join us at Jackson's." With a good-natured punch at Briana's sore arm, he added, "We'll strip you down and see what you're good for."

Darnier cracked out laughing.

Briana turned, reddening, and led the way out through the press of men and odors and noise. It was all she could do to keep from conjuring up the vision Darnier hugely enjoyed of her stripped to the waist at Gentleman Jackson's Boxing Saloon.

# Chapter 16

## Trials and Triumphs

"Three new gowns apiece?" queried Briana, viewing the array in Chalandra's chamber.

Mrs. Milburn turned guiltily from the bed where mother and daughter had six frocks arranged with various accessories. "Not three apiece, Briana. I only have two—this orange one and that royal blue. You told us to order from Madame Yvonne what we required," she asserted, giving Briana a direct stare. "We have many invitation cards."

Briana had meant only for the balls. Taking a deep breath, she spoke carefully. "How can I keep up this house if you are sending me extra dressmakers' bills I haven't authorized? Or correct me if I mistake: are you paying for these gowns yourselves?"

As the two women looked at her blank-faced, Briana's vexation grew. She snapped, "You'll hardly need this many evening gowns in Warwickshire!"

Mrs. Milburn drew up her bosom and looked disbelieving. "Are you suggesting we go to our home in the country while you are here frolicking about London?

Why, what ungratefulness! We kept you for *fourteen months* without complaining about the burden you added to our household. Mercy sakes, but things never work the other way round, do they?"

Briana said, "You cannot pretend I was a monetary burden on you at Milburn Place, for I gave you my decorating money. Try to understand that I alone cannot finance an entire social season for all three of us."

She could see Mrs. Milburn liked this not at all. She and Chalandra were both counting on Briana's money to raise them up the social ladder.


That evening Mary grinned broadly as she tied Briana's lace-edged evening slipper. "Wouldn't the ton turn inside out if they knew you was the handsome man bowin' to them last night?"

"I only pray no one discovers that fact," Briana said in a faint voice while trying a white mask edged in tiny pearls over her eyes.

Mary secured its satin ribbon and covered it with Briana's dark curls. "That's impossible, my lady. Why, look at your bosom now!"

Briana peered down, and then looked up at her elegant reflection. At that moment Chalandra breezed in, a look of envy crossing her features. Briana's creamy charms were lifted to perfection by the new corset she wore, but Yvonne's advice to Chalandra had been to keep her corsages high as possible and to use the bosom friends, for even a push-up corset gave her nothing to display. So Chalandra, arrayed in another stiff-standing transparent Betsie embroidered with gold sparkling thread, made sure she would be visible. She had chosen bright red as her color for the Brocco Ball, with a matching headdress *la toque de ninon* ornamented with a spray of ostrich feathers and a golden butterfly placed in the center of her

171

forehead. Its sparkle matched the threads in her gossamer scarlet gown. Brown curls framed her dainty face, and cornelian pendant earrings swung with every nervous move.

"Briana, can you help me with my mask in the carriage? I cannot abide putting it on already—it's so hard to see."

"You mean you cannot abide for our escort not to see you," said Briana, smiling tolerantly.

"You are a vision!" expelled Rex when he had complimented Chalandra and her mother on their costumes and had liberty to turn to Briana descending the staircase. The vivid peacock of her gown set off her dark hair and fair skin. Her sleeves were enormous satiny puffs with sheer oversleeves gathered at elbow and wrist. A heart-shaped bodice and a slender skirt hugged her feminine figure, the hem a triple flounce caught up at the sides with silk roses. Her hair was lifted à la Madonna in silky curls while the mass fell down her back. At her crown she wore white roses Rex had sent that afternoon.

Tonight his evening coat of midnight blue velvet gave his eyes mysterious depth while the light streaks in his wavy hair matched an ivory marcella waistcoat to perfection. "Lady Briana, Miss Milburn, Mrs. Milburn, you will stun the town tonight with your irresistible artillery," he concluded, "as sure as bullets from a loaded pistol."

Briana's smile felt pasted on. Tomorrow morning she must pull the trigger for real. Could she possibly forget long enough to relax during this ball?

Mrs. Milburn said in a regal voice she had learned to affect, "Sir Reginald, you provide us such an escort that we will be forever envied by the rest of the ton. Do take my daughter's arm; this is all so new to her. Shall we depart?"

Briana cast Mrs. Milburn a wry look. They had had no

words since Briana discovered the extra gowns. Mrs. Milburn wore one of them now, a royal blue crepe with van dyked hem. She had to bend her head to fit through the door because of the turban of blue satin embellished with towering yellow plumes. Briana knew Yvonne had had fun creating that costume, adding that cascade of blue and canary swansdown accenting like a peacock tail the Grecian bend of the train. Mrs. Milburn had no idea she appeared ridiculous.

On the slow ride to Grosvenor Square, Chalandra sat opposite Rex, hanging on his every syllable. Briana let them talk. She felt loath to have her relations enter Brocco House. Inexplicably she felt it should have been her privilege for it was the house where Darnier had whisked her in under a parasol and from where she had escaped with him yesterday and the days before dressed in gentleman's garb. She realized that she looked on the duke of Brocco's house in town, as she had in the country, as her sanctuary from the Milburns.

Now its secretive portals were flung wide to the chilly autumn evening; the hall chandeliers threw highlights onto the rows of gleaming carriages halting to expel masked ball guests by the droves. It was reported to be the event of the Little Season, if not of the year, for tonight Society would clap eyes on the newest duke of the realm. And Darnier would be in evidence, sighed Briana. Something told her he was relishing the idea of this ball, and a niggling feeling kept bothering her about it, but she knew not how to explain it.

"How does that Darnier dare to get dressed up like everybody else?" scoffed Chalandra as soon as they made it into the ballroom. Briana saw his waves of neatly cut black hair above a pristine collar. He wore such an inky black coat that it had to be velvet.

"Do you see that decorated man with Darnier?" asked Chalandra in an awestruck voice.

Briana blinked. "Yes. It's Wellington."

Chalandra's excitement soared. "It is? Oh Bri, you must introduce me instantly! How do I look? Mother, it's really Wellington! I've been living and dying to see him! Briana, please, *please* let me leave off this provoking mask, and take me over to him!"

Briana laughed. "Chalandra, no one makes introductions at a masked ball. Can't you just ogle him and wait?"

Wellington's mouth curved in response to something Darnier had said, and both men looked around the grand ballroom that was filling fast with chattering people. Briana, like Chalandra, stared at the two tall men in their eye masks. They looked like a pair of conspirators enjoying a lark.

When the duke of Wellington caught her eye, he lifted his champagne glass, saluting her across the expanse of heads.

Chalandra gawked from him to Briana and back. Briana hadn't dared boast of her dance with the hero at Almack's, especially as she had been told flatly by Emily Cowper that there was no chance the Milburn women would be considered for an *entrée* after that chit's behavior at the Channing ball.

Rex returned from the side table where he had procured mints. "You so surpass the other ladies, Briana, that all those men are agog."

"Well-bred men do not look precisely *agog*."

"That should tell you why they quiz you so."

Chalandra caught that, and turned away, popping a mint into her mouth.

"I must say you know how to pick up a sagging spirit," laughed Briana.

"Now, why have your spirits been sagging?"

"Because I fear that the greater portion of this society is depraved, and that there is not a man amongst those," she gestured, "with pure motivations toward women."

She accepted his arm and turned to see what he would say.

Rex, pleased by her action which omitted him from her sentiments, regarded her fondly through his mask. Presently he asked, "What must a man do and be in order to win your approval, Briana?"

She spoke the first thought that came to her. "I would like to believe there is one gentleman in all of London Society who is God-fearing enough not to consort with the demi-monde, for example." Briana wondered: had she gone too far?

"Men only do so when their hearts are not engaged," replied Rex.

"I wish I could believe that," returned Briana with a sigh. My father loved my mother—so I thought, she added to herself.

Their private words came to an end with the flourish of a trumpet. The unusual reception by only porter, butler, and footmen had the ball-goers in an unprecedented state of expectation. Word spread that the new duke of Brocco was on his way down to his ball. People positioned themselves to view the grand staircase. Briana held her breath; Chalandra lowered her mask.

Slowly descending the marble steps came a man leaning on Darnier. There *is* a duke, thought Briana, staring with utter fascination. Her first sight of him below the white arch was thin legs in black breeches, a white embroidered waistcoat, stiff cravat, and a black coat with no jewels or embellishments. His brown hair was sparse and combed forward with Macassar oil; his face remained covered with an embroidered white mask with a sketch of whimsical features in black thread.

Briana's amazed eyes moved to the manly form supporting him. Darnier looked magnificent. His moustache was newly trimmed and went well with the silver eye mask, making him look like a satyr. Briana felt her heart swell when she saw the flash of white as he smiled. But, as she realized, the recipient of his breathtaking salute was Miss Cordelia Landers.

The duke of Brocco raised a gloved hand to the upturned faces. Trumpets flourished again and echoed round the spacious rotunda. My, what pomp, thought Briana.

The shrouded duke then leaned against a pillar and motioned to Darnier, who addressed the guests with a brief welcome. Darnier added, "His Grace the duke of Brocco has a special programme planned for the evening. He wishes to choose, as was done in medieval tournaments, a queen of beauty to lead his ball."

The duke nodded. Why wasn't he speaking? Briana knew he had a voice.

"Fairest of the Fair is the name of his contest," Darnier explained with a good-humored look at the duke. "Without further delay, I request all unattached ladies to present themselves in the Pearl Salon."

There were gasps of surprise all around.

Mrs. Milburn gave Chalandra a push, saying audibly, "Chalandra, my dear, that means you."

"It means you, too, Mother."

Mrs. Milburn preened but declared she would not enter a contest meant for young ladies. There followed a bustle of persons urging young widows forward, and spinsters who felt themselves too long on the shelf.

"Aren't you going?" Rex asked Briana.

"I'd truly rather not!" She watched the strange duke limp with Darnier's help down the steps and through the high arched door of the Pearl Salon. Trepidation stole across her. Darnier had said the duke was commencing his campaign. Did he plan to find his duchess in this way by examining every woman like horseflesh at Tattersall's?

"You should definitely go," insisted Rex. "You will look amiss if you stay here although I'd be relieved to

176

keep you under my protection."

"I suppose, as His Grace's guest, I had best humor him. I admit I'm curious to meet my employer." Tucking her hand in Rex's, Briana followed him through the married couples and various and sundry others who watched their daughters and sisters nervously moving into a line. She passed the duke of Wellington, returning his smile. To Rex she whispered, "Is the duchess of Wellington here?"

"I very much doubt it. Some men like to go out without their wives." He amended his statement. "But they cannot love them as they ought." With that, he relinquished her arm and left.

Servants emerged from all corners to serve up trays of liquid refreshment. Musicians on the highest landing struck up a Haydn sonata which was soon taken up by the orchestra in the ballroom so that music seemed to swell from every quarter and swirl down again from the rotunda. Briana saw Miss Landers, resplendent in a golden, tiny-sleeved gown and necklace of topaz, chatting confidently to other ladies in line. My, but she had a becoming blush. She wore a gold and ebony comb in her crown knot and a tiny gold lamé veil.

A shadow fell between Briana and the chandelier. Turning, she encountered a deep purple coat. Protruding from a high cravat was the firm jaw of Lord Fitzroyal. His bruises from that night at Vauxhall had turned yellow-green. Briana's mouth went dry as she saw the half-healed gashes she had inflicted on his cheek with the crop. There could be worse under that mask.

With a lurch of her heart, she said, "My lord, I am glad you're here. In case you've not yet received my letter, I wish to apologize for what I did to you in my shock at what my innocent little cousin had led you to believe . . ."

"Yes, I received your charming missive," Lord

Fitzroyal said with a bow. "I, also, wish to say something to your passionate but repentant ladyship." She was startled by his strangely banal tone.

He moved closer. "Your cousin Radcliffe will have a chance at living if you will but welcome me back to your house . . . back into your house, most delectable Briana."

She drew back in alarm, then remembered she must not vex him further. "I am certain, Lord Fitzroyal, that my cousin is frightened by what occurred, and her mother will not allow you to call on her daughter again." Briana turned away, her temples pounding.

"But you, Lady Briana, can admit me. It is you I want." She felt his hand through the sheerness of her sleeve, and her skin began to crawl.

"I said I'll spare Radcliffe," he reiterated, "if you will be my . . . my *friend*," he said, meaning dripping from the word.

How Briana wished Darnier stood at her side to hear this! Fitzroyal insinuating himself into *her* boudoir! "You dare to offer *me* a *carte blanche?*" she blazed under her breath, her eyes piercing.

A footman approached her. "Your mask, please," he said respectfully. The line of women had dwindled so that it was her turn next.

Lord Fitzroyal hastily untied the bow of her mask. Briana was galled that he dared to do so. The footman thanked the peer, and Briana moved furiously into the salon, feeling Fitzroyal's lustful eyes penetrating her. It was all she could do to shake off her anger and concentrate on meeting the duke of Brocco.

She found herself facing him seated in a music room furnished in pearl-colored silk and gilt. Nothing could be seen of His Grace's eyes as the mask shadowed them, but she could feel his stillness as he observed her standing in willowy poise at the end of the table. Furor at Fitzroyal had forced her chin to a becoming lift.

"Good evening!" barked the duke after an awkward pause. So he did have a voice tonight. "Who is this?" he asked of Darnier.

Briana's eyes widened. Didn't he remember her from the peephole at Brocco Park?

Darnier, bent over an open ledger, grinned in his most amused way. "Lady Briana Rosewynn, Your Grace," he said, writing it down.

"Good evening, Your Grace," she said. She sank into a curtsy.

"Turn around!" said the duke, motioning.

Briana lifted her dark brows and stared at his mask as she pivoted, her lips parted with incredulity.

"Good teeth," said His Grace.

Briana huffed in surprise. "Would you care to check my age by them, Your Grace? Then you might discern whether I am past the green filly stage."

A surprised guffaw issued from behind the mask, and Darnier shouted in laughter, then clutched his forehead as he scratched with his pen.

"Tart one," the duke said aside. "Next!"

Darnier leapt to his feet to usher Briana out.

Briana could not stop her flow of irony. "*Pardonnez-moi* for my tartness, Your Grace, but I have never been rounded into a paddock before—"

"And you're not tame, are you?" He seemed to be grinning.

"Well said, Duke." She turned regally and strolled out the far door. Once outside, she said accusingly, "Are you enjoying your duties this evening, Darnier?"

"Incredibly. And I congratulate you on your repartee. No one else dared to talk to him."

"Not a word?"

"I heard a few 'good evenings' in timid reply; I think your cousin said she was charmed."

"'All my faults in thy black book enroll,'" Briana quoted ominously. "He'll never let me finish the duchess's rooms now."

"Not to worry, your ladyship. He needs those rooms decorated badly."

"They will be decorated badly," she said with a short laugh, "if I'm halted at this point. Would I had but kept my tongue between my teeth where it belongs—must you laugh, Darnier? The most horrific thing occurred just before I walked into that room."

Darnier's eyes behind the silver mask fixed on her troubled face. "Tell me."

Briana's bosom rose. "Fitzroyal had the audacity to propose I become his—his—" The humiliating word failed her.

In disbelief, Darnier sighed, "No!" and Briana could feel her anger pervading him.

"Our only chance is tomorrow morning," she said.

"Darnier!" barked the duke from within the salon.

Briana was compelled to whisper, "How do you do it, Darnier? He is the veriest ogre!"

"I'll tell you one day. Just keep away from Fitzroyal." Watching her eyes, he lifted her lace-gloved hand and kissed it. The prickle she felt from his moustache sent her floating across the marble floor in what she would have called insipid transports in any other female.

The single ladies clustered, awaiting whatever His Almighty Grace would do with them. Briana was not about to mingle there as if she, too, were in dire hopes she would be chosen. She made her way toward Mrs. Milburn's yellow and blue plumes, but Lord Fitzroyal stepped out of a knot of persons and bowed.

"Lady Briana! Your face, I see, is as blooming as the rest of you." Rising from his bow, he leered down at the rest of her. "This was a clever idea this duke had, leaving all covered up but the faces worth seeing." He chuckled and lifted the last champagne off a passing tray and offered it to Briana.

"No, thank you. Champagne is not . . . one of my vices." Spying Rex, Briana encouraged him silently to come to her rescue.

Lord Fitzroyal insinuated, "What, my tender young thing, *are* your vices?"

Rex said conversationally but with eyes hard, "Are you bent on behaving unkindly to this lady?"

"I didn't mean to be unkind. To this exquisite? Never! Tell me, madam: is your cousin Mr. Radcliffe here tonight?"

"I don't know if he planned to come or not."

Fitzroyal's look circumnavigated the room from his vantage point of six feet and three. "I don't see anyone of his build—yet."

"May I give my cousin a message from you should he not show?" Briana asked pointedly. "I may be seeing him."

"How so?"

"I commune with Radcliffe quite often of late."

As Rex was locked into polite words with an old dowager, Fitzroyal said, "By the way, Lady Briana, one of my men saw your cousin Radcliffe shooting at Manton's yesterday. Practicing up, he was. Why, my pretty, should I turn tail?"

"Because I intend talking him out of shooting you," Briana retorted. "Furthermore," she added, looking touchingly sad, "if dear Radcliffe is hurt tomorrow morning, I shall go to the Continent and enter the nunnery where my aunt has been content for thirty years. I—I could not be happy in this life without Radcliffe, whom I've been close to all my life." She squeezed her eyes shut and emitted a sob, hand covering her mouth.

Fitzroyal cleared his throat and looked uncomfortable.

181

Rex came and drew Briana's other hand through the crook of his arm. "It appears you've upset her ladyship with your rough speech, Lord Fitzroyal. Do apologize."

Fitzroyal said, "Lady Briana, I wish nothing but the best for you. But recall that the suggestion I made earlier still stands." He gave her a comprehensive once-over, and Briana ground her teeth.

Darnier moved through the crowd, his mask reflecting light from crystal chandeliers. "Sir Reginald," he said, "His Grace asks for your help."

Rex cocked his head and folded his arms. "Why must His Grace always call on me when I'm conversing with Lady Briana, hmm?"

Darnier bowed to Briana with a grin, and soon he and Rex could be seen recruiting the duke of Wellington. The three men disappeared into the Pearl Salon.

Through the crowd came Mrs. Milburn, having of late gone to check up Chalandra's appearance before the big event. "I suppose you're well into the jitters, Briana," she said.

"Not about anything occurring here."

"Briana, how luscious you look!" called a feminine voice, and Mrs. Milburn turned. Sally Jersey, detaching herself from a knot of men, was resplendent in a lemon yellow gown and bejewled headdress. "Why are you not with the others?" she demanded, expertly drawing Briana aside.

"I wish to stay where the duke of Brocco cannot scowl at me."

"Scowl at you? Why?"

"I've mortified our host. He called me tart."

Sally's eyes grew large. "A *tart?*"

"No, I *was* tart," retorted Briana, laughing.

A trumpet peal heralded the return of the duke leaning on Darnier followed by his assistants, the duke of Wellington and Sir Reginald Channing.

"They're having a high halloo over this," scoffed Briana, eyeing the three striking men whose thoughts were fixed on womanly charms.

Lady Jersey said behind her fan, "The older they get, the worse they are about young flesh."

Briana watched in exasperation the hopeful faces upturned as Darnier led Brocco to the thronelike chair on the landing. "His *trône d'amour*," indicated Briana, sending Sally Jersey into delighted whoops.

"It's a good thing Prinny isn't here," that lady quipped presently, "or His Grace would have to place another throne higher in the gallery."

Briana laughed and nodded.

"Ladies and gentlemen," said Darnier to the guests, "His Grace wishes to recognize the first of his chosen Fair Ladies. As we know,

> Lovely faces
> Full of graces, and
> Heav'nly charms
> Create alarms!"

There was appreciative laughter and applause from many men. Briana felt helplessly frustrated with Darnier. Why must it be he presiding over this?

Lady Jersey could never keep silent. "Now *that* is one exquisite piece of man," she said, her eyes rapt. "Who is he, do you know?"

Briana was obliged to supply Darnier's name and office. The latter information seemed not to scotch the older woman's interest one whit. On the contrary, a dreamy smile played on Lady Jersey's lips.

Presently she pointed her fan sticks. "It looks as though our Sir Reginald has the honor of fetching the lady. What if he can't find you, Briana? Do I have to push you to the forefront?"

"Lady Jersey! He is certainly not looking for me." Nevertheless Briana stepped behind her merry companion.

Rex carried a bouquet of lilies and approached the new and seasoned debutantes, the sprinkling of widows in turbans who had dared assert themselves into the running, and the spinsters who knew they had no chance. He bowed in front of four ladies in gowns of blue, ivory, gold, and red. Briana heard a shriek of delight. Her eyes widened in amazement as the one to emerge on Rex's arm was Chalandra. She held the lilies proudly; her face positively radiated with triumph.

Mrs. Milburn, her chin tipped high, stepped into their path. With plumes bobbing, she threw her hands apart, bestowed a dramatic kiss on her daughter, and then delayed them further to bestow some congratulatory words on Rex.

"That woman!" snapped Sally Jersey. "Ohhh, how could this duke be so shallow as to pick such a little snit? Alack, *pardonnez-moi*, Briana—they are your relations!"

"Say what you wish, madam. I find this whole farce detestable."

As Chalandra, earrings dancing, gained the landing where the duke of Brocco sat, Darnier announced to the crowd, "Miss Chalandra Milburn!"

She curtsied low to the duke, then with her high Betsie glistening from the chandelier's blazing light, she inclined her turban to the audience below in the most queenly way.

Briana groaned. There would be no living with her—or her mother—after this.

As if commanded by thought, Mrs. Milburn swept to Briana's side. "Well!" she said in high victory, drawing looks, "my little Chalandra did it! Don't you agree she's the loveliest in the room? Just think: *she's* the choice of the duke of Brocco!"

Briana smiled in agreement. Lady Jersey coughed and fanned.

Mrs. Milburn added in a fierce whisper, "You do see the necessity of gowning her marvelously now, do you not? After this, Briana, we may make her a brilliant match if we keep her costumed by that Madame Yvonne."

Briana sighed.

Two trumpets blasted for Darnier's next announcement. "His Grace the duke of Wellington will choose our next Lady Fair."

Lady Jersey shot a superior look at Mrs. Milburn, then winked at Briana.

As the duke's hawk nose passed in front of the crowd, Briana felt herself heating. Something about this whole exercise was intolerable. "I'm leaving," she whispered to Lady Jersey.

"No, you're not!" And that lady grasped Briana's hand and pulled her back into place.

"I can't stand this!" Briana whispered through her teeth.

"I can't either," returned Lady Jersey, all the while fixing her bright eyes on where the duke of Wellington moved slowly through the array of headdresses and fearful, hopeful faces. A buzz of comments rolled through the crowd when a golden veil emerged from amongst the young ladies. Briana's heart sank. It was that pretty woman Darnier liked who was bestowing her springlike smile up at Wellington as he escorted her up the marble steps.

"Miss Cordelia Landers!" pronounced Darnier. He had undoubtedly used his influence with Brocco in choosing this one.

Briana fought a consuming need to flee, but knew that to move now would look to all like a pique of jealousy. She was not upset that Miss Landers had been chosen, she told herself. It was the way Darnier's smile welcomed

185

that beauty. Yes, that was it.

Cordelia, in her shimmering gown, curtsied before the duke of Brocco and took her seat, radiating poise above the crowd. Chalandra vied for attention between the grand arches, and aimed her red-lipped smile often at the duke of Wellington.

Three trumpeters sent dancing peals around one another, commanding attention, which was quite unneccessary as all eyes were glued to the landing to see what could possibly transpire next. Darnier received a paper from the duke of Brocco, as he had before the other announcements. He turned to the crowd. "His Grace the duke of Brocco wishes now to recognize the Fairest of the Fair."

Chalandra's mouth dropped in insulted surprise. Miss Landers cocked her chin in a gracious, attentive manner.

A beautiful auburn-haired lady was urged by friends to the front of their group. All eyes followed as Darnier descended the steps with a third bouquet of lilies.

Mrs. Milburn declared, "Ah-ha! They'll have a brunette, a blonde, and a redhead."

Darnier moved amongst the plumes. Briana's heart thudded when he paused before the lady who was surely the choice. The lady curtsied.

Briana whispered behind Lady Jersey's fan, "Now that this is settled, I'm going for some lemonade." Lady Jersey took one look at Briana's stricken eyes and let her go.

Slipping into the corridor, Briana saw a French door open at the end. Fresh air beckoned as the musicians launched into a grand fanfare in the ballroom. Rushing onto the little terrace below the library, Briana gripped the stone railing and breathed in gulps of air. She knew what was wrong; she could not bear to watch Darnier bestow the kind of attention he had given her on someone else.

She knew that thoughts like this made her selfish—

despicably so. Darnier was the duke's employee after all, and what on earth could she *do* with him? He had been kind enough to take her wish for adventure to heart, and had offered himself as her means to gallivant all over London in the guise of a man so she could have the taste of freedom and the education she wanted. Likely it was only his intention to show appreciation from the duke for her decorating.

But she couldn't forget that he had kissed her in this very house—that window right there—and tomorrow morning, he would be her second in the duel. He would do his utmost for her safety, she knew that. After the duel, she must never reach out for his help again.

Briana knew in her heart that men such as Darnier were often the kind society women took as their lovers. She had heard Sally Jersey sigh. Darnier would likely receive many offers this night.

From somewhere deep within her, a well of despair rose unbidden, and sent tears sliding over her eyes. There was a sound, and through the sparkling blur, Briana saw a tall figure of a man striding toward her, followed in the distance by Lady Jersey. Briana stumbled down the steps from the terrace and would have run away if there had been a place to go.

"Lady Briana!"

She could not answer him. Why must Darnier find her in tears again? What must he be thinking?

"Briana, you are wanted in the ballroom," he said gently. "Lady Jersey wants you to return."

"Have you already picked the Fairest and all that?" she queried.

"Yes." He came down the steps.

"Haven't you duties in there?" She motioned to the house from which the musical number continued in its building crescendo.

"Yes, I'm afraid I do; so let's go in."

Briana shot Sally Jersey a resentful look for telling Darnier she had left.

That lady seemed unaffected. "Briana, I have learned that it never pays to desert a social function of any kind. No matter how discreet you might think to be, someone always notices you've left, and in many cases, with whom. You have not gotten away with this, my dear girl."

Briana tightened her fingers around the plush of Darnier's velvet sleeve and forced her chin a fraction higher. When they entered the ballroom, her heart jumped to see all faces turned expectantly to her. She looked up at the thrones. One was still empty. Chalandra's hooded eyes widened sharply.

Briana felt Darnier give her a nudge. When she looked at him in consternation, he indicated that she ascend the stairs.

"No!" she gasped, leaning against him in her wish to escape. Gazing up at the duke sitting immobile on his throne, she saw a glitter behind the narrow mask slits "Never tell me," said Briana, fighting for her poise, "that he liked being sassed?"

Darnier chuckled. "The duke enjoyed it. But you don't look pleased to be the Fairest."

"I'm not, Darnier!"

"But you won't run away, will you? I would look the fool prowling after you again."

Briana picked up her skirts. As she ascended the steps, a great cheer went up. The duke of Brocco rosé with Rex's aid, and Briana saw the duke of Wellington signaling Miss Landers and Chalandra to their feet. Poor Chalandra!

Briana's knees shook as Darnier, with a firm grip on her hand, led her to the duke. She curtsyed, still clinging ludicrously to Darnier's fingers. If she let go, she was certain she would fall backwards down those stairs.

The duke barked, "Finest of them all!" and then he plunked back to his velvet throne.

Darnier shouted (or so it seemed from right beneath him), "I present to you, our guests, Lady Briana Rosewynn, the Fairest of the Fair!"

A smiling sea of faces and thunder of applause honored Briana. Music swelled and crashed as Darnier led her to the throne at the duke's right. Her gown caught on the arm, but Darnier whisked it away, preventing her from landing hard on the gilt back.

Pink tinted her cheekbones. "Thank you!" she whispered, shooting him a grateful look while Miss Landers and the others looked on.

"Brace yourself, dear lady," Darnier whispered near her ear. "His Grace requires a kiss."

Before she could react, Darnier called, "Now, before the Dance of the Fairest, the duke would like all his guests to unmask."

Wellington's famous face appeared. He winked at Briana.

Chalandra shrieked. Miss Landers, too, looked horribly startled.

Briana followed their strange gazes. Instantly she felt a gasp rise in her own throat. The duke of Brocco had removed his mask. He was hideous.

Not only was one of his eyes smaller than another by dint of a scar slanting across eyebrow, lid, and cheek, but his nose appeared to be pushed in in an odd manner.

Briana felt her head swim. But she determined that the awestruck silence that had fallen amongst His Grace's guests should not prevent her from showing the poor man some respect. He had hidden since the war, and she now understood why he had refused to admit her at Brocco. Fighting for his country had given him permanent battle scars.

The duke sat unmoving, but his defensive eyes took in

the expressions of his Beauties. "A kiss!" he barked suddenly. Then he smiled as at a joke, an action which only allowed half of his mouth to move.

Briana's middle turned over, but she stood with resolve. Not looking at Rex or Darnier or the duke of Wellington or the ladies, she bent and kissed the duke on his cheekbone. "Thank you, Your Grace," she managed, "We are truly grateful to you for these honors."

"Thank *you!* You're the best of the lot!" he rasped.

Miss Cordelia Landers had turned white beneath her rouge, and was stumbling on her hem as she moved to bend and brush her lips across the scarred cheek nearest her. Briana and everyone else knew she could not have moved to the other side without offending the man. Cordelia reached for Wellington's support immediately, and began to descend the staircase, whitefaced.

As Briana wondered what to do, Darnier mouthed "Wait," so she stood respectfully and watched as Chalandra, pasting on an angelic smile, put her red gloves on either side of the Duke's face and planted a kiss right on his misshapen mouth.

Briana lifted shocked eyes to Darnier.

His eyebrows shot up and his moustache twitched.

Chalandra, steeped in her role, sighed and said, "Your Grace! You have totally captivated us with this display of your good taste."

The duke of Brocco leered at her. "Flattering me!" he spat. No one failed to see the swat he administered to her backside as she turned and took Rex's arm. She cast a look as coy as could be over her Betsie.

"Go ahead, Darnier," cackled the duke, motioning impatiently. "Dance with my Fairest for me. Can't quite do it yet," he muttered, casting Briana a longing look from under lowered brows.

"Thank you, Your Grace." Briana descended in a haze, her hand through Darnier's arm. What an ordeal!

Perhaps these moments just beginning were repayment for the trepidation she had gone through.

Darnier smiled, his autumn-colored eyes warmly beholding her. "Well done, Briana," he said sincerely. "Tell me," he added after her silence (wherein he made her weak in his arms as he masterfully maneuvered her to the middle of the floor), "How would you fancy becoming a duchess?"

"A *what?*" Briana's head drained.

Darnier looked down at her, and she saw mischief brewing. "That way we could, perhaps, continue our little . . . ah . . . escapades."

"Our little escapades must cease!" hissed Briana, stiffening. Then she said, "They will die a natural death after I am laid to the ground at daybreak."

"You must not court disaster," Darnier admonished severely, drawing her closer and causing her heart to skip. "You will live to . . . to marry well," he finished.

Miss Landers and Wellington, followed by Chalandra and Rex, were waltzing around them, the gold and red gowns swirling with Briana's peacock. She missed the beauty of the scene, for looming over her fairy-tale ball came a dark cloud of suspicion. She sought Darnier's eyes and held them. "Darnier," she said ominously, "are you courting me for the duke?"

His lower eyelids deepened in that dear amused way she had seen on several memorable occasions. "I—" His look wavered. "Deuce take it, Briana; if I said no, I'd be lying to you."

Briana halted in her tracks. "*Darn . . . you!*" she screamed, and slapped his dear, handsome, traitorous face with a muffled impact of her glove. She streaked in painful humiliation past Chalandra's startled giggle and all the gaping faces. The musicians tactfully ended the number and began a new one.

The white-hot knowledge of what he had said flashed

in her head, and was soon over. Hadn't she suspected this for some time? Oh, how she wished she were back in Wookey's kitchen.

"Briana, what did he say to you?" came Rex's whiplike voice and his footsteps in a great hurry.

"Oh Rex!" she wailed. "How could I have done that to the duke of Brocco's secretary? Likely everyone thinks Darnier proposed something illicit to me on the ballroom floor!"

"Didn't he?"

"No. Not exactly that."

"Then what on earth did he do?" Rex wore the look of one about to flee and spring on the infidel at the first syllable of proof.

"He admitted to courting me for the duke!" she uttered, her outrage bringing tears to her eyes.

Rex stared at her, a strange speculation transforming his features. Doubling his fists, he stalked away toward the ballroom.

Briana started after him, only to see Darnier meet him in the corridor, thrust him aside, and appear dark and towering before her. She backed into a tiny sitting room where she bumped into a chair in trying to close the door. But Darnier slipped inside after her. "Briana, you have every reason in the world to be vexed with me. I'm sorry. And the duke is a bumbling, conniving wretch, is he not?"

Briana stared at him, wrinkling her brows. "Then why do you continue to work for him, Darnier? Doing such cork-brained things for him?"

Darnier passed his hand down over his mouth as though wiping away a helpless laugh. "I beg your pardon, Briana, but why I do it has nothing to do with your situation. First of all, you must get home at an early hour tonight in order to be awake for your assignation at half after five. Secondly, you and I should patch our quarrel and return amicably. Can we do it?"

Her lashes fluttered to rest on her cheeks, and in embarrassment she nodded.

"Thank you," he said. "And thirdly, you are requested by His Grace to eat supper with him which commences after the third dance."

Briana barely heard. Over the lump in her throat she said, "I'm sorry for my ghastly behavior toward you, Darnier. Will you forgive me?"

He took the one step forward which made it possible for him to wrap her in his arms. "You are all forgiven, surely, by God above as well as by me below. Now, can you forgive me from your heart? Don't cry—you've got to return to that blasted ball!"

As he clutched her face in his hands, he suddenly covered her lips with his. Briana's senses reeled in loveliness as Darnier fervently explored her feelings. In turn he gave her a staggering assurance of his desire for her, and Briana was never more happy or shocked or dazed.

Streaking immediately out the door, she collided with a servant, and sent a crystal bowl of sweetmeats sliding off the tray to crash on the marble floor. Heads in the doorway turned.

Briana smiled as though she had had nothing whatever to do with the servant's mistake, and held out her hand graciously to Darnier looming in the archway.

As they danced, her heart palpitated. Darnier crushed her once so close against his chest to avoid her collision with another couple that she knew he felt her heart racing. How was she ever to live through this evening?

He said, "Thank you, Briana, for your kindness to me. I will never forget it." The dance was concluded. He bowed very low to her. Something compelled her almost to curtsy, but she settled for a touch of thanks on his forearm.

She was instantly claimed by Rex, and it was a relief to

breathe freely again. He demanded wryly, "What caused you to make up with Darnier?"

"He admitted to his mission and I forgave him. He also pardoned me for my public display." Briana forced a smile for Miss Landers dancing by in the arms of Darnier, then took a deep breath. Why oh why should that perfect peach of a woman be privileged to feel his arms about her, too? Briana wanted to rip and tear. She smiled brightly up at Rex.

"You are a truly gracious lady," he observed with an incredulous shake of his head. "But Briana, if you don't want the duke proposing, hadn't you better be a little less charming?"

"What should I do—strike him, too?"

"I would suggest returning his gifts, to begin with."

"Yes, he has given me too much compensation for my decorating services. The extra money must go back tomorrow." I better send it tonight, thought Briana, for I may not be alive tomorrow.

Before the evening was much further spent, Briana had reason to despair of Chalandra's ever learning sense and decorum. She fluttered about the duke, declaring he was charming her to death. Briana had a whiff of which way the wind blew when Chalandra sank into the chair at his left at table, though Cordelia Landers had been designated for the spot.

Briana, on his right, received a good share of his gravelly comments. She managed to reply in cool politeness to his abrupt questions about her late parents. She was loath to tell His Grace anything, and felt every question a probing into the circumstances of his prey. Horrors! Did he think he had set her decorating her own future rooms?

"I am relieved you found my designs acceptable," she remarked when she felt him looking at her over a glass of Madeira. Did he know she had heard him say to get her fribble out of his sight?

"I—yes! Acceptable! More than that," he returned, gulping and eyeing her up and down.

Briana shuddered. A grotesque man like this courting her through his handsome secretary! A brilliant attempt, but there was no way she would ever marry the duke of Brocco, and as soon as she finished her task for him, that would be the last contact she would have with him.

"I would so like to see all of this palace," Chalandra was saying, cocking her chin in her palm and smiling with her eyes. How could she gaze at his face so? My, but she was a consummate actress.

"Glad to show you!" barked the duke.


"Well, Sir Reginald," said Mrs. Milburn on the carriage ride home, "have you pinched yourself tonight?" Her hand swept mainly over her daughter and lastly included Briana. "Imagine all the other men's envy at you taking home two of the Fairest in all of London— which means England, of course. Do you suppose all the other titled men will call you out?"

Rex sat back and crossed a leg over, laughing politely. "I can hardly believe I'm not living some wonderful fantasy. But, Mrs. Milburn, you neglected—out of modesty, I believe—to include yourself in my good fortune."

Into the silence in which Mrs. Milburn tittered and tried to figure whether Rex was roasting her, Briana said to her cousin, "At least you weren't bothered by Lord Fitzroyal tonight; or were you, Chalandra?"

"Oh, but I was! He said he would *try again* unless you, Briana, would consent to ride in the park with him. Talk about two-faced! I gave him the worst stare you ever saw!"

Mrs. Milburn said throbbingly, "*Go* with him, Briana!

195

That man has caused intolerable humiliation to my Chalandra already, and unless you placate him—" Looking suddenly at Rex, she changed her words. "He has made such a nuisance of himself over my daughter that Briana had better take him off her trail at once since Briana's the one who introduced them in the first place. Well, Briana?"

With a clutch of dread, Briana said, "I will see him first thing in the morning."

When they alighted in lantern-lit Berkeley Square, Rex whispered, "I beg a private word with you."

Briana, therefore, lingered with Paget, asking him rather ludicrously for any letters that might have come in while she was at the ball. Mrs. Milburn and Chalandra slowly wound their way up the stairs with curtsies and good-byes for Rex who pretended to be leaving.

"Would you like a glass of something before your journey home?" Briana asked him.

"The very thing, Lady Briana. How kind."

Paget said, "Shall I summon Miss Snivelton, your ladyship?"

"I am sure she is abed, Paget. You may cover for her." Briana threw open the diminutive library doors where Paget promptly lit a half-dozen candles in the sconces.

Wondering what Rex would have to say to her, Briana perched on her chair behind the table and pulled out the drawings she had done for new window dressings for his front salon. "Will this do?" she asked, determined to be convincingly employed when Paget reappeared.

Rex studiously pored over the sketches, murmuring about a new sofa table with brass inlay and gilt mounts. When Paget set long-stemmed goblets on the table and retreated to the hall beyond the open door, Briana handed a glass to Rex. "Thank you for your escort tonight," she said. "I appreciated your support."

Rex jumped up and came around the desk, kicking the

door nearly shut as he did so. He pulled her from her chair and held her round the shoulders so her face was within inches of his. His dark eyes glowed. "You may have my support forever, Briana," he said, "for I want you to marry me!"

So Briana's night of astonishment was not over yet. With her eyes straying to Rex's mouth which obviously hungered for her, she blushed becomingly.

He bent his head.

"Stop!" she gasped, laughing to cover her panic. She backed out of his grasp, and, endeavoring to appear in control, planned to say something. But what on earth could she say?

"Briana, the seconds tick by! Why can't you answer me? Have I really surprised you?"

"I find no proper words, Rex. I—I find you a wonderful man and yet I must know you longer before we speak of such things. . . ." she trailed off. Her mother appeared in the background of her mind urging her to accept such a titled, wealthy, and charming gentleman.

Rex breathed, "Ah yes, more time is what we need. Some time alone together would do it." He smiled secretively and ran eager fingers up her cheeks, grasping her head and pulling it to his shoulder.

"Would you care for more wine, Sir Reginald?" came the butler's concerned voice from behind the door.

"Dear Paget!" exclaimed Briana, flustered. "Yes! And some lemon tarts." She resumed her seat like a bolt of lightning while Rex took his, grinning at her in a lingering manner. She hoped her cheeks would cool. How could she handle this? What did she want?

"If you accept, you'll never have to worry about Brocco and Fitzroyal and all that," said Rex, raising an eyebrow and sipping his wine.

"And all—what?"

"All the provoking favors you perform for your cousin

197

and her mother, for instance. Why don't you send them packing to Warwickshire? You shouldn't have to dance to their piping."

He looked so comically stern that Briana laughed helplessly. Was she really laughing and having a highly improper coze with a gentleman who had just asked her to marry him and whose blood raced for her, when in a few hours she would have to don men's clothing and grip cold steel and face her destiny?

A proposal of marriage now! She felt as though she were living on the brink of reality, for why, when she dropped her lashes from Rex's straight nose, did it turn bronzed and slightly crooked in her mind's eye?

Heaven help her! The longing she felt when Rex presently kissed her good-night was not for a continuance, but for the scratch of a moustache on her skin.

# *Chapter 17*

## *The Duel*

When Rex's team clicked away down the moonlit street, Briana entered the chamber of mirrors which used to be Chalandra's. Briana could not like the room, but had taken it for her own after the hidden staircase incident. "Mary, are you still up?"

The lamp on the table lit the golden fringe of Emmaline Clifton's bed hangings. Mary was nowhere within sight or sound.

Briana tossed her reticule on the bureau, pulled the roses from her hair, and loosened the combs. As she stood massaging her head and stretching in languorous aftereffects of her evening, she saw a movement of the fringe. "Poor Mary, you fell asleep waiting for me," she said, flicking the white and gold chintz aside.

With the flash of a ruffled cuff, a burly hand locked around her arm and pulled her until she landed on a man's large body in her bed. Briana gasped and screeched, "What are you doing here?", only to be rolled onto her back and pinned down by a broadly smiling Lord Fitzroyal. "How dare you!" she quivered in wrath, pushing up against his heavy bulk.

"I have come to seal our bargain, dear Fairest," he said, his breath hot and reeking of brandy. "No, don't fight me. Listen to me, Lady Briana—I wouldn't dream of shooting the dear cousin of my own wife."

Briana's lungs felt ready to burst as she glared into his hungry face. *"Wife?"* she spat up at him. "Who would marry a venomous lecher like you? Get off of me at once or I'll make you forever sorry!" She struggled in futility to free her hands and in desperation screamed, *"Paget!"*

"You hush, my lively morsel!" Lord Fitzroyal covered her mouth with his beefy hand. "Your servants must not be woken. Not until I can tell them that I've tasted all of your delicacies." With a grunt, he moved himself more firmly onto her, crushing the peacock satin.

In real alarm at her immobility, Briana prayed with all her might. Then she bit his thick finger with her fine strong teeth.

He swore, hastily binding her mouth shut with his other palm. His eyes glittered. "Don't anger me, my Fairest," he said low, pulling the bed curtains with his free hand, leaving them in a glow of muted light. "You do want to save your two cousins, don't you? Or have you changed your mind, hmm?" he murmured near her ear, then bit the tender flesh below it.

What horrid sensations! Briana, pinioned by his weight, was unable to bear his assault an instant longer. She doubled up her knees under the ripping tightness of her petticoats and gave a mighty lunge.

Fitzroyal jerked and gasped. Obscenities issued from his throat as he writhed away from her.

"Paget!" Briana screeched again, trying to free her flounces.

The butler must have heard the first time, for he burst through the door, his tired eyes rounding at the sight of her rolling off the bed, Fitzroyal ripping at her sash.

Paget had a poker from the fire in his hand before Briana's bow had been pulled loose. He positioned himself carefully and cracked the iron down with a precise blow, putting a halt to all Lord Fitzroyal's plans.

Thereafter, chaos reigned. Between the bed curtains, the large man in purple velvet lay unconscious. Briana, with a flushed face, snatched at Paget and hugged him in sobbing gratefulness.

Anselma hurried in, red eyes blinking. She dropped her shawl, exclaimed, "Oh my *stars!*" and fell into a heap. Mary, horror-stricken that she had been in the washroom while this occurred, jumped to do Paget's bidding by running to rouse the footmen.

Chalandra wandered in, her hair webbing about her. "Not *him* again!" she shrieked. "Oh, *kill* him, Briana!"

"Hush! Come help me tie him up."

When Mrs. Milburn peered in and was suitably voluble over the lusts of men, she poked Anselma into consciousness mainly because she was blocking the doorway. The footmen, half-clothed, took action at Paget's orders to secure the intruder with strong cords, not these bed tassels, and deposit him—where should they deposit him, madam?

Briana bid them put him in a hackney. When it was called and Lord Fitzroyal had shown no signs of coming to, Briana, observing the colored lump rising on his temple, wondered for an unsettling moment if Paget hadn't done away with him.

"He'll come round soon enough," said that worthy. He supervised quite calmly the footmen conveying the heavy lord down the stairs and toward the front door.

"For heaven's sakes, hide him with parasols!" Briana called after them. When Mary and Anselma jumped to do this, Briana told Paget, "Advise the hackney driver that this man is drunk and must needs be deposited back on the steps of Brocco House."

"Why Brocco House?" inquired Mrs. Milburn.

Briana said coldly, "To prevent scandal to my name, of course. By placing him there, we may contrive to make people think he's been there drinking the duke's punch all night."

Mrs. Milburn's mouth had a funny look about it. Briana detected a tinge of triumph, or plans, or something.

"Mrs. Milburn," she said evenly, "don't even dream of breezing this story about town. If you say a word, even one little hint that Lord Fitzroyal has been in this house tonight, I'll have your trunks packed before you can gasp."

"Well! I don't know how you could ever *think* I would do such a thing," Mrs. Milburn huffed.

Briana showed Anselma and her incredulous relatives the new lock which was truly in place on the outside of the hidden door, and they all decried the despicability of peers who were too clever for locks.

Chalandra said, "You can sleep in my room—I mean, what really is your room, Bri."

"Thank you, but since the man is trussed off senseless, I doubt he'll have the power or inclination to return. If the footmen move my armoire in front of the door, I'll at least have a loud crash of warning if he dares to try again."

Mary pressed a cool wet cloth to Briana's forehead, whispering, "Send them away and I'll bathe you, dear." Briana was surprised to see tears in her eyes.

"Mary," said Briana when the door clicked, leaving the two of them, "I must have my riding suit. Yes, the gentleman's riding clothes."

"*Now*, my lady?" Mary asked, stupefied.

Briana took out her timepiece. A quarter to three. "I'll lie down for an hour, but you must, absolutely *must* wake me if I fall asleep. I have to leave by this staircase at five o'clock, Mary, or I am dead."

"Dead?" she gaped.

"No, not dead precisely," Briana said, a clutch of the possibility looming close. "But Mr. Radcliffe will have no honor left, and neither will Lady Briana Rosewynn if I don't leave this house by five."

"Oh," said Mary. "You've gotten deep into this man's identity then, my lady." Her voice carried woe, but she ministered to Briana's bedtime needs and saw her mistress at last with dark hair spread across the pillow and her nervous eyelids trying to calm into a much-needed rest.

When Briana, at five minutes to five, pushed her moustache onto her upper lip, she hoped it would stay, for she was perspiring in small beads which she had tried her best to wipe away.

"Mary," she said nervously, "go watch for Mr. Darnier, and run up and let me know the instant his horses enter the street."

Mary was soon back, breathlessly saying, "He's comin', Lady Briana, it's him in a hired coach! Whatever you're about, oh my lady, God go with you!" Her voice broke.

Briana hugged the maid quickly and whispered, "Thank you. Now make a pile in my bed, close the curtains, and tell Anselma I'm sleeping until I wake and no one's to disturb me because I've had such a dreadful night."

She heard Mary lock the door as directed. Briana felt her way down the long flight of narrow stairs. The door at the bottom opened between the basement walls, for she could hear the clatter of pans from the kitchen, then it led underground past small grates of air and weak light to the door which Briana had discovered opened into the basement of a pump house surrounded by high shrubs.

Darnier's hired coachman slowed the pair and Darnier

opened the door with a creak, and reached out his hand for Briana to leap up. The horses stepped into Davies Street, as their objective was to avoid notice.

"How are you?" asked Darnier, leaning toward her to begin tying her cravat.

At his sure touches, Briana felt better. "I've had an hour of sleep. Oh Darnier, you cannot imagine what happened last night! I'm dying to know if you found any baggage on your steps."

"You doubtless mean Lord Fitzroyal."

Briana told him the upsetting events of the wee hours.

Darnier, eyes intense beneath a black frown, said he had indeed been told Fitzroyal had fallen and banged himself up badly and been sent home. Furor at what the cad had done deepened Darnier's frown and his jaw muscles moved.

"What if he doesn't show this morning?" ventured Briana, nervously smoothing her buckskin breeches.

"We shall see. For now, we should concentrate on what we do if he does." Darnier was quiet, thoughtful, and very, very handsome to Briana's view in the dark coach interior, his squinted eyes expressive of deep deliberation. She wondered if he had been up worrying all night, for he still wore his ball clothes and had an opera hat on his head, and had thrown a greatcoat of many capes over his shoulders.

As they rounded the corner of Gower and Great Russell Streets, Briana clutched the strap and said, "I have never seen a duel, nor have I known anyone who participated in one. I am supposedly upholding my family honor, but I feel somehow that I'm throwing away any honor I ever had." She sighed. "What if someone reports us? Couldn't I be thrown into prison?"

"You won't be. I'll take care of you."

That sounded well to her ears. "Do you have the pistols?" she asked with a stab of her heart as they came

204

in sight of Montague House.

"Here." Darnier nudged a box with his boot heel.

"Darnier," she said as they passed the grand edifice and continued to the park beyond, "why is this place called the Field of the Forty Footsteps? Is that how many steps Fitzroyal and I must take between us before one or both of us fall?"

"Briana, you must not fall; you must shoot faster than Fitzroyal, remember?" He directed a confident look at her. "As for the story: in the 1680s two brothers dueled here over a girl they both loved, and both were killed. Tradition has it that forty of their footprints could still be seen after several years, and no grass would grow in the field or upon the bank where the lady sat to watch them fight."

"Oh Darnier, my heart is not working properly!" whispered Briana.

He reached out and took both her hands in his. "Dear Briana! Of course it's not. But you'll be fine; just keep a cool head and pretend with all your will that you are Radcliffe. Stand sideways, as narrow as you can be, and be quick to present and fire."

Briana nodded solemnly, remembering his careful drilling.

The coach halted beneath a towering oak, so tall the top could not be seen in the swirls of dark fog. It seemed to Briana as if the sun would never grace the English skies again.

"One is always afflicted with the jitters before one performs well," said Darnier, giving her shoulder a reassuring squeeze.

Briana felt like throwing her feminine self on his mercy and begging him to deliver her from this frightening circumstance. But she desisted, knowing she could never let Darnier feel obliged to take her place against Fitzroyal. Furthermore, if she came through well,

Darnier would be exceedingly proud of her.

The coachman let the steps down with a clank, and Darnier got out and paid the man, asking him to return in less than half an hour.

Praying to God, Briana strode with Darnier across the wet grass beneath dripping branches bereft of leaves. The high dome and smoking chimneys of Montague House rose in eerie splendor through the mist. Briana felt a bitter surge of regret, and her stricken gaze lifted to the rugged profile beside her. Oh Lord, she added fervently, let Darnier be blessed with a happy life, and let us meet in heaven. . . .

"What were you saying?" he asked, bending to her.

"I was just hoping," she whispered, "that we meet in heaven. Oh Darnier, I'm scared!"

At that, he turned her face toward him and would have gathered her close, but a rattle of wheels arrested them both. "Fitzroyal arrives. Can you dry your tears?"

Briana lowered her hat brim and did so, then watched two men emerge from a hackney hired to give them anonymity even as Darnier had taken precaution. Briana's heart thumped loudly at the sight of Fitzroyal's second, Dr. Clewes, with his bulging brown bag.

Darnier murmured, "We didn't call in another surgeon for that is Clewes's profession."

Briana pushed at her loosening moustache and swallowed hard.

"Good morning, isn't it, Radcliffe!" called Lord Fitzroyal with a wealth of sarcasm. He looked ghastly with his bruises discolored and no attempt made this morning to cover them. She wondered how much of a headache he had after Paget's use of the poker.

Briana said in a level tone, "I see you're late. My cousin had some doubt as to whether you would show."

"Whether I would show?" scoffed Fitzroyal. "Little does Lady Briana know but that I fight this duel rather more because of her than for that traitorous Emmaline Clifton. You're welcome to Emmaline, by the way. But I reckon, Radcliffe, that you'll have little use for her unless you survive my ball."

Drawing off her clammy gloves, Briana said caustically, "I did nothing to attach your Miss Clifton, of that you may be certain. But if I die by your hand, you will also kill your chances with Lady Briana Rosewynn." She turned away, knowing she would say no more but leave the rest up to God.

Darnier, with the pistol case under his arm, gravely addressed Dr. Clewes. "Shall we walk off the paces and set the midpoint?"

That done, Darnier and Clewes were soon heads together over the pistol box. While they loaded the guns, Fitzroyal kept slapping his gloves against his hand and eyeing Radcliffe narrowly.

Briana walked about, hands thrust deep into her coat pockets, hoping she appeared unperturbed. Her heart constricted as she saw Clewes adjust his spectacles and measure gunpowder. The next time she turned he was handing a pistol to Fitzroyal.

The peer made a show of checking it, saying with forced joviality, "Can I trust a man who can't see without his spectacles?"

Briana adjusted the waistcoat which fit tightly over her bound bosom and to which her breeches were buttoned. She heard a click and looked up with a start. Darnier had finished loading her pistol.

As he stood, he tripped on his greatcoat, lost his balance, and reached out for support from Clewes, who, in staggering, lost his spectacles. With fast footwork, Darnier both prevented Clewes from going backward and the pistol from firing.

Amidst apologies to the doctor, Darnier presented Briana with her pistol. She was encouraged by his look as he whispered, "You can do it, Radcliffe."

"Come on—come, come, let's get on with it!" called Fitzroyal.

"I must find my spectacles," shouted Clewes, stooping.

"Right there," Darnier pointed.

Briana saw the glint of gold wires, but although Clewes looked right over them, he could not see them. She picked them from the wet grass. "They're here, Doctor," she said, then stared to see only a jagged shard of glass left in one of the wires.

Clewes snatched them, but when he positioned them around his ears, a puzzled look crossed his face, and he poked his finger through the denuded wire and declared the glass was out.

"I beg your pardon, Doctor," Darnier said when he heard this. "I guess I stepped on them. As soon as this business is over, I'll be glad to accompany you to have some new ones fitted, at my expense, of course. Is it all right with you if our principals begin? I'm afraid if we don't end this soon, someone will come by."

"By all means. I've already loaded the pistol, after all," said Clewes.

Darnier said, "Can you tell me, Doctor, is Fitzroyal in the same position as when we counted out?"

Dr. Clewes squinted and said, "The darned thing is, I can see up close if I have to attend to a wound here today, but without my specs I can't tell where Fitzroyal *is*. Better have them both pace it out again from midpoint."

"Good idea." Confidentially Darnier added, "If you can't see well, perhaps it would be wise to stay over there near the hedge and out of danger. Your expertise may be needed very shortly if I interpret the look on Fitzroyal's face. Frankly, it worries me. I don't suppose he consented to stop this madness?"

"I tried to persuade him, Darnier, I—"

Fitzroyal called, "Clewes, what's keeping you? This is no time for exchanging pleasantries. Come, Radcliffe, I grow impatient to put a ball into you."

"I remind you, gentlemen," said Clewes, "that you have agreed to one shot only. This affair will end after that. Now shake hands."

Briana forced herself to stride forward, to grasp Fitzroyal's hand formally, and to say as Darnier had instructed, "God be with you."

His lordship grumbled unintelligibly in return.

To Briana's sudden dismay, she felt her moustache slip.

Fitzroyal fixed his keen interest on it. He burst out with a jeering laugh. "What's happening, there, Radcliffe—eh?"

Flushing, Briana pulled both sides off and thrust them into her pocket. She muttered, "Can't grow one of my own."

"Witness what a milksop! This should be easier than I thought," crowed Fitzroyal, grinning at the seconds.

Briana threw up her chin and tried to look fierce.

Darnier looked chagrined.

Clewes had seen nothing of this. He called as loudly as he dared: "Backs together now. Twenty paces. Begin!"

In prayer, Briana whispered, *Thy will be done!*

As the doctor counted in stentorian tones, she took long strides, each step removing her as far as possible from Fitzroyal.

"Halt!" called Darnier through the murky fog.

Poising on her twentieth step, Briana's quick backward glance showed Darnier under the walnut tree, his opera hat held respectfully before him. He gave her a quick nod, then resumed his watch on Fitzroyal.

As Briana's heart hammered, her finger slipped in the cold trigger, wet from the increasing drizzle. She shifted the heavy barrel, but the angle was wrong and it was too late to rectify it when Darnier's commands came like whiplash, one after the other.

*"Turn! Present! Fire!"*

Briana whirled, lowered her tense arm, and aimed at Fitzroyal's white cuff. She pulled the trigger. With the kick came two loud reports.

She staggered. Through the smoke cloud that exploded from her barrel, she saw Fitzroyal fall, knees bending, arms groping. She squeezed her eyes shut and heard a thud.

Time seemed to stop. Briana knew she was still standing, still alive. Through a glaze of horror she thought, *I've killed him!* Her head pained in fear.

Darnier came running through the swirling pockets of mist, collapsing his opera hat and thrusting it within his coat. "See to Fitzroyal, Clewes! He's down!"

The doctor hefted his bag and strode across the field.

Briana felt the mesmerizing sensation of the world tipping and grass rushing to meet her face in a wet assault. As she landed, a bolt of white-hot pain coursed through her right arm. She cried out, wavering on a brink of whirling strangeness.

A tweedy cape brushed over her hand, the pistol was drawn quickly from her slack fingers, and she heard Darnier exclaim, "Briana! You're hurt! Oh God in heaven, how could this happen?"

He moved her arm gently, but she cried out.

"You need laudanum, and a good dose of it," he said, "if I'm to pull this bullet out of your forearm. Dr. Clewes is bound to be occupied some time with Fitzroyal, deuce take him."

A bottleneck connected with her teeth as Darnier lifted her head. After gulping, she moaned, "Darnier, I shot him! I should not have . . ."

"Hush," said Darnier, folding back her sleeve and slathering wet lint over her skin. "You did exactly the right thing. I'm supremely impressed. What's more, your father would be proud, and so would your mother, I suspect."

How like Darnier to try to lighten this catastrophe. He added, "And Fitzroyal is hardly dead; merely in a vile taking over being hit first. Can't you hear his bellows?"

Briana protested, "My pistol trigger was wet, and at the last second I couldn't get a sure grip. Where did I hit him?"

"In the leg, by the looks of it. Now close your eyes and let me remove your coat. Try to be as quiet as you can, and as brave as you just proved yourself to be, Lady Briana, and I'll remove the ball."

She took a deep breath as she lay beneath the London sky, the pinpoints of rain pricking her forehead like a cooling benediction. The laudanum was working on her senses, and coupled with her steady deep breaths, made the probing at her forearm bearable.

"We can thank God that the bullet went through without breaking a bone," Darnier said at last. "There was nothing to remove but linen and wool."

Briana touched her throbbing arm and felt the stickiness. Darnier lifted her hand away and cleaned it. "I don't want that doctor to come and discover you're a woman. Where is that blasted hackney?" His relief was apparent when the sound of wheels squeaking into the lane produced their vehicle. He lifted Briana carefully off the ground.

Depths of blue darkness blanketed her eyelids, and she knew she was slipping away from him.

# Chapter 18

## The Hole in the Hat

*"I can't breathe!"*

Something clamped Briana's chest unbearably. The sound of wheels over cobbles soon became jolting reality. "I can't *breathe!*" she repeated.

"Why can't you breathe?" came Darnier's clipped voice from the vicinity of her ear.

"My—my—" A knife of pain reminded her of her arm, now clumsily wrapped in what appeared to be her cravat. Her good hand was at her breast before she realized she couldn't complain to Darnier that what constricted her was her bound bosom.

"I should've thought of that," he said under his breath. He laid her back against the squabs, and before Briana could fully waken from her laudanum-laced sleep, he unfastened her shirt, button by button.

She jerked in surprise as he inserted a knife between her breasts from the underside of her bandeau, cutting it with a rending sound.

Shocked as Briana felt at the feel of his hands and the cold blade of his knife, the action freed her, affording instant relief. "Oh, thank you," she sighed.

When she looked at him, a hot blush stole up her cheeks. Darnier's sights had narrowed on her shirt front.

"Lady Briana, I must cover you," he said roughly, reinserting one of the shirt buttons and deftly securing it.

Briana clutched away the falling bandeau from around her waist, insisting, "Darnier, please—*no!* It's far from proper for you to—"

"You must let me help you; your arm must be kept still until I get you to bed."

Briana's hair fell over her mortified face. She saw her wig and hat on the seat. "Thank you for carrying me away from that . . . that nightmare," she said. The throb in her arm was forgotten as she looked at his black brows and lashes so near.

Darnier, intent on his task, inserted the third button, causing Briana unbelievable thrills from the slight movement of his fingers. To her chagrin, he must have sensed her reaction for he began to quote:

> Then nature said, "A lovelier flower
>    On earth was never sown;
> This child—"

He halted, clearing his throat, looking away.

Briana knew the rest of Wordsworth's lines, and they swam through her head:

> This child I to myself will take;
>    She shall be mine, and I will make
> A lady of my own.

Darnier leaned past her to look out the window. His unshaven jaw was so near that Briana felt an urge to run her finger along it, to feel whether it were soft or rough.

She was startled to hear him say, "I cannot sit here

213

looking at you any longer without kissing you, Briana."
His lips, heated and heavenly, closed around her own,
kissing her as a man starved.

Briana reveled long afterward in the remembered scent
of his skin, the awesome sweetness of his mouth, the
willingness she had felt deep within her to kiss him in
return. At the time, the coach shuddered to a stop.
Darnier, with a wince, pulled away.

With her head and heart in turmoil, Briana panicked,
trying to cover herself. She snatched with her left hand at
the collapsed opera hat slipping out of Darnier's
greatcoat, and held it in front of her.

"I'll call an umbrella for you," he said just as the
Brocco footman opened the door. Darnier stood to
protect her from view. He gave orders to the footman,
then turned back and discovered Briana's consternation.

She held up the opera hat. She could see the morning
light through a hole in its crown. "What is that?" she
asked, her heart beginning to pound.

"Briana, I had to do it."

"What on earth did you do?" She stared at him, her
mouth going dry.

"Hid a third pistol in my hat and shot Fitzroyal
through it."

"*What?*" She stared, disbelieving. "I thought *I* put a
bullet into him!"

"Briana," he said quietly, "you had no bullet."

Briana felt all at sea. "But I had to have! My pistol
fired."

"It fired because I put powder and a wad in it, but
didn't you find the kick lighter than normal? That's
because there was no ball."

"So I didn't shoot Fitzroyal at all? *You* did! Through
your hat." She sank back, the magnitude of what he had
done overwhelming her. He had made sure; he had
guaranteed her safety by taking such a risk. "Oh, what if

214

he suspects, Darnier? Did Clewes see your barrel smoking?"

"He couldn't see," said Darnier simply.

Briana sat up, her eyes alive. "Darnier! Did you crunch his spectacles on purpose?"

Darnier bowed his head. Before Briana could expostulate in wonderment at this unheard-of breach of the code of honor, a bonnet appeared around Darnier's elbow, and Anselma looked in.

"Stars of the Milky Way! It's *Lady Briana!*"

They were thoroughly caught; no doubt remained in either Briana's or Darnier's mind that Anselma could make nothing else out of her mistress's half-open shirt front or her tumbled hair than the worst of all possible explanations.

"Miss Snivelton," said Darnier, quickly pulling the woman inside the crowded carriage and onto his knee, "we need you badly!"

Briana nearly giggled at Anselma's countenance.

"For what?" the spinster queried, her eyes darting about, not daring to look at her mistress's condition.

"We need you to keep Lady Briana safe from scandal," said Darnier in a hushed tone. "She has done something very noble, and has been hurt into the bargain, Miss Snivelton. I shall rely on you to nurse her until a doctor can be had."

Anselma instantly exclaimed in great outrage at Briana's bandage and her men's clothes.

"Dear Anselma!" Briana expressed in relief. "I'll explain it to you later. But pray tell us what brings you here to Grosvenor Square at this hour?"

"Don't you realize, Lady Briana, that Chalandra is gone? Yes, gone! I thought sure you had come after her."

Briana exchanged a puzzled look with Darnier.

"Frances, let me read Chalandra's note that so upset her mother. I came here to chaperone you home, thinking you had sped after her without waking me. So many problems! But is Chalandra here, Mr. Darnier?"

"At Brocco House?" he asked, opening the door and setting the duenna onto the cobbles.

"I don't suppose you realize, Darnier, that your master sent Miss Milburn a letter of assignation, I mean to say—invitation." Anselma grew red uttering such words.

Briana could see Darnier wondering, as she was: an invitation during the night? He removed his caped greatcoat, and placed it on Briana's shoulders, buttoning it over her hurt arm. As Anselma protested, "No, let me!" he twined Briana's mane of hair tenderly round his hand, fixed its slipperiness at her crown, and crammed the wig over it, attempting to view his work as a success. "It's no use. Get the umbrellas," he called over his shoulder.

Briana laughed weakly as he lifted her down, but sobered when she felt the heavy bulk of two pistols inside the greatcoat and heard bottles of laudanum and such clanking in the pockets. She was carried by Darnier, under careful cover, into the marble hall of Brocco House where servants were cleaning up after the ball.

Could Chalandra have kept an assignation with His Grace after coming tamely home from the ball? Briana's mind filled with uncharitable thoughts.

While Anselma clucked over Briana and was suitably awed at her confession of participating in a duel with Fitzroyal, a maid was sent by Darnier to bring a feminine frock and other necessities. He had tipped off the maid to resume the role of Miss Jane Attington, cousin of the duke, thus putting Briana's presence in Brocco House in a respectable light.

Darnier reappeared a half-hour later in the suite of rooms where Briana lay against muslin pillows in a draped French daybed. "The doctor is on his way. Miss

Snivelton, with your leave, I must speak with Lady Briana alone."

Anselma looked ready to protest, but when he added, "It's important and I'll only be a minute, Miss Snivelton," she scurried out.

"I found Miss Milburn," Darnier said flatly.

Briana sat up. "Where was she?"

"Playing the grand piano for him."

"For the duke? By herself?"

"Yes. I've summoned her here."

Chalandra appeared in the doorway, clad in a white gown, hastily donned judging by the ill-tied sash. "What are *you* doing here?" she queried, glaring at Briana in bewilderment.

"Me! What are *you* doing here?"

"I thought I was coming to breakfast." Darnier left the room with a backward glance. Chalandra undulated to a looking glass and pulled a comb from her bodice.

"Answer me!" shouted Briana, wanting to shake the smug little thing until she snapped in two. "What are you doing in this house, at this hour, by yourself with the duke?"

Chalandra tossed up her chin. "I am going to marry him," she said loftily.

"Marry *him?*" Briana closed her eyes and clutched her forehead. The man's horrible visage swam before her vision. Seeing Chalandra's determined pose, Briana said, "Mmm-hmm, I see. You think that to be a duchess would be the epitome of wonders—and wouldn't your mother be proud? You have therefore tossed your reputation after the first duke who clapped eyes on you. Coming to see him tête-à-tête in the middle of the night! How could you, Chalandra?"

Chalandra tossed a tress back and examined her skin in the mirror. "No one will know if you don't tell," she said.

"How about all his servants?"

"Darnier can hush them."

With a heavy heart, Briana asked, "Do you expect to be happy if you snare such a husband for yourself?"

Chalandra's cool pose came to an end. With arms akimbo, she marched toward her cousin, threw down her comb, and cried, "He will give me clothes and jewels . . . and carriages, and this house! And Brocco Park will be mine, too. Why would I pass up all that?"

"Tell me, Cousin," said Briana calmly as Chalandra sank to the hassock, "tell me what he said."

Chalandra cradled her crossed knee, straightened her little back, and declared, "He said I was the most desirable creature he had ever met, and he asked if I would come here to keep him company for there was no way he could sleep anyway for thinking of me."

Briana rolled her eyes. "So you took my carriage and came here like some courtesan. How could you so stupidly throw away respectability?"

Her cousin made no reply. She fiddled with a ruffle on her skirt.

"How I wish you had told me, Chalandra. Didn't you realize his intention? Did His Grace try to take advantage of you?"

"He exclaimed at how beautiful I am, and . . . But I couldn't quite *do it*, Briana. I—I played song after song for him instead," she finished with a tremor.

Briana's heart couldn't help but soften in spite of her exasperation. "That is a relief! But Chalandra, what are you going to do? You are utterly and thoroughly ruined!"

"No, I'm not! Not for long. I'm going to marry him." Briana saw the unmistakable determination which had, in the past, brought results.

"Even if you do," Briana sighed, "come here and tell me how you'll be able to put up with such a man night after night, year after year!" She knew she must put it bluntly, for it was reality Chalandra was playing with.

218

Chalandra rose to her feet. "When I am married to him," she declared, "I will not let him near me."

Briana was all amazement.

Fiercely Chalandra admonished, "But he is not to know that until I am the duchess of Brocco, do you hear? For me to marry him is the way out of this 'ruin' as you call it, but it really is my making, for by this means I can become a duchess of the realm and do just as I please."

Briana could not believe her ears.

A drumming sounded on the door. "Who is it?" Chalandra cried.

"Darnier," came the deep answer.

She rose, looked archly at Briana and said, "There is your answer to your 'night after night, year after year' question: Darnier. Can you think of anyone more suited to the role?"

Briana's breast rose in overwhelming emotion. She watched Chalandra swing the door wide and smile up into Darnier's handsome face. The nerve, the gall! So infuriating was the thought that Briana met Darnier's questioning eyes with blazing blue rage.

# Chapter 19

## Snaring the Duke

Back in Berkeley Square, Mary and Anselma fluttered round Briana, bathing her and lamenting over her wounded arm. They had whisked her in before Mrs. Milburn awoke. Mary wept and implored Briana not to make her bring out the men's clothes ever again.

"No, Mary, I won't," said Briana. An hour later, she went in search of Mrs. Milburn and found her in the breakfast room. Briana laid before her what Chalandra had done.

"What do you *dare* to fabricate to me!" Mrs. Milburn's eyes nearly bored holes in Briana's resolve. "My Chalandra returned from the ball with us, and you know it."

"But what I told you is true, also. I have just had the disgrace of fetching her home from His Grace's house in Grosvenor Square."

Mrs. Milburn's mouth twisted. "I cannot and *will not* believe such a thing! Pooh, you're just trying to do her a damage ever since last night's argument."

"Our argument last night was my trying to warn

Chalandra against a man like the duke of Brocco—and your trying to insist that I was motivated by envy. Now I tell you that His Grace's mischief and your daughter's rashness have resulted in a tête-à-tête of many hours' duration. If you choose not to believe it from me, write to Darnier and have him come and tell you. Or, ask your daughter."

Mrs. Milburn stated, "Of a certainty she is still asleep in her bed."

Briana was so fed up with the woman, she quit the room. What was worse, a rising fear had intruded upon Briana's confidence. What if Darnier would uphold Chalandra's plans? He might think it best for her to marry the duke of Brocco. How long had Darnier and Chalandra had private words? He had escorted her out of that salon on his arm, had he not?

Briana picked at breakfast in her own room pondering all that had occurred. She shed a few tears looking down at the foggy square, and regretted ever coming to London. She powdered her face a bit and went out to the gallery in time to hear raised feminine voices below. And just coming in the front door, removing his tall hat, was Rex.

Briana, with long sontag sleeves, had succeeded in concealing from Mrs. Milburn that she had an injury, but she had to be careful in her movements. She therefore gave Rex her left hand and said, "A timely arrival. I was feeling a little lonely for friends."

"I must talk to you, Briana. You look tired from the ball and all your fame, but gorgeous in spite of it. Was it taxing?"

"Yes, rather." She invited him into the breakfast room since Mrs. Milburn vacated it. She motioned for Paget to bring more coffee.

"May I kiss you?" Rex asked immediately the butler's steps receded.

Briana started. The sound of Mrs. Milburn and Chalandra shouting at one another resumed. Briana smiled ruefully, saying, "Pardon them. They have things to discuss."

Rex smiled. "And so do we." He trapped her against the silk-covered wall, and sank his sculpted lips onto hers.

"Oh Rex!" breathed Briana in alarm.

"I love to hear you sigh my name like that." He obviously felt it expressed passion. At the sound of Paget's measured tread, Rex whisked her into the nearest chair and dived to the carpet at her feet as if he had been lounging there worshiping her without hope.

Briana laughingly said, "I'm glad to see you're prompt, Paget, for this gentleman must be raised from his ridiculous abasement."

"Food and drink should do it, madam," said Paget, setting the tray on the table. He bowed and said, "Miss Snivelton will be with you directly."

At that he slipped out, and Rex lost no time in crawling to her side and gazing burningly up at her, his chin resting on her knees. "Confound your servants!" he said. "Come riding with me." He took her hand and kissed it.

Briana thought what a charmer he was, what attention he would give her, how nice he always looked, and how right their marriage would be in a social sense. But she did not want to discuss wedlock with the dear man when another man's face kept cropping up in her mind.

She said, as Anselma walked into the room, that she would go riding with Rex, providing it was a vehicle and not horseback, and found herself whispering to Anselma in the hall that they would be in a phaeton and amongst other people, and that yes, she would take good care not to move her arm. Anselma conceded that an open carriage must be considered acceptable for she had seen numerous men and ladies riding about so in London.

Which caused Briana to reflect, when she and Rex were wheeling down Rotten Row, that the closed carriage rides she had experienced with Darnier had culminated in the most shocking occurrences. She knew she had been hard on Chalandra in her advice, especially since she felt no better than Chalandra in her own behavior.

Rex finally asked, "Was it something I said, or are you drinking in the fascinating scenery?"

"I'm thinking," she murmured.

"Of my proposal?"

A wistful smile touched her lips.

"What is your concern, Briana?"

All that had occurred at Brocco House following the duel a mere five hours ago now colored Briana's every thought in regard to herself and Rex. She asked what she knew to be an indelicate question, for she had to have reassurance. "Is it truly possible for a man to cease visiting other women—the kind we ladies are not to know about—when they fall in love and marry?"

Rex's jaw muscles moved in what could have been amusement.

"Is it likely, Rex?" Briana insisted.

He pulled up his team at the iron fence before Apsley House. Under the hood of the phaeton, he gave her a long look and took her hand, the one that ached, and held it with a tightening grip. "I cannot speak for other men, but for myself I say: I love you, Briana Rosewynn, and from the moment I saw you in Warwickshire, I have wiped the very thought of other women from my life."

She returned his smile blindingly, and it was said by the duchess of Wellington to the duke as they emerged from their fanlighted doorway, that there was a happy couple in the high-perch phaeton. Likely they were shortly to be married, but she would hate to see that lady's smiles diminish as the years went by.

Therefore, when Briana noticed the nation's hero he was scowling. She raised her parasol to him and his

223

duchess, and saw a smile transform his face. Rex looked irritated, but waited for the Wellesleys to reach the phaeton.

The duchess was attired in pale dove with violet ribbons, and looked to be unsure of herself under her hanging brow curls. Wellington presented the ladies to one another and declared, "Lady Briana was the Fairest of the Fair the other night at the ball you missed, my dear. She has certainly taken Brocco's fancy."

"Please, Your Grace—" began Briana, smiling apologetically at the older woman.

The duke's lazy eyes livened. "You do not care for the old dog, do you, Lady Briana? Rex, have you set out to keep this tender flower from his reach? Take care! The duke, our *friend*," he punctuated, "may have somewhat to say about it."

Rex's chin firmed. "He may be a friend of mine, but he does not dictate to me."

"Ah, look who comes! It's—Darnier," declared Wellington, lifting a hand to the striking dark figure on horseback.

Briana turned uneasily. Darnier was splendidly mounted on a chestnut with black mane, himself clad in a black cape and beaver. There was something intense about his countenance which Briana noted had much to do with his brows nearly meeting. Doubtless he was displeased to see her out and about so soon after the duel.

"Good Day, Your Grace," he bowed from the saddle to the duchess of Wellington. "Lady Briana," he added, lifting his hat to her. "How is your health?"

"Better, thank you." A rush of guilt assailed her to be seen with Rex after Darnier's passionate kiss with her entire neck bared in the coach. All were looking at her, so in a false-sounding voice she added, "How nice it is to see you, Mr. Darnier. Would you like to ride with us along the Serpentine?"

"Thank you, madam, but I must regretfully decline as I am here to see the duke."

Wellington watched this interchange with keen interest. Rex tapped his riding whip on the floorboard.

Darnier moved his horse to Briana's side of the phaeton. "I did, however, call by Berkeley Square to deliver this book of lamp designs for you, but was told by your good butler that I might run into you here."

Briana received the book he withdrew from his coat. As she thanked him, the pages divided to reveal a leaf. It was freshly picked from a yellow horse chestnut.

Rex looked at it with a blink.

Briana knew not what to do.

"My Lady, how that got there you can only guess," murmured Darnier, picking the leaf away after she had gotten a good look at it. "It must be from a branch near the dam of the Westbourne. I was noticing them as I rode by, and pulled some off. I believe those trees would be in their best beauty early in the afternoon, for the sun would light the leaves well. You might like to paint them before any more fall."

When their eyes connected, Briana conveyed her understanding. He murmured an adieu and joined the duke and duchess who were mounting horses.

As Rex gave his team office to trot, Briana asked, "How does Darnier know the duke of Wellington?"

"I believe Darnier met Wellington, or saw him, in the war," said Rex. "Now he's just doing Brocco's business. Brocco is getting set to introduce betterment of military conditions when he takes his seat in the House, and Wellington is advising him."

Rex returned to the subject closest to his heart. "Will you promise, dear Briana, to think and speculate on what a dashing, happy couple we will be?"

With a touch on his arm, Briana said, "Yes, Rex, I will certainly think about it."

She would give it her serious consideration as soon as she could chase Darnier out of her mind.

"You may think you have snared the duke, but what if you haven't?" came Mrs. Milburn's voice from the music room when Briana arrived back in Berkeley Square. "Woe befall you, Chalandra, if he's playing you false! If this gets out, you'll have no choice but to be my lifelong companion."

Chalandra coolly replied, "Oh no, that'll never be the case, for I can catch a husband anytime I want. By the way, I'm amazed, Mother, that women like the one who lived in this house before us don't have more beauty or grace than they do, and yet men flock to them. I'll have no problem gathering proposals, for wasn't I just proclaimed a beauty in front of all Society?"

Mrs. Milburn, Briana could hear, halted in her pacing. "What do you know about the woman who lived here? Was that Lord Fitzroyal's mistress?" she lowered her voice to ask.

"Yes. Miss Clifton," Chalandra said. "Why, she cannot even speak properly.

"Miss Clifton? Not the one Fitzroyal visited by that staircase? Never tell me you've met, not to mention been *conversing* with that smutty woman!" shrieked Mrs. Milburn.

"Why yes, she called here an hour ago while you were out with Mrs. Wipplingote."

"What did she want? How dare that woman come to our door?"

Chalandra drawled, "She was asking for a Mr. Radcliffe. I must say I was astonished, Mother, that men of stature keep women of such lack of finesse. I'd certainly show a little more—"

226

"Chalandra! You're talking about kept women! Do hush!"

"Anyway, I saw Miss Clifton looking around the hall at Briana's changes. I asked her who this Mr. Radcliffe was, and she said never to mind; if he didn't live here she wouldn't bother us further. But she did say that Lord Fitzroyal had muttered something about catching up with him here. Likely somebody Briana met. I questioned Miss Clifton if she was a friend of Fitzroyal's, and she said not anymore! I told her he has been often in this house of late."

"Chalandra!"

"She said we wouldn't see much of him in coming days since he was stuck to his chair now that he couldn't walk."

"Couldn't walk?" echoed Mrs. Milburn.

"He was injured somehow. Unless that's an excuse for the way Paget hit him over the head," Chalandra finished airily.

Briana's heart stilled, then lurched. She left her eavesdropping and tiptoed upstairs to say a prayer of thanks for her deliverance by Darnier in the duel, and to add a petition that Fitzroyal might be able to walk again. It would be awful to see the man crippled forever even though he might have very well done the same thing to her given a split second more in which to do it.

Briana shook her head at her domestic situation. It was apparent that Oonagh Milburn had lost control over her daughter's actions. Briana felt her own helplessness in guiding Chalandra. The occasional camaraderie they had enjoyed at Milburn Place seemed to have slipped entirely away since the ball.

Chalandra expeditiously checked the multitudes of flowers Paget crowded upon the hall table, the floor, and the stairs. When the occasional bouquet arrived for her, she was quick to broadcast the news by discussing the man who sent them in voluble tones to her mother. If only Chalandra could acquire a decent husband. But so far the cards attached to her posies came from undesirables as far as Briana could connect faces to names.

At least one of her own floral gifts was in that category, for Lord Fitzroyal had sent her an enormous spray. Briana sent them to the kitchen and out of her sight. Others arrived from gentlemen Briana could not remember but who thanked her for the dance or congratulated her on her "crown," as one put it. The duke of Brocco sent a spray of white lilies in a crystal bowl with a card that said, "The Fairest in All the Land." Briana felt strongly tempted to send them back.

# Chapter 20

## Betrayal of the Heart

"Anselma, I want Mary and that's final," repeated Briana that afternoon as, outside her chintz curtains, the sun rose high. The light would soon be as Darnier had said, slanting in beauty through the yellow leaves of the horse chestnut tree.

"But, Lady Briana, Mary is too *young* to adequately chaperone you!" protested Anselma. "Furthermore, I have nothing other to do, for I finished netting that reticule and I cleaned all your brushes."

Mary's face remained expressionless in her triumph as she tied the red sash beneath Briana's ear and gave the fashionable bonnet a tilt.

Anselma added sourly, "Mary has to press your fichus, and she has that rent to mend in your yellow spenceret, and—"

"Dear Anselma!" said Briana, rising to say confidentially, "My real reason is that I would very much like for you to keep an eye on Chalandra. If she leaves the house again, go with her. If she refuses your company, follow her. Since she and her mother have locked horns, who

229

knows what she'll do?"

Anselma, with tight lips, nodded and accepted the office of spy. "What am I to do if I have to chase her somewheres—then what?"

"Send a message to me here. Or if the case seems desperate, go to Brocco House and tell Darnier. You acted very prudently this morning, Anselma, and I'm grateful to you."

Anselma waved her hand in deprecation, and went to check on Chalandra's activities.

Mary fitted a red pelisse over Briana's white sleeve as gently as could be, and they were both shortly ensconced in the Rosewynn town chariot. "My Lady," Mary entreated, "I'm scared your wound will never heal if you don't lie abed. You have been going somewhere constantly since yesterday before the ball."

"Mary, I've had an important summons. You must aid me in this, and keep my confidence. When I alight, drive round the park slowly and then come back for me."

Darnier was waiting, throwing spiny pods from the horse chestnut into the water of the Serpentine. Quite unobserved at this early hour, Briana walked through a scatter of leaves and leaping squirrels to where branches of swaying yellow leaves reached over the glittering water.

Darnier's pupils widened as he turned and saw her. He said:

> She was a Phantom of delight
> When first she gleamed upon my sight . . .

Briana knew she blushed; she who was not in the habit of blushing. Darnier had meant for her to see that very poem in her Wordsworth—he had!

"Who, may I ask, is the phantom?" Briana parried. "You appear in the most unorthodox places."

"So do you." He smiled, a refreshing, private smile that did all kinds of strange things to her heart. He added, "I don't deserve for you to meet me after all I've put you through, Briana, but I'm glad you've come."

I shouldn't have, she thought, for he was so appealing. Oh, the ache in her heart . . .

"Would you prefer to walk?" he asked.

"No, thank you." The world was suspended, warm with leaf-filtered light and the distant splash of ducks in wavery water, and she did not wish to move an inch. Her time here in this cocoon with Darnier would not last long enough.

"Good. It pleases me, also, to stay here. I feel I must beg your mercy, Briana, for I couldn't stop myself from . . . kissing you."

"Please!" Breathless, she plunged on. "I know I'm wicked to say so, but I want no apology. Please don't talk of it." Leave the memory the thrill that it was, she cried to herself. In hot confusion, she turned away. What was she to do with this servant who had admitted to courting her for his master? Darnier was far more to her than anyone's servant could ever be.

He tugged another pod from the tree and threw it into the water where they watched it disappear, then bob to the surface. "Do you ever wish to reappear as Radcliffe again?" he asked, lifting a dark brow mischievously.

Briana had an instant's urge to gallivant with this man again. "Tell me more," she said, and they both laughed.

"You see," he said, "I've already toyed with the idea of sending word to Fitzroyal that Mr. Radcliffe died, but—"

"From an arm wound?" inserted Briana. "That would be stretching belief."

"And it would be no fun," Darnier added as the clincher.

A smile tugged at Briana's lips. "However, if people believed it, I would have good reason to cut his lordship and refuse his company."

"But there would be no reason to do so. He would have to quit the country. On the other hand, it isn't like you, is it, to cut someone?"

Briana gazed at Darnier, unaware of what a vision she was with her dark hair escaping the confines of red ribbons, her black-lashed eyes eloquent. "I can't lie to Fitzroyal, saying my fictitious cousin died from his bullet."

"You don't surprise me."

"Do you know what's happened to him? Emmaline Clifton has been at my door talking to Chalandra, saying Fitzroyal cannot walk."

"I visited him to see the damage. He has a splintered shin bone."

"Oh no."

"I feel responsible but not sorry, Briana, for it had to be he, or it would have been you."

Unsteadily she said, "Darnier, I will always be thankful for what you did for me."

"And I will never cease to admire what courage you displayed on that dueling field." He came around the tree and absently opened a chestnut pod, dropping the nut into her hand. "Last night I heard wind of a certain party," he said in a new tone. "A party planned for tomorrow night, and to which I should take you to complete your education. If you think you can manage another little adventure? Hmm?"

"Dressed as a buck?"

"Of course." Darnier's lower eyelids deepened. "Shall it be as a rakishly injured Radcliffe? Or will I be obliged to bleach your eyebrows and procure a red wig?"

Upon reaching her doorstep, Briana's arm throbbed,

but the physical discomfort was overridden by anticipation for the next night's mysterious doings. They had agreed that Darnier would call for her at ten o'clock.

More tissues and vases of scented flowers greeted her arrival. Anselma pointed out that she had moved many into the drawing room, front salon, library, dining room, and every other spot in the house which could accommodate a vase. Briana thanked her and took the letters and invitations to peruse them in private.

Velvety red and white roses came from Rex with a card that said: "Red for love, white for hope."

Briana sighed. What should she do? She unsealed the card accompanying a generous spray of camellias. It took her aback, for it bore the duke of Wellington's crest. His sharp scrawl read:

Lady Briana:
    Be careful, my dear. You could break a heart.
                                    Wellington

What did that mean? Her pulse hastened as she stared at the words. Surely he didn't refer to his own heart . . . ? Did he think she was leading him on? Surely he had more savoir faire than that.

Briana puzzled over those words, as, with some pain in her arm, she wrote notes of thanks and acceptances to various invitations. All she could finally think of writing to Wellington was:

My lord duke,
    My thanks for the exquisite camellias. I mean to break no hearts. I have met no man with one so brittle.

She chewed the stalk of her quill in deliberation before

233

she dipped it and wrote to Rex:

Dear Rex,
    Roses are my favorite, as you know:
    You may be my favorite—time will show.

She felt better for having given him hope without acceptance. She would give his suit serious thought until she knew in her heart of hearts that he was the one for her.

"Anselma, come with me to Hatchard's," Briana called as her duenna emerged looking weary from her vigil over Chalandra, who had been trying on new accessories they had bought that morning from the Pantheon Bazaar. "It looks like my cousin will be occupied for quite a while, and I hope to find a design book on stained glass for the Brocco apartments," Briana explained. Truth to tell, little remained of her former enthusiasm for the project since she had met the duke of Brocco and had heard Chalandra's plan to be the duchess.

Though Anselma chattered on their ride through streets clogged with vehicles, Briana was lost in her thoughts. So much concerned her. On top of her problems was the perplexing fact of her own willingness to gad about with Darnier when, in her mind, she mulled over the possibility of a betrothal to Sir Reginald Channing.

How it galled her that Chalandra, who had treated Darnier so shabbily before, now had designs on his person. She had doubtless discovered that ladies of the aristocracy, not only doxies, had male companions while loveless marriages kept them socially aloft. Could this opportunistic arrangement really be what little Chalandra would pull off?

A thousand pricks of jealousy tormented Briana as she pictured Chalandra running her slim little hands across

Darnier's bronzed cheekbones, ruffling that thick, crisp hair. "Oh! I'll murder her!"

"Murder who?" demanded Anselma, startled beyond measure.

Briana fumed, "My cousin!"

"Is that really necessary, Lady Briana? What would that accomplish? You would still have Mrs. Milburn to contend with."

Laughing hopelessly, Briana sank her head back to the squabs. "Anselma, I don't know how much longer I can field my cousin's hijinks."

"I know how it must bother you, Lady Briana. All the servants are talking of nothing else after Mrs. Milburn shouted at Chalandra this morning."

"I'm sure poor Chalandra has ostracized herself from high society which, to be truthful, she never had a prayer to enter. But if her latest conduct is voiced abroad, she'll be snubbed everywhere, and I'm sure I don't know where she'll end."

"Well, I fear there is nothing you can do more than you've tried already," said Anselma stoutly. "Let them that make their beds lie in them."

As long as they lie in them without Darnier, added Briana silently.

Her arrival at the fashionable Hatchard's created quite a stir. No sooner had her crested vehicle halted in the street than it was voiced like lightning that Lady Briana Rosewynn, just entering the bookseller's, had been declared Fairest of the Fair at the most stunning ball in London. Caricatures of "His Grace the Invisible" were plastered in shop windows and newspapers, his visage rendered into frightening attitudes by sundry artists. Three beauties were always depicted coquetting around the monster.

"Lady Briana! Just look at how famous you've become!" exclaimed Anselma, looking from one shop window to another where crowds perused the pictures.

Briana groaned. "There will be no more Almack's for me, I fear."

"Nonsense, my lady. I am sure His Grace's choice was right, even though he is a terribly voluble and eccentric individual. Now I am thankful to God I have never seen his face if he looks that diabolical."

"Lady Briana! I can scarcely believe my divine luck," sang out Major Quentin, he of the park and Vauxhall. "My congratulations! I didn't get a chance to dance with you at the ball for the tight squeeze around you, but perhaps at the next one?"

Briana greeted him genially but kept her reserve, remembering when he had leaned over her shoulder at Vauxhall thinking she was a man, and pointed out the wanton women.

He seemed not to notice, his spirits were so high. "Another of the Fair is in the next room reading the newspapers," he told her. "I didn't expect to see the Fairest on my way out."

When Briana had disengaged herself from the effusive major and other people gawking or accosting her with congratulations, she entered the newspaper room. Miss Cordelia Landers stood there with Darnier. Briana felt turned to stone as he kissed Cordelia's hand, replaced his beaver, and smiled as he turned and walked out a far door. Miss Cordelia watched him in stillness, then lifted her hand, gazed rapturously at a sparkling ring on her finger, and raised it to her cheek.

"Good afternoon, Miss Landers," said Briana calmly.

Cordelia spun in surprise, then flushed and said, "Good—good day, Lady Briana!"

There was something new in Cordelia's eyes, sparkling like the stone on the hand she was trying to hide.

"Is that a new ring?" Briana asked. Cordelia bit her lip but lifted her hand, trying to hide it from others. Fresh gold glinted around a diamond and rubies. "How pretty," Briana commented while her head began to pound.

Cordelia's voice dropped as she tugged on kid gloves. "Please take no more notice of it, Lady Briana. I—I must keep it a secret for a while."

"You must?" Briana wondered if her face were noticeably ashen.

"Yes. It is a betrothal ring, but, you see," she whispered, "the man I love has not yet gained my father's consent."

Briana could not look at Cordelia's troubled radiance any longer. She turned to draw a newspaper off the table, saying, "I can see where that could be trying. Who is your fiancé?"

There was a short silence. Miss Cordelia glanced over her shoulder, then said, "I'm truly sorry, Lady Briana, but I cannot say just now."

"I see. Forgive me for asking. I wish you every joy. Good day. I really must be going."

"Lady Briana, stay a moment. I want to say that I agree: you *are* the most beautiful lady in all of London; on the inside as well as on the out."

This was too much for Briana, who felt miserable and mean and ready to cry. She made a beeline for the front door.

Anselma raced after her, casting looks back, wondering what that golden-haired woman had said to send Briana into the boughs.

After wading through the crowd around her chariot and directing her cursing coachman to drive home, Briana felt her arm hurting and she knew she was depressed to the core, and weary besides.

"That wasn't much of a trip, was it?" said Anselma, peering back at Hatchard's facade. "Except I've learned how adored you are in this city already, my word! Did you see what you needed in the newspaper? Did you go to look at the reports about the ball?"

"No, nothing of the kind. I felt I couldn't go searching for books when my arm had begun to bother me. I just wish to go home and to bed."

"Poor Briana! I should never have let you come out."

Briana slept for five hours. The languid feeling still permeated her bones as she stretched her good arm. "Have Mrs. Milburn's guests arrived yet?"

"Yes, six women, and some of them chattering too loudly, I'd say," quipped Mary who frowningly laid out Briana's evening wear. This array consisted of black kerseymere knee breeches, black silk stockings with embroidered white swords, kid pumps, velvet waistcoat, and a nip-waisted evening coat with silk lapels.

"Come, this is likely my last escapade, Mary, so I want to look all the crack. Can you tuck this shirt deeper into my breeches?"

There was disapproval in Mary's countenance as she poked and smoothed, but she did not express it any longer in words.

# Chapter 21

## An Eye=opening Engagement

"Do you think I should write a note of condolence to Lord Fitzroyal?" Briana asked as Darnier tied her cravat *à l'Americain* in the light of the coach lanterns.

"Do you wish to?" he asked, looking amused as he raised her chin to tie the knot which would keep the stock high.

"I think I should say something to the effect that I hope Radcliffe has not *killed* him."

Darnier laughed. The happy sound and the glimpse of his handsome teeth made Briana feel his magnetism. Here was another potentially risky situation. "Go ahead," he mentioned as the hired carriage jolted along, making his precise work difficult, "but he may take it as a 'come-hither' message, and then you shall have him neck and crop whether you want him or not."

"Say no more," shuddered Briana.

Darnier sat back and surveyed her. "Complete to a shade. All you lack is a quizzing glass," he said, fingering his of gleaming silver. "Would you like to use mine?"

"Will I be wanting to quiz anyone?"

"Likely you may," was his unrevealing reply, and he removed the glass on its chain and handed it to her.

Briana scrutinized him through it. How strikingly he had dressed in a burgundy coat with white breeches, black waistcoat, and a cravat tied in intricate perfection with a touch of the rakish. She could have gazed for long minutes at his black hair and brows and moustache above the splendor of his raiment, but he playfully reached as if to snatch the glass away from her eye.

"I say," she drawled in her Radcliffe timber, "what *is* that style called?"

Darnier replied, "The Oriental, sir. I quite admire yours."

"You cannot have my valet," she quipped, then stopped. Her guilty thoughts had flown as if to Chalandra and Cordelia: you cannot have my Darnier. Hurriedly she joked, "Would sitting like this be acceptable wherever we are going?" She lifted an ankle to her thigh and assumed a dissipated scowl, her wrist—the one not in the sling—supporting her temple where black locks fell. She had seen Lord Byron depicted so.

"You'll make the ladies swoon to death."

"Ladies!" groaned Briana. "Oh no!"

She was stabbed by the fear that had deluged her in Hatchard's. "What ladies? Anyone you know?" Casually, she ventured, "Will Miss Landers and her circle be there to see through my disguise? I sat rather close to her that night of the ball."

"No, I don't expect to see Miss Landers where we're going."

"Did you know she's wearing a new ring?" Briana watched him closely, pretending not to.

Darnier's brows lifted. "Yes, I did," he murmured. "So you've seen it? What did she tell you about it?"

"That it's a secret engagement ring."

"Ah, that's what I understand as well. Now here we

240

are, just around this corner; we must alight in a hurry, Radcliffe."

Briana felt sickened. Was he being evasive? "Where are we going?" she asked, correctly positioning her top hat while Darnier paid the driver.

As they strode along the flagstones, Darnier said, "After the Brocco ball, I received an invitation to a *petit souper* at a house where you will never, ever go other than tonight."

"Why not?" she asked. "Won't I like it there?"

"That is something I will be very interested to hear," he said. Briana was taken aback by his tone of solemnity. He kept his head lowered although it was quite dark, and before he raised the knocker, he said quietly, "This is the house of Amy Sydenham, one of the Dubochet sisters."

"Not Harriette Wilson's sister?" Briana squeaked in horrified astonishment.

"Shhh. The same. Now do compose your features into that wicked scowl which even I cannot quite emulate, and you will live through it all. Remember: you wanted to be savvy to what occurs in places where you cannot go. Now concentrate on fooling *these* women."

The porter conferred with Darnier who produced his invitation and relinquished his hat. Briana carefully removed hers and followed him into a dimly lit room full of pianoforte music and fragrance and laughter. When her eyes grew accustomed, she found herself under observation by a woman with a lovely mane of curls, an attractive but rather prominent nose, and a lively eye. She was wearing a shockingly décolleté gown with the appearance of nothing between herself and the pink silk.

When she appraised Darnier, whose look paid homage to her charms, she smiled beautifully. "You must be Mr. Darnier of whom I heard recently. You were quite visible at a recent ball at Brocco House, I believe. I'm Harriette. Who is this? A friend of yours?"

241

And so Briana was presented to the notorious Cyprian, the queen of the demi-monde, that fascinating Harriette Wilson. Miss Wilson did nothing to disgust other than show off her voluptuous bosom and tiny waist, for she apparently had men by the dozens courting her for favors and had no need to send out other lures.

"A-a-my! Does that feel nice?" bawled an old man rubbing the arm of a dark-haired woman sitting with him on an ornate divan.

Briana looked askance.

The woman leapt to her feet and streaked to Darnier's side at the punch bowl. "Are you the duke of Brocco's man?" she asked, intently eyeing him.

"Yes, Mrs. Sydenham, I'm Darnier. This is Mr. Radcliffe. I'd like to thank you for your invitation."

Briana made her bow; not low, however, for she couldn't pay respect to a woman so notoriously clad as was Amy in filmy peach and fingerless gloves.

"Mr. Radcliffe is new in London, and I have decided to show him the fairest sights. You and your sisters were a must," Darnier threw out easily although Briana knew very well he could not call such a coarse-featured woman attractive. "Has supper begun?" he asked genially.

"It is just, and we must go in. This way, gentlemen," Amy said effusively, drawing Darnier by the arm while she clucked over Briana's tied in a black sling. When she heard that Radcliffe had been hit in the arm during archery practice, Amy looked suitably awed and led them to the sparsely laden table.

Food was obviously not what people came for. Laughing and coquetting guests meandered in from the drawing room and parlors. Briana was embarrassed yet fascinated to watch real Cyprians flirting. Taking the plunge, Briana whispered, "Tell me how much they sell their favors for!"

"Harriette can command a hundred guineas for an

evening of her brilliant company," Darnier replied, his mouth curving. "Or so I've been told."

Briana gave him her most withering squint, and he laughed aloud.

Amy could be heard telling her footmen to douse the lights except for the few candelabra on the tables, and Briana soon had little worry over being recognized. The dinner was quite ordinary but for the witty conversation taking place in Harriette's corner of the table, and the general jollification of the men with their lustful intentions.

Briana was annoyed to find most of Darnier's attention commanded by the young, self-possessed sister called Sophia who seemed to agree with everything he said, repeating him in such effusions as, "Oh yes, I think that Lawrence is the very best artiste, I've always thought so." Before long Briana heard her telling the man on her right, "I agree entirely—Goya has the best eye and the greatest talent, to be sure."

Briana watched men she had danced with caressing these women, and she began to feel sick. How could she ever dance with them again? Eyeing Alvanley's progress, she knew she would flatly refuse.

But she was not to know how sick she could feel until the *petit souper* was at an end and the parlors and drawing rooms had been thrown open. Droves of men arrived shortly after the eleven o'clock hour.

"I am ready to quit this place," she muttered distinctly as she strolled with Darnier to a salon long and narrow and full of shadowy couples and a buzz of low conversation. From somewhere she heard a shriek of Harriette's happy laughter.

"Come, Mr. Radcliffe," said Amy, materializing at Briana's elbow, "I overheard you! You must not entertain any idea of leaving—why, you just arrived. Sophia insists on singing for us and Harriette, I suppose, must play." She cast her sister a venomous look. "Her new spark just arrived, so I wonder if she will be induced to leave him. I shall go tell her to get her playing over and done with. Do sit there, Mr. Darnier and Mr. Radcliffe. I shall be back in a whisker."

Darnier said the polite thing, and with a raise of a tentative brow, motioned Briana to take the chair Amy had indicated. Sophia came by and took the chair next to Darnier who was certainly the handsomest man in the room, and Briana found herself presented to the irritating Sophia.

Briana asked her, weren't there four of them? Whereupon Sophia pointed out her sister Fanny, the one with fair curls and the face of an angel. She looked puzzlingly innocent to be in such a nest as this. To think that these women entertained peers and were treated with such tenderness by them while their ladies at home dared not even speak such women's names.

Amy returned directly, pushing up her bracelets. "Some bottles of rare champagne are being brought in. Harriette says we're to—well, I might as well announce it to all the room." She clapped her hands. "We have a friend whom we hear is betrothed," she declared with lashes batting, "and you know, gentlemen, what kind of a celebration that calls for!" She giggled amidst the halloos and cat calls. "Do drink up!" she advised all and sundry.

Briana reluctantly accepted a glass, but sipped from it only when she wanted to escape the foolish feeling of sitting in a place she didn't want to be. She made no effort to be agreeable to the gushing Sophia or the unrefined Amy. Darnier, however, seemed to enthrall them both with no exertion at all. But they must have been wearing on him, for he reminded Sophia she had promised to sing.

"Harriette!" cried she, jumping up. "Leave your knight for one instant and play for me!"

Darnier rose, also. "Shall I turn for you?"

As he motioned for Briana to follow, she did so, moving with dignity, knowing she and Darnier drew looks as they always did; such an arresting pair they made. While Sophia shuffled wildly through her music sheets and Darnier made a selection, Briana heard a low laugh which sounded familiar. It compelled her to take a few steps out of the circle of light to see who sat behind the plants in the dark corner.

There, with his arm around Harriette's abundant curls, a champagne glass in his free hand, was Rex!

Briana groped for the quizzing glass. It was really Rex.

Harriette, noting Briana quizzing them, called gaily, "Do you play, Mr. Radcliffe?" A joke, as Briana's arm was in a sling.

"No, Miss Wilson," she said with a valiant effort, "but I can assure you that others do!" She whirled on her heel before Rex could lift his quizzing glass, and strode out of the rooms, her pulse pounding in her temples.

*Rex!* What was the world coming to? Her handsome, honorable Sir Reginald Channing, he of the honest smile—bestowing that and more on a queen of the demi-reps!

Briana, streaking for the door, dodged the duke of Wellington who was handing his hat and cape to the porter. "Say, what's your rush, stranger?"

She escaped him and leapt down the steps, falling off balance because of her bound arm. She ran down the dim street past parked carriages and chatting grooms until she raised suspicions and was grabbed by the collar.

"Let go!" she raged at the huge Charly.

"You thievin' or what?" he growled, tightening his hold.

Darnier approached on a run, calling, "Let him go, good man. He's no thief; he's with me."

Briana marched angrily on, Darnier keeping step and handing her her hat. She marveled at the gall of the man who had devotedly decreed he was through with other women since the day he had seen her in Warwickshire.

"Lies!" she sobbed, "All lies!" She covered her distraught face as they turned the corner into a gang of young men on the spree. They turned and stared at the gentleman in tears, and hooted saucy comments.

Darnier took her by the elbow and steered her out of their way. "Go ahead," he urged, "you were saying?"

Briana had never felt so choked or so furious or so betrayed. "Never tell me that Rex was the one celebrating his betrothal!" she expelled, leaning her head back against a wall, cradling her arms and closing her eyes in pain.

"That's what I heard."

Briana opened her eyes. "Who is his fortunate fiancée?"

In the gaslight, Darnier looked at her in surprise. "I thought the fiancée herself would know that, Briana. Oh confound it! I begin to see what he's done." Darnier took her by the good arm and led her on, for three ladies of the streets had spied them and were advancing *en force.*

Briana asked between deep breaths, "When did you hear about this betrothal celebration?"

"Yesterday in White's when I went looking for Fitzroyal."

"In *White's?*" she repeated, aghast. "Does all of London think I am engaged?"

"I don't know about all of London yet, but I don't understand, Briana, because Rex himself told me that he had his future happiness fixed with you."

Indignantly Briana shouted, "I have not entered into any engagement!"

"You haven't?"

"No!" Briana jostled angrily through a crowd of riffraff.

Darnier snatched at the bridle of a hackney horse, and

the coachman halted. "Come, Radcliffe," Darnier gestured her in. His jaw muscles were working, and he appeared to be deep in thought.

"Take me home!" cried Briana.

Darnier stood up to confer with the driver.

Pulling off her itching wig and yanking out hairpins, Briana sobbed, "You were right! Never have I been so educated as on these outings with you! I have learned never, *ever* to trust or believe a man again!"

Darnier whistled in surprise. "That is partly what I hoped to accomplish, but not so generally as that, Lady Briana."

"Well?" she questioned imperiously through her tears. "Can you name one man I know who is not lying or deceiving me in some way?"

"No, I can't," admitted Darnier in frank regret.

She cast him a smoldering look. He, too, was guilty. She wished she were dead.

"How is your arm?" he asked.

"Fine!" She hugged its painful throbbing to her bound chest and pressed her nose to the window. Let the wheels rattle her head senseless. Naiveté had been better than this knowledge she now possessed. "Do you go to that house often?" she asked, stifling her urge to cry.

"No. In fact, my only other occasion in entering that portal was to seek out someone with whom the duke had business."

Oh yes, indeed, thought Briana, but she wanted so desperately to believe him. "I see that all of the pinks of the ton make that house their second home," she sniffed.

"Not *all*, Briana," Darnier corrected her firmly.

She asked pointedly, "Did you enjoy your evening?"

"No, I heartily did not!"

"Then why on earth did you take me there?"

"This may have been wrong, Briana, but I wanted you to see what you were getting into."

She sighed into her trembling fingers. Feature that. What wisdom this Darnier possessed. As she lifted the quizzing glass on its chain from around her neck and returned it to him, she said humbly, "You were right to do so."

She saw Rex's arm around the locks of Harriette and her eyes blurred with hot tears all over again. "Oh Darnier!" she cried, "I cannot bear for the world to be like this!"

"I know," he murmured. "Will you tell me please: do you love Rex, Briana?"

"No, I do not!" As she collapsed into hopeless tears, Darnier pulled her head onto his shoulder and said softly, "Cry as long as is necessary, dear little Radcliffe."

She realized before too many more minutes of pressing her cheek into his fine coat that Darnier was sincerely suffering for her in her disillusionment.

# Chapter 22
## Confrontations

"Sir Reginald is not at home to callers yet, your ladyship."

"I must see him," said Briana. "Bring up my card. And have your footmen carry in these crates." She spoke firmly to the porter but her heart thumped painfully in her breast.

Was she sadly romantic? Was she hoping to live in a world of good and light which did not exist even with people one held as friends and believed in? Did she expect to be happier than her own mother?

For the half-hour Briana directed Rex's servants in hanging his new curtains, Anselma fidgeted about the salon trying to help Briana by arranging blue and lilac vases on mantel and tables. Briana moved every one again in order to balance the colors, and ended up speaking sharply when her duenna reached to adjust a statuette. Briana had told nothing of her real reason for coming here, but Anselma could feel tension, and kept darting her worried looks.

At last Rex strode in, his face clean and shiny, his hair

waving damply, and his eyes lighting on Briana despite his obvious lack of sleep. "What a wonderful surprise, Briana!" he cried warmly, grasping her hands and smiling. "You reward my undeserving eyes at such an early hour. Why, look at this room! It's character has completely changed. Amazing!"

"Yes, how it has," she said dryly. "Leave us now, Anselma."

Briana lifted her dark lashes, searching Rex's expression. No sign of conscience. He smiled at her just as admiringly as before. She wanted so badly to believe last night had been but a bad dream, but very low, she replied, "Yes, undeserving."

A look of puzzlement crossed Sir Reginald's face. "To what do I owe this unlooked-for pleasure?" he continued, directing a glance at Anselma watching from the hall. He closed the door and came to lift Briana into his arms.

"Stop right there!" she cried, throwing his hands off.

"Stop what, my dear?"

"Touching me, calling me your dear! I can never consider marrying you now," Briana finished in a whisper, turning her face into the crook of her arm as she sank to the sofa.

"Briana! What on earth has brought this on? What are you saying?"

"You've brought it on, Rex! And I was gull enough to believe your word!"

"What word?"

"That since you met me, all desire or thought of other women has gone out of your head forever."

"But it has!" he cried stricken.

"*No, it hasn't!*" Seeing his extreme puzzlement, her head reeled in doubt but she deliberately removed his fingers from her arm and said, "You see, Rex, I was there last night."

An expression of the most incredulous blankness crossed his handsome features. In a diminished voice, he asked, "You were . . . *where* . . . last night?"

Rising dramatically and gathering up her sketches, Briana said, "I was where you were." She shot him a glistening look.

"Briana, do not keep me in suspense! Where were you, and whom did you mistake for me, I wonder?"

Briana took a deep breath. Could she have been wrong? "Do you recall a young man with his arm in a sling whom Harriette teased about playing the pianoforte?"

Before he could prevent it, astonishment jumped into Rex's eyes.

Dying inside as she watched his face, Briana said, "You will say it was unfair of me to spy on you. But it was beyond my wildest dreams to see you there, believe me."

With those soft words, she removed herself from his slackened grasp, summoned Anselma, and hurried to her carriage. Her hands were shaking. She could think of but one haven: Darnier.


The missive read, in Darnier's hand:

> The duke of Brocco provides his carriage to convey Lady Briana Rosewynn to Brocco Park to oversee the decoration of his future duchess's apartments. Can Lady Briana be ready to depart by eight o'clock tomorrow morning?

"Anselma, have Mary pack me a trunk." Briana handed the letter to her duenna.

Mrs. Milburn entered the library, asking, "Where are you going?"

"Back to Shipston with all my decorating paraphernalia. I must see that project to a close."

"Can you take Chalandra with you?" Mrs. Milburn asked almost courteously. "After all, she will want to approve the final setup of those rooms."

Briana tried to cloak her choking thoughts. She knew Chalandra was best out of London at the moment, and sensed Mrs. Milburn's silent plea. "If she can be persuaded to come," said Briana.

That afternoon, Briana received a letter from Rex accompanied by an exquisite porcelain urn full of red rose buds. He begged her forgiveness and asked for another chance.

Briana wrote back:

> I would give you another chance, dear Rex, if I could bear to live in a state of distrust with the man on whom I pledge my fidelity. If you had been truthful in your words to me and to Society, and had not tried to hide your visit to Miss W, there might have been a ray of hope. May you find happiness.
>
> Adieu.

Briana found herself wracked by a desperate feeling of loneliness as she lit the red sealing wax and watched it drip onto the paper. How could she go through life without a husband who loved her, only her? She knew she could never willingly put herself into the position which her mother had endured during those months in Bath separated from her husband, and likely knowing full well that he had another woman in London.

*Not I!* vowed Briana, pushing her crested seal firmly into the wax. Let me live and die a spinster first.

On that cheerful note, she looked up and saw Anselma standing there. Without a word, Briana put the missive into her hand for dispatch. Briana sought out Chalandra and made plans for their trip back to Warwickshire. Her cousin seemed tractable enough after an initial pout about leaving London. At her mother's pointed suggestion that she approve the duchess's rooms, Chalandra assented. "But only for a se'nnight," she stipulated.

Mrs. Milburn could not be budged from Berkeley Square. If only Briana could hit upon some easy way to dislodge her relations permanently.

A note from Wellington arrived as Briana oversaw the packing of the lamps. As she cracked the ducal seal, she wondered what he had thought of her declaration that she had met no male heart so brittle it could break.

Dearest Lady Briana,
    Have you discovered who loves you?
                                        Wellington

Stymied, Briana stared at the words. It couldn't be he—could it? Remember his bantering at Almack's while he looked into her bodice, Briana bit her lip. He loved to look, that was certain. She recalled his presence at the Brocco ball without his wife. Then she thought about how uninteresting his wife looked. Trying to be logical, Briana wondered how she supposedly could have discovered Wellington loved her if she hadn't seen him since his last missive? No, it must be Rex he referred to. And there he was mistaken.

Chalandra burst into the hall and ran across the marble floor in unaccustomed haste, snatching Briana's hand and pulling her into the library. She slammed the door.

"What on earth—?" Briana asked, staring at her flushed cousin.

"Something strange is going on!" gasped Chalandra. "Cordelia Landers's father just left Brocco House in a traveling coach. With him he had the duke, but His Grace looked to be *tied up!*"

"Really, Chalandra," said Briana, "how ridiculous.

253

More importantly, what were you doing in the vicinity of Brocco House?"

"I was going—I was going to meet him!" Chalandra threw back. "He sent me a letter saying I can go away with him, and we will marry. But, Bri, I couldn't reach him because Mr. Landers took him away! Oh, I saw the duke's eyes through the coach window, but he looked helpless to me. What could be happening, Briana? We must get Brocco back! You have to help me!"

With her dark brows gathering, Briana said, "Did you think to ask at Brocco House?"

"Yes, but the butler, that giant black-haired terror, looked down at me like a mountain and said his master was not at home to visitors."

"Did you explain what you just saw?"

"Of course! But he acted as though I were some little child telling tales. Then he practically shut the door in my face!" Chalandra's fists clenched and her eyes were enormous.

Briana could not ignore Chalandra's genuine panic. "Before you go chasing after him, Chalandra, tell me: why has he never once come calling on you if he's so interested in marrying you? What worries me sick is, why must you have him? You will not have a happy life despite all his money. Please give this some sober thought, Chalandra, before you knowingly ruin the rest of your days."

Chalandra allowed Briana to hug her fervently, but could not quite return it. Mrs. Milburn's corset creaked as she leaned to look in through the door she had quietly opened. Chalandra instantly flung it wide and ran out past her mother.

Mrs. Milburn jerked her gaze back to Briana. "What were you telling her?"

"Not to ruin her life."

"You are no doubt trying to ruin it for her!"

"How?" asked Briana. "By warning her against her own folly in chasing a duke whom she admits is repulsive to her? Mrs. Milburn, what kind of a mother are you to push your child into the arms of such a beast?"

"Push!" she scoffed. "I'm not pushing her! You know very well that he is after her, and you try to twist the whole affair around because you are probably irked it isn't you who have snared a duke. A *duke*, Briana!"

"A duke indeed." Shaking her head sadly, Briana said, "Pride! All your efforts are for glory and possession, to make others envy you. I cannot think of one person who will envy poor Chalandra if she marries His Grace of Brocco. I pity her already being pitchforked at him by you, likely for your own gain. It is nothing to you to urge your daughter into wedlock with him, Mrs. Milburn, for *you* will not have to climb between His Grace's bed curtains."

With that, Briana left Mrs. Milburn filling her lungs. "She's *not* going to Warwickshire with you!" she shouted up the stairs.

At the door, Paget was doing his tactful best to send someone away since Lady Briana was "that moment at her dinner," he said.

"Who is it, Paget?" She knew with a sinking heart that the visitor could not have failed to hear their raised voices.

As Paget moved aside, she saw that Fitzroyal had shoved a walking stick into the doorway and was now gaining entrance. The stick turned out to be one of two shoulder-supporting crutches with which he propped himself, and his left leg was bandaged heavily judging by the swell beneath the nankeens and hose.

"Good evening, Lady Briana, may I come in?" he called, his voice quite unimpaired.

Briana descended the few steps in statuesque calm. "Good evening, Fitzroyal," she said. "Paget, do open the front reception room for a few moments. I cannot request that Fitzroyal pull himself up these stairs."

"Thank you for your kindness, your ladyship," said Fitzroyal.

As Briana passed the butler, she tugged his sleeve, signaling him to stay in sight.

Lord Fitzroyal lowered himself into a wing chair. "It is good of you to admit me," he said. "I have come to explain to you that I did not mean to mortally wound your cousin, Mr. Radcliffe, but as I have not seen him or discovered his whereabouts through the usual channels, I am come to appeal to your aid."

"And what can I do for you?" asked Briana, smoothing her skirt.

"You can tell me if he is he still alive, or must I flee the country?"

"I doubt that my news would bring about the action you mention," said Briana with courage, "but Mr. Radcliffe is in fact dead, for I have laid him to rest early this morning."

Lord Fitzroyal started visibly. With his closely set eyes pinned on her, he repeated, "Laid him to rest?"

"Yes."

Seeing Paget in the shadow under the stairs, Briana turned her back to the butler and unbuttoned her sleeve at the wrist.

Fitzroyal's eyeballs were bulging with the need to hear more, but she deliberately rolled up the lace cuff until a bandage appeared below her elbow. She raised frank eyes to him and gestured. "Voilà: your bullet wound, my lord."

He jumped up, then fell back into the cushion at the pain he had caused himself. "What in thunderation?" he gasped, staring from her arm to her face.

Briana covered her wound. "Lord Fitzroyal," she said softly, eyes lowered, "I wish to forgive you for this, and

256

most importantly, beg your forgiveness for the injury I caused you. My trigger was wet, it slipped, and I did not shoot where I intended."

"*You* did not shoot—? *You?*" Fitzroyal gobbled.

"Yes, me," said Briana. "I was afraid you'd discover it when my moustache fell off. Now, do tell me what I can do to ease your suffering." She pointed innocently to his incapacitated leg.

"Nothing! I—I cannot believe it! Lady Briana, it cannot have been you!" He looked so overtaken with stupidity that Briana fought to keep her lips from curving.

"Then—hang it from high heaven!—you didn't kiss my Emmaline, did you?"

"I *certainly didn't!*" returned Briana with loathing, darting a pained glance toward her butler.

Fitzroyal sank back like a sack of beets, eyeing her through stubby fingers pressed to his forehead. As he considered all the events in this new light, he grew more and more astonished. "That turban and beard at Vauxhall! A lady like yourself—!"

Briana laughed. "Not quite a lady, am I? But I'll thank you to keep this quiet—quiet as the tomb—and I will not put about town the story that Mr. Radcliffe succumbed to your bullet. Are we agreed, my lord?"

Fitzroyal could see that his chances at winning the lady of his dreams were at an end. When Briana held out her hand, he took it. She did not, however, allow him to kiss it.

"A braver, more fiery woman have I never encountered. Agreed, Lady Briana. Ah, what might have been! If only I had not been so wild over you. I came here today to apologize for everything." Lord Fitzroyal said the words with effort, his eyes downcast. He raised them curiously. "Why did you do it, dress like a man and all? Ah, I see I am not to ask."

"No, you are not to ask," affirmed Briana. "And I will not ask you why you broke into my bedchamber, first after Chalandra, and then after me."

"I am despicable," said Fitzroyal gruffly. "Not to worry, my dear lady, I shall never inflict myself on you again nor will I sully your names by speaking of my perfidy."

"I think better of you already," said Briana generously.

# Chapter 23

## The Duchess's Rooms

Briana could hardly believe her eyes early the next morning. Before the sun touched the Brocco traveling coach parked in Berkeley Square, she saw Rex reining in his gelding beneath the plane trees. Stepping back out of the carriage, she crossed the cobbles to the central lawn to greet him.

"Briana, I must speak with you," he said in a restrained voice. As he eyed Darnier, the latter bowed politely, bidding him good morning. Rex's brows lowered, and Briana knew he bore Darnier ill will for taking her to Amy Sydenham's house when he knew Rex would be there.

Briana invited him into the house. Anselma scrambled out of the carriage, but her presence did not stop Rex from taking Briana into his arms as soon as the salon door closed.

"Briana, I must have you! Please forgive me and forget what's gone before. For you, there's no one else, is there? As for me, I've been anguishing over what happened, and I've learned my lesson. I vow, I *promise* I'll never go near

259

another blasted woman again! How in God's earth can I make you trust me? Oh, beautiful Briana, give me another chance! I want you so badly as my wife!" He shook in despair.

"I have forgiven you, Rex, from my heart. But I cannot marry you because I have discovered through all this that I *can live without you.*" She paused, letting that weighty truth sink in. "Therefore, it is not love, but it was admiration and your charming ways which drew me to you. I'm sorry, dear Rex, it is not enough. I cannot marry you."

He groaned, closing his eyes.

Anselma sniffed.

"Then whom will you marry?" he asked.

"Please don't look distressed. There is no one on the horizon for me. Maybe I shall never marry."

Turning to prop his elbows upon the mantel while he gazed into the empty grate, Rex said heavily, "There is someone I know who loves you." He looked sideways at her. "Other than me," he qualified.

"You and Wellington both," Briana uttered in puzzlement.

"We both what?"

"Seem to think that someone loves me. Who is this mysterious lover?"

Rex came close, looked down at her from black-brown eyes full of heartfelt regret. "I must desist from telling you again how much *I* love you, and just bow myself out of someone else's way. I won't pave his path for him, but heaven knows, he is a better man than I." And he pulled her hand to his lips, kissed it with touching misery, and strode out into the pink dawn.

Anselma's wet eyelids blinked rapidly.

With a lump in her throat, Briana watched Rex's blue coat disappear behind the plane trees.

"My dear Lady Briana, you have broken Sir Reginald's heart, but you must have good reason," evoked Anselma, blowing her nose. "Oh, you must not weep! We are leaving on a journey. Here, let's find your handkerchief, here it is. Come, come, those big Brocco horses look impatient, and Darnier is wondering what we're about staying in here so long. We want to reach Milburn Place before nightfall so we don't have to stay at an inn."

As Briana nodded and dried her eyes, they were able to shade her condition with her bonnet brim so she reached the carriage in unimpaired dignity.

An upper window of her house opened. Chalandra leaned out and waved. Briana grasped that this was for Darnier's benefit although her cousin called, "*Au revoir*, Briana! Be back soon and save me from this boredom."

"Yes, Chalandra. Just be sure you stay good and bored until I return." But Chalandra was already calling a sweet good-bye to Darnier.

Briana reviewed the distasteful revelation Chalandra had made last night. Cordelia Landers had called while Briana was out, and Chalandra had spoken with her alone.

About that interview, Chalandra had said vehemently: "I swear I'll have Darnier's company more than Cordelia ever will!"

"What, pray, do you mean by that?" Briana had asked.

"She thinks she's going to marry him. I'll show her! When I marry the duke of Brocco," proclaimed Chalandra, "I shall have Darnier escort me all about London, and he shall be mine more than ever that twit's!"

Briana, in sinking spirits, had asked weakly how Chalandra was certain Cordelia was marrying Darnier.

"I saw her ring, and she said her father doesn't want her to marry someone without a title, which is true of the

261

man she loves, and especially not a man who fought against the French. I hear Mr. Landers is French and bears a grudge for his slain relations."

Now, from the carriage door, Briana could hardly stomach the scene being played out in Berkeley Square. Her cousin, fetching as could be, posed with bare arms on the sill and flirted at Darnier.

A hired footman ran into the square and, searching the numbers, halted in front of Briana's house. She sent a Brocco footman to inquire what the messenger's business was. When she held it before her in the form of a sealed missive, Briana saw it was addressed to Miss C. Milburn.

Briana looked up and caught her cousin actually blowing Darnier a kiss before she pulled the windows in. Darnier touched his hat, and turned to Briana.

"Do you know this hand?" she asked, thrusting the letter at him. Endeavoring to squelch her irritation at what just passed, she said, "Should I give it to Chalandra and leave, or do you suppose I should wait and see what it's all about?"

Darnier said without hesitation, "Leave it for her, and don't give it another thought. It will give her something to think about which may alleviate her boredom."

Briana realized he knew something about it, but was distracted from her pondering when she saw Apsley House looming before them in the early sunshine. "Why are we going this way?" she asked Anselma.

Her question was answered when Darnier dismounted and said he hoped Briana would pardon him but he had a message to convey to the duke of Wellington. "It's a draft of Brocco's first speech to the House. Wellington has promised to review it."

"Is it about betterment of conditions for our men in uniform?" Briana asked. "Rex mentioned that you were doing a great deal of study for the duke to help him prepare."

Darnier looked like a trapped rat. "That's what it is, and yes, I have done a little work on it."

After she had seen his broad shoulders disappear, she sat and worried her bonnet ribbons. She saw a housemaid pull back some drapes, and somehow that spurred her to action.

"I'm going in," she said to Anselma who was crocheting, "I must have a quick word with His Grace."

His Grace was apparently an early riser or expecting Darnier, for he was breakfasting, his butler informed her. Briana sent in her card. The butler returned, summoning her in. Anselma sat stiffly on a chair in the hall, disapproving of ladies' private words with dukes, but she was becoming noticeably more tractable.

Darnier was on his way out, and turned to stare when Briana breezed in.

Wellington strode across the bow-windowed room to where she stood, looking fresh in her yellow muslin and gray French hat festooned with camellias. Rising from his bow, he said, "Had you not come in, my eye-gladdening paragon, I would have come out to you. Darnier tells me you go to decorate Brocco Park. Do sit first and share my kippers."

"Thank you, no, Your Grace. But I would like to talk for one brief moment about a letter which you sent me."

"I believe I know which one."

"Why did you write such a thing?"

Wellington's round, hooded eyes looked frank, but he smiled. "Because I think it's time your lover's game was up."

"I don't have a lover!" she protested. Then she asked curiously, "What is his game?"

"Ha, ha! Ah yes, you know no gentleman who

263

qualifies. Let me see, how can I put this? Are you one to follow your heart, Briana, or are conventions all to you?"

"Conventions? *Me?*" If he but knew!

He crossed his arms and walked closer. His smiling appraisal of her as he searched for words caused her uneasiness. She put it into an exclamation. "Your Grace, not *you—!*"

The duke laughed. "Oh, that prospect is infinitely pleasing, but no, I would never offer you, my dear, a carte blanche. Heaven's gates, but you are charming! No, I am not after an illicit liaison with you, dear angel. But someone who has not been quite truthful with you is desirous of making you his own, and I must say I could not wish a better man a more victorious end to his campaign. However, it will require not only a great deal of forgiveness on your part, but also a sense of humor, which I happen to know you possess. You're puzzled? Ah well, for a while yet."

Briana could not figure him out. Her eyes glistened with emotion as she implored, "Your Grace, I must have a moral man! I can forgive, certainly, but I must also trust."

"Yes, Briana, you must trust."

As the Brocco carriage rolled out of the city, Briana's muddled thoughts moved to the contemplation of Rex's appeal that morning. How could she look at his visit to Harriette Wilson with a sense of humor? There was nothing remotely funny about it. "I don't *trust* him!"

"Who's that?" asked Anselma.

"Rex. Forgive me, but I need an ear to talk to, and it may as well be yours."

"I would think so, since I am the closest person you have. Well, Sir Reginald is a handsome gentleman, that I'll grant him, and well connected; but if you don't trust him, then that's that."

"Why do you say that so assuredly?"

Anselma's cheeks pinkened. "I didn't trust a certain handsome captain, either. The woman who did marry him came to grief. I knew I did the right thing in those days, although to you, Lady Briana, and to everybody else it must appear I'd be better off married."

Briana's concern focused on her duenna. "What kind of grief did the woman have?" she asked.

"The captain's wife went to join him on the Continent last year after the war was over. She found another woman living with him in camp. I suspected he'd be that way."

"How? What made you suspect?" pressed Briana.

Anselma cleared her throat. "Minutes after he left with promises to return and marry me, I saw him from my upstairs window. He . . . he patted the laundress hanging clothes and gave her a kiss. That did it!" Anselma jerked at her crocheting.

Briana felt a sudden compassion for her gray-haired duenna. "So from that you knew he couldn't be true to you?"

"I knew."

Darnier, riding sometimes ahead and sometimes behind the luxurious traveling coach, drew alongside and asked Briana if she would like to stop for luncheon in High Wycombe. When she assented, Darnier bade a liveried outrider gallop ahead and bespeak a private parlor in the best inn.

Anselma, who had studied him the while he leaned toward the window catching Briana's words, declared, "Now *there's* a man. Trustworthy, I'd say."

"How can you know that?" asked Briana thinking of his proxy courtship.

"I just know. If he ever marries, his wife will be his only one and mighty happy, too I'd say, by the looks of him."

"Anselma, you're wistful!" Briana teased.

With a heavy sigh she said presently, as the countryside sped past, "He's reportedly betrothed to Miss Cordelia Landers."

Anselma was incredulous. "I cannot believe it!" she kept exclaiming, and her crocheting suffered and she had to pull out stitches and begin again. During their meal at the bustling inn, she put herself forward by saying to Darnier that she had heard he was about to be married.

Darnier set down his goblet, wiped his lips with a linen cloth, and said, "Miss Snivelton, who has told you that?"

Anselma pinkened, but she said, "My sources must remain sealed. I am not a tattle-monger. But Mr. Darnier, I would like to know if I am to wish you happy."

Briana sat breathless.

"I want very much for you to wish me happy," he said. "But whether I marry is not at all certain at this point." He returned to his sirloin.

Briana blushed as if she herself had pried into his affairs. The betrothal must be true, but Miss Landers was having trouble gaining her father's consent.

With aching heart, Briana shot unseen glances at him. She knew that, never in days to come, would she know another man to equal Darnier in noble presence or kindness or—what was his most attractive quality?—ah yes: his joy in living. She would never forget his love of ridiculous adventure. He was not technically a gentleman, but he most definitely was one in thought and deed even though he flouted conventions, laughed with dukes and conspired with maidservants, schemed with bootmakers and cheated at dueling.

All those things and more, Briana realized, he had done for her. The enormity of his sacrifices in time and effort caused her to put down her fork and look at him in wonder tinged with sadness.

"How can I serve you, Lady Briana?"

She dropped her lashes, remembering with a rush the kiss in the Brocco House library and the incident when he ripped out her shirt buttons and cut her bandeau. "I—I need nothing." She knew that was not true. Now she wished herself otherwheres than sitting across the table from the man whose devastation of her heart was complete.

Ensconced once more against the plush squabs, Briana heaved a great sigh.

Anselma remarked, "That Mr. Darnier attracts women without trying, I'll say that for him." She went on rhythmically crocheting her green lace.

"And who, pray, is attracted to him now?"

"You are, Lady Briana. Now, no need to look that way at me. I keep mum about such things as these, but I can't help but notice that he looks at you, too."

"Anselma!"

"Begging your pardon, but 'tis nothing to be ashamed over. You are lovely as lovely can be, and all the men, gentlemen or otherwise, look at you and admire. It renders me proud."

Briana rolled her eyes. Then she met Anselma's, and they shared a laugh. It felt rather nice.

When the coach halted at the top of a hill, Darnier asked with apologies if he could ride inside for a while. Briana could see as he dismounted that he moved with difficulty. "Are you in pain, Darnier?"

"A tight muscle, nothing more. I appreciate your concern and hope I won't disturb you ladies."

Anselma instantly disclaimed, and her cheeks reddened as she bustled to sit next to Briana, leaving the backward seat to Darnier.

"Miss Snivelton, must you scurry away?" he protested

267

as he lowered himself, smelling of outdoor breezes, into her place. "I had hoped I could snatch this chance to sit at your side," he entreated. "Must you crowd your mistress so? Better return to snuggle by me."

Anselma dropped her ball of thread, uttering confused syllables.

Briana shared a laughing look with Darnier but rescued Anselma by saying, "I am not crowded in the least, and I should watch how she makes this lace. By the way, did His Grace receive the extra money back?"

"He did."

Briana plunged on, for she felt this was the moment to ask, "Will you enlighten us, Darnier? Is the duke now near his wedding day? Is that the reason for hastening my decorating?"

"He has found the woman he means to propose to, but please keep this your own private knowledge until His Grace finds himself accepted."

"Certainly." Briana took a long breath. So Chalandra was nearly there.

At dusk, they arrived at Milburn Place where Anselma insisted they stay, although Darnier repeated that the duke had offered the guest wing at Brocco Park to Briana and herself.

Wookey, who had not been expecting them, was set into a flurry of orders for the kitchen maids, and was clearly full of reasons for existence again. Briana asked him how he would like to cook for her in London, and he surprised her mightily by accepting the post. Briana's maid, Lucy, was in tears of joy for she was hired, too.

The next morning at Brocco Park, Briana found herself thinking of Chalandra with more and more concern. She pictured again the hideous face, the raucous way Brocco had given Chalandra a clout on her derrière, and the pure deception Chalandra practiced on the duke with her fawning and her flattery. With each leaf Briana painted into the mantel border, she felt outraged that her cousin would call this room her own.

Sighing at the vast differences in people's views, Briana made a careful touch of golden white to highlight a leaf. She knew she could do no more for her relations to prevent their foolish plans. Very likely she would see Mrs. Milburn moving in like a flash with her daughter. That was one good thing: Briana would have her town house to herself.

Early that morning, Briana had entered the mansion and had found the duchess's apartments empty and cleaned as she had directed. She supervised Brocco footmen in the laying of the new carpets and the hanging of the curtains and pictures, and then the bed was returned to the room by all the men in the house save Darnier. Briana had to physically put her hands on his waistcoat and beg him not to lift anything or his pulled muscle would be worse. He complied with humor and a bow, and left her to her miracle-working.

Briana and the housemaids, with rods and ladders, embellished the bed with its lace and silk. The effect was cheerful, airy, and elegant. Briana positioned the new chairs brought in from the baggage coaches, then the cushions, the lamps, the vases, and fashion dolls; and after four hours' work, had transformed the room into a frothy fairyland so appealing she knew Chalandra would be in dithers of rapture when she saw it.

Then Briana drew the curving stringcourse of flowers and leaves on the wall to frame the oval mirror and continue down over the fireplace. Since luncheon, she had painted a foot of it into life. Anselma left the chamber, for she could not abide the smell of paint. She adjured Briana to keep the windows wide.

Darnier walked in from the gallery. "Briana, you don't

have to paint all of those yourself, do you?" he asked, looking with interest at the roses and leaves and ribbons in shades of pink, rose, mint green, and French blue. "Pardon me, but now I see why you must. No one else could do it quite like that."

"Thank you, Darnier."

"And what are you thinking of, to make you so sad?" he asked.

"Of Chalandra. She's marrying our employer, but she doesn't love him, and probably never will because—" She left off.

"Because why?"

Briana rushed her words. "Because she wants a lock on that door." Embarrassed, she pointed to the connecting portal in which her stained glass bouquet had been installed. "The duke is not to be given a key."

"She told you that?" asked Darnier quickly.

"Why do you look almost amused?" Briana's anger returned at the kiss Chalandra had blown at Darnier. "Perhaps I should stop behaving in a ladylike, stupid fashion, and say what I think."

Urged Darnier, "By all means."

"Then I imagine you are not surprised at what I said because you are the one who will have a key to this chamber!"

Darnier halted in swinging a bed tassel. He looked at her, his expression utterly blank.

"Won't you? Can you deny that it's your plan?"

From the corner of his eyes, he studied her. It took her aback when he said, "No, I can't. You see, it's time to tell you that I plan to come to this room *often* when—"

"Oh, I *knew* it!" Not wanting to hear another word, Briana, incensed beyond bearing, swiped her paintbrush at him, halting his speech and leaving a green slash across his cheekbone. "Chalandra's right!" she cried. "She *does* get everything she wants! The duchy of Brocco—and you at her command! How can you be that way, Darnier? I thought more of you than that."

Through the ringing in her ears, Briana heard Darnier say in an odd tone, "Do you really think the duke of Brocco is courting Chalandra?"

Afraid, she clattered down her palette and stared at his paint-streaked face. She threw him a clean rag. "If not, then *whom is he courting?*" Her eyes narrowed dangerously.

"Another of the Fairest at his ball."

As realization dawned, Briana breathed, "Of course! It's Cordelia Landers of the new betrothal ring." Following her relief, Briana's mind grasped the worst aspect of all. Her glare grew in intensity as she fixed it on Darnier's handsome face. "And you are going to visit her when she's the duchess! You despicable, philandering man! Ohhh . . . what wickedness! I hate every one of you!"

As she raced away, Darnier snatched her in a whirl and pulled her back. "Who do you hate?" he demanded.

"Every one of you men! No heart for women or their feelings!" With her eyes blurring in tears, she cried, "Chalandra was as fresh and witless as I am! She thought *you* were the one about to marry Miss Landers."

"Me? Marry Miss Landers?"

"Naturally." Briana tried to struggle away, but could not without losing her dignity. "The clues were all there the day she showed me her ring as you were leaving Hatchard's and she gazed after you so adoringly. Now it becomes clear: she will marry the duke, but you will visit her in this room I'm preparing. Well, don't expect me to paint another leaf on a wall that's going to watch adultery!"

"Briana!" cried Darnier in an amused, shocked tone.

"You're wrong about Miss Cordelia and me. A congratulatory kiss on the hand was slim evidence, wasn't it?"

It wasn't so slim, thought Briana, the way you were leading her around at both balls. With her heart hurting terribly, Briana amended her statement. "Cordelia said her betrothal was a secret, and told Chalandra her fiancé was not approved. She said he used to be in the army and her father didn't approve of anyone who fought against the French. But this doesn't bear talking of if I was wrong, and she's to become the duchess of Brocco instead."

"This subject does bear talking of since that, also, is not the case." Darnier drew Briana firmly to the sofa and pushed her gently to sit in it. "Without further delay," he said, tugging the knot out of his snowy stock and loosening his collar, "I must ask you a very important question."

She watched him, fearful at the change in his tone. He lowered to one knee before her. The rustle of Anselma's old petticoat meant that party was listening avidly in the antechamber.

As Briana looked at the play of feelings apparent on Darnier's handsome countenance, she was filled with her own tangled emotions. Putting a cool hand to her forehead, she was unable to sort between Darnier's declaration that he would cuckold his employer, and the singing relief she felt that neither Chalandra nor Cordelia would be receiving Darnier into their chambers.

"You must hear me out, Briana. You mistake too many matters, and it's all my fault."

She swallowed against the lump in her throat and waited for him to continue.

"Miss Landers," he said, "is hoping to marry Major Quentin. Yes, Major Quentin. Not me, not the duke."

"Oh," Briana finally said. "Now I remember seeing

272

him leave Hatchard's that day. But Darnier, Cordelia very definitely stared after *you*."

Darnier smoothed his moustache. "Possibly because I gather I was the first person to encourage her to marry the man she loves and not forsake him for the title her father decided he wanted for her. She was so torn between her father's pressure and Quentin's love, that I spent some time working on her courage. Did I do the right thing, in your opinion?"

Briana's heart skipped and she said, "Yes. Yes, you certainly did."

"But don't think that I'm all good, Briana. I must now expose myself for the wretch I am," he said, "and tell you that I want to come often to this room if you, Briana, will marry the duke of Brocco as I've desired you to do all along."

Briana gasped. *"What did you say?"*

"I should've explained, Briana, that he loves you to distraction, beast that he is."

"A beast is too good of a name!" she cried. Her hands made fists and her eyes sparked. "But you are even worse!" she shouted at his dear, handsome face while her heart shattered.

Darnier winced, obviously having worded his proxy proposal all wrong.

Briana rose furiously, her skirt ruffle fanning the sketches on the floor. "How dare you think I would even listen to such a despicable proposal! Just because I paraded around London with you, dressed as a gentleman? That doesn't mean I'm not a lady in my heart!" A sob choked her and she amended, "Well, maybe it does!" and ran blindly for the door.

Darnier blocked her way, pulling her to him by her good arm. "I'm very sorry. Of course you're a lady. But Briana, you don't love anyone else, do you?"

She pierced him with a sparkling look and rushed out past Anselma.

"Yes, Mr. Darnier," cried Anselma indignantly, "she does!"

On the curving staircase Briana halted in shock.

Darnier asked, "Who is it?"

"*You*, you stupid fool!" Anselma informed him, her voice rich with feeling.

Briana stumbled in sheer panic. Anselma had said *that?* Briana's head heated with mortification, and she had to lean over the rail for support.

Above and out of sight, her duenna continued, "Mr. Darnier, you are a nine-days' wonder! How can you behave so doltishly, teasing Lady Briana so? You know nothing about how to treat a woman as upset as she is, and more's the pity!"

"You're absolutely right, Miss Snivelton, I said the worst things possible."

"But I'd rather see her make a grand mésalliance with a basically superior man as you are than see my Briana wither away into an old maid!" And with that emotion-filled statement, Anselma's boots clumped onto the stairs.

Briana fled. With her gown impeding her, she sped from the honey-colored mansion of Brocco Park and down the gravel lane, plunging into sun and shadow, as she ran down the majestic lane of oaks, the air cooling her flaming cheeks. When she gained the woods, she crunched through a sea of leaves and ran on, bursting into the copse where Darnier had left her book of Wordsworth with his first message and those poems.

Now it was he who had tried to waylay her, but it was no phantom of delight, but a phantom of fear which pursued Briana. She could not deny what that blasted Anselma had told him: she did love him, she loved him to distraction! She burned with resentment at the sight of other women hanging on his arms, she missed his wit and fun in her quiet hours, and she wanted his strong hands pulling her close to him again—even now. Oh, the misery of being wooed by the man she hopelessly loved, all for his purpose of turning her over to that raspy hermit, the duke of Brocco!

It didn't help matters to hear that Darnier desired her. She had felt it when he gazed at her through those ebony lashes the time he picked the ant off her breast. Of course she wanted him, more shame to herself, but for Darnier to think she would even consider such sin was hurtful in the extreme. Is this what had come of all her reckless cavorting about London with him? She shed tears and pounded the ground.

# Chapter 24

## The Broken Window

Hearing a crunch in the lane, Briana hauled herself up in fright. Through the leaves she saw Darnier and Anselma coming down the hill.

When she had dashed past the hedge and arrived breathless in her old room, Briana turned the key in the lock and threw herself onto the window seat where sunlight weakly warmed her tear-dampened face. Pushing a wet tendril back, she heard Anselma's creak on the wooden steps, and braced herself for the knock. It came.

"Lady Briana, may I come in?"

No answer would move from Briana's throat. Despite that traitorous duenna's insistent hammerings on the door, Briana would not let her in. She was too furious with her.

When Lucy scratched softly on the panel about four o'clock that afternoon, Briana let her in with a whispered admonishment not to let Anselma know.

"Oh, I won't, your ladyship. She's real worried over you, though. And Wookey sent a message. He says Mr.

Darnier was here asking if he can call on you tomorrow morning."

Briana turned away, clinging to the bedpost.

"Will you see him, my lady?"

"No!"

"Very good, your ladyship, I'll say so; but do eat up this splended gleany and chutney or Wookey'll think 'e can't cook a man's shaving water."

"Thank you, Lucy. I'm for bed; my head aches."

It still ached the next morning. In her dreams, Darnier had been running after her trying to persuade her to give up her loaded dueling pistol but she had run headlong for Rex's outstretched arms, falling before she reached him. When she gazed up from lying on the ground with an injured arm, Rex had both of his about Harriette Wilson, and he smiled in pity. Wellington stood aside saying "Did you discover who loves you?"

"No one loves me!" Briana exclaimed, awakening herself. She heard a scratch on her door.

Splashing tepid water on her eyes, Briana clutched her aching head and admitted Lucy with the breakfast tray. Briana shut the door and locked it as Anselma sped up the stairs calling, "Lady Briana! Please, I pray of you, wait! Let me come in! I absolutely must speak with you!"

Briana had Lucy ask what it was that Anselma found so dire at such an early hour.

"Mr. Darnier is here! He wants to see Lady Briana!"

Briana sipped her coffee and burned her tongue. "I do not wish to see him."

"I believe you are mistaken about him, Lady Briana," called Anselma urgently. "You can trust him— you can."

"Trust him?" shrieked Briana. "Consider this conversation at an end!"

A half-hour later, as she put out her foot and Lucy

laced up the black ankle ribbons, a sharp sound hit the gable's window frame. "What's that, Lucy?"

"I don't know, unless a bird hit it."

Briana went curiously to the window seat and peeked out on the herb garden. She glimpsed a tall beaver above the dark brows of Darnier just as a pebble rattled the glass of the small pane. She jumped back with a little scream. "That despicable man! Throwing stones at my window now!"

She hoped he hadn't seen her. The nerve of that Brocco secretary, wanting to make her his mistress! Barring personal desire, the very fact of her titled birth should have nipped such exalted notions on his part.

As she sat in defiant nonchalance at her vanity a quarter-hour later, Lucy curled the falling hair from Briana's elegant crown arrangement into *tire-bouchons*. Briana's thoughts turned traitorously and without warning to Darnier tying her cravats in dark carriages.

There was a loud crash, a tinkling of glass, and a missile sailed into the room.

"What on earth—" Briana voiced. Wind rushed in through the gaping window pane. On the carpet rolled a stone with paper tied around it.

"Lands sakes, my lady!" Lucy dived for the bundle. "This is addressed to you!"

Briana strode to the window. Through the broken jags she eyed the spot where Darnier had stood. The herb garden was empty but for a robin hopping in the rosemary.

"Let's see that, Lucy." When Briana finally managed to cut the string off with scissors and open the wrinkled paper, she sank to the bed and read, in Darnier's unmistakable slant:

My Dear Lady Briana,
    If I write lines from Wordsworth instead of my

278

own, perhaps my chances are better that you will read this.

The hermit sits alone.
. . . But oft, in lonely rooms, and 'mid the din
Of towns and cities, I have owed,
. . . sensations sweet,
Felt in the blood, and felt along the heart;
And passing even into my purer mind,
With tranquil restoration:—feelings, too,
Of pleasure: such, perhaps,
As have no slight or trivial influence
On that best portion of a man's life,
. . . little, nameless, remembered acts
Of kindness and of love.

Briana's eyes prickled with tears at the beautiful flourish he had made after that word with a heart entwined with leaves on a vine. She read on:

Please come down and talk to me. Tell me all you feel against me. I wish to hear it deservingly, and pray you will allow me to voice my reasons and beg your forgiveness.
Your most obedient and most wretched servant,
Darnier
Duke of Brocco

Her sudden intake of breath brought Lucy running from the armoire. "What is it, Lady Briana? Is someone dead?"

Briana lay back speechless, lifting the paper and staring at the words. She shook her head, which pacified Lucy, but a pounding began in Briana's temples as she wondered why on earth she hadn't realized the truth before . . . So how—?

Later she hardly recalled setting a white, lace-crowned hat on her head, for her heart was singing: he was courting me for himself! Oh merciful God, he was courting me for himself!

Smelling the fresh morning breeze in through the shattered window, a joyful, shaky laugh rose within her, scattering her despair.

Lucy said, "I'm glad it made you that happy, then, my lady. But what do I do about that there window?"

"I don't care what you do about it. Poke the rest of the glass out if it amuses you. But first I must have your help to leave this house."

Five minutes later, the stairs creaked. Lucy motioned Briana to come on down. As the maid tiptoed across the dim hall, her capped head swiveling in both directions, she kept motioning and Briana gained the front door.

Afraid of being seen by Anselma, Briana left the leaning Tudor house on winging feet. As she nearly reached the stand of oaks, something caused her to look back.

Anselma stood at the kitchen-garden gate. Her arm came down hastily, as though she had raised it with a prepared outburst. Expecting a shout, Briana halted in full view, feeling guilty for having denied her duenna admittance or speech for so many hours.

Oddly, no challenge issued from Anselma's lips. She just stood there in expectant stillness, and Briana was astonished when her chaperone lifted her hand and waved. Puzzled, Briana waved in return, then proceeded until she gained the copse. There she saw Darnier.

He stood between two towering, mossy oaks, removing the black beaver from his head. He looked exceedingly fine in a forest green coat and black pantaloons tucked into glossy boots. As Briana flashed a look back, she saw Anselma's smiling face, and realization dawned that her duenna had been *signaling* to Darnier. Imagine that.

With thumping heart, Briana gazed at the man she loved: Darnier, the duke of Brocco. How could she have taken him for a servant? Why had he pretended to be one?

His milky white cravat lifted on the breeze as he ran toward her and pulled her into his arms. The roughness of his jaw caressed her cheek, and her heart swelled at the flooding message of his tight arms enfolding her.

"Darnier! Oh, Darnier!" she cried. "I love you!"

"Briana, darling, you cannot love me," he whispered in wonder, his lips against her cheek. "I have been so bad to you. But I am wildly thankful that you have said you do, for I've been praying to God in heaven that you will marry me. You see, I have loved you thoroughly since the day Rex found you here."

Bursting with joy, Briana's beautiful eyes filled with tears.

"Is that a no?" asked Darnier in alarm.

"No, my Darnier, it's a yes!" she said with a catch in her voice. She had called him hers out loud. Reveling in the magnitude of her most secret dream exploding into reality, Briana smiled, for Darnier was trailing his lips down her neck, murmuring, "My Briana! My sweet duchess, I'll make it all up to you. All the pain you've suffered will be replaced."

"It is replaced already," Briana gasped. All this heavenly closeness in addition to the consideration, the rakishness, the fun that life with Darnier promised. Between a kiss and a breathless laugh, she remembered to thank God.

"Come away from the view of our watchful Miss Snivelton. Will you ride with me to Shipston? We can request our first banns read on Sunday."

Briana nodded, and soon she was nestled next to him in the backward seat of a very tame landau with the tops lowered. She felt a sense of having been lifted into another world where coachmen drove lovers on sunny, crisp days, and devastating men with dark waving hair and sun-bronzed cheekbones kissed one's temple with the heavenly prickle of a moustache.

She sighed against his lapel, emerging from such glory to sneak a peek at the driver tooling the white pair down the hill. Then she sat up straight. "Who on earth was that horrid, shouting man we all thought was the duke?"

"Ah yes. Do you mean here or in London?"

"What do you mean by that?"

"Well here," said Darnier, chuckling, "since I had to keep you from an audience with the duke, I just denied you admission and went into the room and shouted at myself."

"You didn't!" Briana was astonished into an incredulous laugh. It grew funnier the more she thought about it.

Darnier grinned sheepishly. "When I wanted to have a ball to proclaim to the world I had found the most beautiful woman in all of Europe, I was in difficulty. I had to find a bogus duke."

"A bogus duke! Where does one find such an animal?"

"I hired him in Fleet Street."

"*Hired* him?"

"I should explain to you why I was obliged to do all this maneuvering. I began my decoy before I ever arrived here at Brocco Park." He drew her closer. "You see, after Waterloo, Wellington sent me to Switzerland to recover from Hougoumont. It took nearly a year for me to walk and ride—but forget all that."

Briana burst out, "I care very much about that! Are you all right now? Oh, you're not, are you?"

Taking her wounded arm tenderly and kissing her fingers, he said, "Nearly so. I was injured, but not irreparably. When I was ready to come back to England, my father died. If that wasn't bad enough news, my distant uncle Brocco gave up the ghost, and I was saddled

282

with the dukedom. I had been given to understand it could befall me in some hazy decades of the future, but my father was in line ahead of me and strong as a battle horse. Never did I dream this would befall me so early."

"Didn't you want to be a duke?"

"No! That is, the money was fine, but the title seemed like a vulture about to land and pick away all my freedom. I had once visited the late duke in London. His style of life, with twenty footmen at table and secretaries and visits from the Regent and all the rest, not to mention his starchy wife who was alive then, all made me feel certain I would be just as set-upon by the multitudes as he was. He thrived on it. I abhorred the thought."

"So you came here incognito," sighed Briana. "How did you enjoy fishing the brook and letting Rex abuse you? As I think back, how could he?"

"Giving those fish to you was the beginning of my real excitement in life. Hougoumont was nothing to the battle that raged within me after seeing those eyes of yours. As for Rex's orders, I didn't take to them well at all," chuckled Darnier. "He took unfair advantage as soon as he saw you. Because I had vowed to keep my identity a secret, old Rex had no mercy. He, like me, recognized a rare treasure when he saw one. He set out with dishonorable intentions, believe it or not, but quickly reverted to wooing you as a gentleman. And, I must confess that my own knees were, from a glimpse of cherry lips, turned to jam."

Briana laughed helplessly.

Darnier pulled his beaver brim low over his brows and looked sidewise at her. "You caused me to do the most desperate things."

"Like what?"

"Like fit you up with breeches so I could have opportunities to gaze at you, laugh with you—"

"Tease and hoodwink me!" cried Briana. "But I still

283

fail to fathom this person—this horrid apparition you say you hired from Fleet Street! Who was he?"

"A cobbler's assistant. He stood outside a shop sweeping my path and quoting from Goldsmith. As you can imagine, I was struck with his handsome visage, and couldn't resist the joke I could play on everyone waiting to fawn over the new duke." Darnier's lower eyelids deepened in laughter. "I asked the apparition if he'd like a temporary position in a great household."

"Oh Darnier! How could you?" Briana looked shocked, her eyes dancing.

"I couldn't resist the challenge. He used to tread the boards, he said, until the war where he was carved up pretty thoroughly by a deserter he tracked down. The theater wouldn't take him back so he learned to be useful to a cobbler. He worked out quite well for me until—"

"Until Chalandra!" Briana exclaimed. "Oh, my poor cousin!"

"Yes, my plan limped along tolerably well until Miss Milburn," Darnier said, looking exceedingly regretful.

Shuddering, Briana said, "Lord have mercy on her—she is convinced she is marrying him and will be a duchess. Darnier, I'm fearful for her. What can we do?"

"I've done everything I can. I sent him off with bulging pockets to Australia. He really was a good sort of chap until he drank too much wine, became cocky, and took liberties in my house. Having performed in Drury Lane in years past, he developed a quick affinity for the affluent life he'd witnessed in the boxes. After his improper invitations to your cousin, I had to have a friend of mine forcibly convey him to the packet at Dover because he refused to leave the country without Miss Milburn. I made him sign an agreement never to come back. If he tries, he'll be liable for double the amount I paid him."

"So that was when Mr. Landers took him away in the

coach? Oh, what will Chalandra say now? What will her mother do? I cringe to think."

"You tried to help them, Briana. Chalandra went to London head over ears on the road to ruining herself. First it was Fitzroyal, then it was my bogus duke."

"Somewhere in there it was Rex, and of recent date it has been you," Briana pointed out.

"Yes, too many hitches developed which I could never have foreseen. The worst part was hurting you." His dark lashes dropped to survey her injured arm cradled tenderly in his.

"Darnier?" said Briana in a small voice after the spoked wheels had turned in silence in the shaded dirt lane. "Why was it necessary for you to deceive me all this time?"

"Because at first when I saw you lying out in nature, I thought it would be heaven to be able to move about freely and let you waylay me again. I planned to catch you more fish and take you and your chaperone for sunset rides to paradise, but that would never work if I were the duke, would it? We would've had to have been so proper."

Briana's laugh rang out, her eyes a-sparkle listening to his suggestive fantasy marred by Anselma.

"Then when I found out you were the lady who transformed my rooms, I knew I had made the most horrendous mistake. Rex, however, went into whoops over my plight."

"I remember your putting a stop to our tea by calling for him about tenants coming. So you did get back at him, Darnier."

"At times. When you said you were going to London and I had seen how Miss Snivelton and your relatives always pestered you, it was obvious to me you needed rescuing. I decided it would be great sport to show you the men's side of life as you wished. You fired my

285

imagination, proving more and more to be exactly the woman I had thought God hadn't made for me on this earth."

As Briana sighed, the landau slowed for a flock of sheep crossing the lane, their wooly backs undulating and their garbled bleats making a comical chorus.

Darnier smiled ruefully. "But I got you into the worst kinds of trouble: your standing at twenty paces with Fitzroyal! I nearly went crazy with fear he'd kill you, although he had agreed not to shoot your midsection. You were so deuced brave, Briana!"

Her heart swelled as she listened to him, as she saw the love in his eyes. She hugged him tightly. "I was only brave because you were there for me." After a pause, she asked, "What about Wellington? He knows you are the duke of Brocco?"

"He and Rex and Quentin and my servants were the only ones in on my secret. Wellington thought it all a famous joke on gullible society. He especially enjoyed the ball; in fact, he encouraged me to go ahead with it."

"Snapping your fingers at the ton, Darnier?" she said, aghast. "What will you do when everyone finds out?"

"Wellington promises me it will be a big laugh. And what do I care as long as I have you? We don't have to go out in society for some time if we choose not to, for we will have a honeymoon to take. Unless you, my dearest, desire to be married at St. George's, Hanover Square?"

"Oh no! Not unless you do, Your Grace."

"All I care, Briana, is that we are lawfully joined. And please!—call me Darnier, or any of those other endearments that have been escaping your lips this past quarter-hour."

"Oh Darnier!" sighed she. "Do you really want me to be your wife? I behave so unlike a duchess."

"Thank God for that!" Smiling meltingly at her, he ran a finger along her chin, saying, "You have shown more honor than any lady I've ever known. Look how you worried about hurting Fitzroyal after what he did to you. And how you care for those ungrateful relatives of yours."

"Oh dear, what will happen to Chalandra?"

"I've had my cobbler write her a letter, the one which arrived in Berkeley Square as we left. Who's overtaking us, Harris?" Darnier asked over his shoulder.

"Looks to be the women from Milburn Place, Your Grace."

"Whip 'em up!" Darnier ordered, and eight white hoofs churned up puffs of dust.

It occurred that, as Chalandra and her mother looked out their post chaise windows, Briana's lace hat was thrown off by a masculine hand, her dark hair stroked back, and her face pulled up into a kiss—all this by the darkly handsome man Chalandra had come hurrying to Warwickshire with to make her peace. For now the Milburns knew he was the duke of Brocco and infinitely to be desired as a husband.

Briana's reaction was to pull away from Darnier when she heard Chalandra call, "Your *Grace*..." in a desperately friendly appeal.

But Briana felt Darnier smile as he continued to kiss her.

The coachman looked over his shoulder and took stock of the duke's interesting occupation. The hoofbeats quickened.

After all, Briana thought, with Darnier's strong arms about her, she could flout convention when there was such a marvelous reason for doing so. Now she had no need to gather up courage to announce this to Mrs. Milburn and Chalandra, for they were at that moment witnessing her scandalous behavior.

"Darnier," breathed Briana, seeing the dust cloud rising high between the chaise and the speeding landau, "at last I feel free of my relations."

"Is that why you are marrying me?" he asked, grinning at her happiness. "Seriously, will you forgive me for all the pain and agony I've caused you?"

She forgave him completely, caressing the raven hair that waved loosely over his ears.

"I have one thing in particular I'm downright ashamed of," he said, his breath against her forehead. Briana tipped back her face and watched him say, "It was something I said. I should have quit trying to make you guess my secret. It was about my visiting the duchess's rooms . . ."

Briana blushed, then flashed a winsome smile. "You may visit the duchess's rooms *often* when I marry the duke of Brocco. You may tell His Grace it is under that condition I will marry him. After all, Anselma approves."